The Treatment

Winner of two O. Henry Awards, Daniel Menaker was a
senior editor at *The New Yorker* for twenty years. Now Senior
Literary Editor at Random House, he lives in Manhattan.

The Treatment

DANIEL MENAKER

faber and faber

First published in the USA in 1998 by Alfred A. Knopf
First published in the UK in 1998
by Faber and Faber Limited
3 Queen Square London WC1N 3AU
This open market edition published in 1999

Printed in England by Mackays of Chatham plc, Chatham, Kent

Daniel Menaker is hereby identified as author of this
work in accordance with Section 77 of the Copyright,
Designs and Patents Act 1988

A CIP record for this book
is available from the British Library

ISBN 0-571-19761-2

2 4 6 8 10 9 7 5 3 1

For Katherine

PART ONE

The Eden of Anxiety

I WAS GOING TO BE LATE. A fat woman in a quilted brown parka—she looked like a walking onion—had kept everyone waiting in the heavy snow at Ninety-sixth and Broadway while she argued with the driver. She was trying to get him to take a transfer from the day before. She insisted, loudly, that a downtown driver had just issued the transfer to her. "It couldn't be, lady," the driver said. His Caribbean accent, his delicate features, the touch of gray at his temples made him seem like an aristocrat with favors to dispense, especially in the presence of the bulging woman and the huddled masses outside.

"I'm telling you not five minutes ago," the woman said.

"And I'm telling you that he couldn't have any transfers from yesterday," the driver said. "They are destroyed each day."

Holding aloft the slip of blue paper, the woman turned around and shouted at the rest of us, bunched up against the snow and wind blasting off the Hudson, "Five minutes ago! Five minutes!"

During the silent glaring that followed, another crosstown bus stopped across the street, and among the passengers who got off were four or five Coventry School seniors, dressed only in sports jackets and slacks and sneakers. In two hours some of them would jostle their way into my second-period eleventh-grade English class, and I would give them farcical interpretations of the first half of *Billy Budd* until one of the quicker ones began to suspect I was putting them on.

"Hey, Mr. Singer," one boy called.

"Hey, Jake, where ya headed?" another shouted, probably taking the weather as permission for impertinence.

If I'd wanted to answer the question, I would have said, "Boys, I'm going to see my psychoanalyst, Dr. Ernesto Morales." And if I'd wanted to amplify, I'd have added, "He's a Cuban, and a devout Catholic, apparently. There's a crucifix in the waiting room and another one on the wall behind his chair. I got his name from the school psychologist." And if I were histrionic, like the fat woman, I would have gone on yelling my plaint for all to hear: "You see, boys, I am in real trouble. My mother died when I was six, on the day before Halloween—Mischief Night, if you're susceptible to ironies, as I know a few of you are when you manage to stay awake in class—my father and I are barely on speaking terms, and my girlfriend left me two months ago. And I'm not going to be head of the English Department next year after all. I told the headmaster that I thought the football coach was too hard on the players, and he didn't want to hear it, so he used it as an excuse not to give me the job."

But no. It would never do even to allude to my problems to the boys. First of all, I wasn't so crazy that I didn't know how boring my plight would be to most people. Even the banality of evil is outstripped by the banality of anxiety neurosis. Second, the kids weren't my friends, and third, even though they weren't my friends, they were all I had left. Anyway, I was sure at the time that I wouldn't be seeing Dr. Morales much longer. He was a madman privateer for whom conservative Freudianism was merely a flag of convenience, and I was just trying to keep him at a distance as I planned my escape—into what, I had no idea. The school psychologist must have been crazy herself.

"How long are we going to allow ourselves to be treated like this?" the fat woman demanded of the wind.

"Come on," I said. "Here." I was third in line, and I reached around the person in front of me and handed the fat woman a token.

The woman snatched it from my hand. "It's not the money," she said angrily. "It's the way we are treated. But obviously you don't care about that. So all right, all right." She put the token and the transfer into her purse and took out another transfer. She turned around, the fabric of her casing sighing against the metal panels of the bus's entryway, and handed the second transfer to the driver.

"Can you beat it?" the driver said to me as I paid my fare.

TEN MINUTES AFTER my session should have started, I pushed the buzzer outside the door of the brownstone in which Dr. Morales's office occupied the rear of the top floor, and he buzzed me in. In the stuffy, overheated waiting room, the white-noise machine was hissing away. The machine could sound like anything—wind in a cane field outside Havana, a wave receding on a beach, a tiger's warning—but today it was just static. I looked out the window, which was flanked by two big flowerpots out of which *Cacti freudii derelicti* thornily protruded. In the backyard of the house across the way, snow was building up on the back of the huge sow.

"Yes, I know the story of this pig," Dr. Morales had said a few weeks earlier. "This was Johnny Carson's house, and he had the statue installed in the yard. And when he moved he did not take the pig."

"It's strange," I said.

"I agree," Dr. Morales said, "but what is even stranger to

me is that you have not mentioned it before now. You have been coming three times a week for how long—two months now?"

"Four," I said. "But who's counting?"

"We shall get back to your anger in a moment," he said. "But right now perhaps you could talk a little about why you did not bring up such an odd thing for such a long time."

This was as far as I got in my recollection of the pig conversation, which had quickly and typically put us at sword's point, when Dr. Morales opened the door to his inner office. He was beaming, as usual, and was bent at the waist at the customary ten-degree angle, in what I took to be sarcastic deference. This upper-body inclination made him seem even shorter than he was. He had on a white shirt and the vest and trousers of a three-piece suit, and his shoulders ballooned out like a miniature stevedore's. Light bounced off his shiny bald head, and behind his straight, heavy, broomlike black beard and narrow mustache, he was smiling the diabolical smile he always smiled.

"Good morning, Mr. Singer," he said in his insinuating way—his voice, as always, even more flamboyantly Spanished in reality than it was in my memory. "Please come in."

"There was this fat woman on the bus," I started out after I lay down on the couch. I told him the rest. "She was probably on the way to *her* analyst," I said at the end. "Life in the city. How can someone let herself get so fat?"

"What do *you* think?" Dr. Morales said.

"Well, I suppose with some people it's just their metabolism or glands or something."

"So you are apologizing for her and for yourself."

"Myself?"

"With this 'Well, I suppose.' This is a habit, as I have pointed out before. You guess, you suppose, you think maybe. You castrate yourself before it happens, what you so fear—that if you display your balls, someone else will cut them off. Pre-emptive self-castration."

"Opinions are testicles?"

"Yes. And so are feelings. You are amused, but this is the case. And people do not let themselves get fat, by the way. Again we have this passivity. They make themselves fat."

"Well, so why do they do it?"

"You must tell me what you think."

"It *could* be physical. They might—"

Dr. Morales dropped some papers on the floor. As he picked them up, he said, "Now we are like—what do you call them?—a champster on a wheel."

"Hamster. But sometimes it must be physiological."

"When it is, it is boring. As boring as this conversation. Unfortunate, maybe even tragic, but boring. The majority are fat because they want to be fat. They feel entitled to have more room and more attention than other people. They talk too loudly and they take up two seats on the bus. They cheave themselves around, and everyone else has to make room for them. And excuses, as you are doing. If you go to the mountain for a hike with them, they get out of breath going up the hill and you have to wait for them. They want attention, and they are saying they should not have to take responsibility for what they do."

Dr. Morales paused. "You are smiling again, I can tell."

"It seems to me so outrageous as to be funny," I said.

"But were you not angry at this woman?"

"Of course. I told you."

"Then why do you laugh when I am denouncing her?"

The office was silent except for the ticking of the wind-driven snow against the windows.

"Maybe it's because it would never enter my mind to go on a mountain hike with a fat person."

"Again the 'maybe.' You disavow your anger, and you do

not have the courage of your own contempt. She is a clown, I am a clown, the entire world is a circus, correct? But even then it is only *maybe* that the whole world is a circus and everyone except you is a clown. I must tell you honestly that I do not know how to proceed right now."

"I did not disavow my anger," I said.

"Ah, but you did, you did," Dr. Morales said. "You presented it as if it were a play and you were a character but in the audience at the same time. You had even a title for it, as I recall. The Life of the City."

"Life in the City," I said.

"Now, really, Mr. Singer, I must protest. You are correcting me and resisting the treatment at every drop of the hat. You do not want intercourse but frottage."

"All right. I was angry at the fat woman on the bus."

"Oh, thank the good Lord Jesus Christ. Why?"

"Because she stole a token from me."

"No."

"She made me late for the session."

"At last the penis goes inside the vagina. But not quite yet with the ejaculation."

"What did I miss? Oh, I get it. Me. I made myself late."

"And at whom are you angry?"

"Myself?"

"Why?"

"Because I was late? By the way, is there a makeup test if I fail?"

"You know, Mr. Singer, you are a gigantic pain in the ass. *Now, again, why were you angry at yourself?"*

"I already said: because I was naughty."

"AND SO AT LAST WE HAVE FINALLY MADE THE BABY," Dr. Morales declaimed.

"But I already said that."

"No, you will have to pardon me, Mr. Singer, but you said first that you were angry at yourself because you were late. The second time, you said it was because you were nowty. Now, do not sigh this way, please. You are an English teacher. You know that the choice of words always matters."

"So I was naughty, like a little boy."

"Exactly." Dr. Morales shuffled his papers.

"When I'm late, I'm always testing you or trying to provoke you."

"Yes, especially if you could express the idea a little less like a quadratic equation, with a little more feeling. You are like a three-year-old who takes down his pants and shows his penis and testicles and anus, all the dirty parts, to see if your mommy will love you anyway, even though you are nowty. You are angry at yourself because you are in reality an adult who has allowed his unconscious to be seen. You also use your lateness to get me off the tracks of your more serious problems and to get extra attention for yourself."

"Like being a fat person."

"Oho! We have engendered twins today. Yes, the fat lady makes passengers wait. You make me wait. You are amused again."

"All your patients probably do the same kind of thing."

"This is guesswork, and in any case, much as you might like to, you cannot throw your arm on my shoulders and talk to me as a colleague about my other patients."

"The guy after me is often late."

"Perhaps he does not have a regular appointment time. You are hunting with blinders and without a license."

"Sometimes when I leave I see him running down the street."

Dr. Morales yawned loudly. The wind moaned around the windows, as if nature itself wanted an audience with him. The radiator behind his chair clanked and spluttered, the noise machine in the waiting room hissed, and the air seemed closer and hotter than ever. At length he said, "Are you not tired, Mr. Singer, from lifting these sandbags and throwing them up against the treatment here? You are only hurting yourself, you know. And the more construction you perform on this wall behind which you try to hide, the more clearly you can be seen."

"Then what's the problem? If it's all grist for the mill, it doesn't matter what I talk about, right?"

Another yawn, this one downright theatrical.

"I guess that to you, people who are fat or late for the ordinary little neurotic reasons must be just as boring as those whose pituitaries have run amok or who get detained by a police roadblock. It must be excruciating for you."

"Nor do I need your sympathy, Mr. Singer. And I do not recall saying that your neurosis was little. You have now succeeded in filling up fifteen of the thirty-five minutes available with dramaturgical exercises, procedural pettiness, philosophical speculation, an attempt to join the New York Psychoanalytic Institute and form a partnership with me, and condescension to the tedium of my practice. Not one mention of the headmaster who has reneged on his promise, not one mention of the woman who left you, not one mention of the joy of teaching, not one mention of the sadness you must feel about your estrangement from your father, not one mention of what you are doing in your sex life these days. I suspect that your being late is in fact not a plea for attention but a reluctance to tell me that you have been masturbating."

"I'm sorry. I guess I was just struck by how boring many aspects of your work must be, and I said what was on my mind, as you are always haranguing me to do."

A long silence ensued.

"You are kind to think of my working conditions, even

when your thoughtfulness is diluted by the guesswork that precedes it," Dr. Morales said. "Perhaps you would like to vary my routine for me by going outside and taking a walk in the snow in the park?"

"Well, you have been yawning and rearranging your papers back there."

"I must congratulate you. You have graduated from being my partner to being my analyst. Shall we go?"

"You're serious?"

"There are no jokes, Mr. Singer."

THE SUN WAS UP high enough behind the clouds to give the air the bright, false-spring light that always marks an hour or two of daytime snowstorms before afternoon arrives and the gloom lowers. The wind was coming from behind us, at the same speed we were walking, and the snow had retired from fine urgency to flaky slowness, its movement more horizontal than vertical, so that as Dr. Morales and I walked to the end of the block we seemed to be moving without moving. He had on a coat and hat so bulbous and red and shiny—it must have been some sort of weird new synthetic fabric—that he looked like a postmodern mountain climber or an explorer or astronaut. He didn't appear to notice the glances he got from nearly everyone we passed, but charged ahead as if he had just caught sight of some lunar objective. I tried to keep up.

We entered the park at Ninetieth Street and went down a small hill. Paths that had been shovelled were already recovered by snow, and the banks stood three or four feet high on either side. We walked in silence for a few minutes, following a course that took us—appropriately, it occurred to me—in a large circle. At the halfway point, Dr. Morales asked, "What are you thinking about?" and I said, "Not much." When we got back to where we had started, I stopped and scooped up some snow, made it into a snowball, and threw it at a tree about fifty feet off. It nicked the trunk.

"What a beautiful day, yes?" said Dr. Morales, beaming at the winterscape as if he had created it himself. "It makes you feel like a kid, no?"

"Yes," I said. "But you couldn't have had much weather like this in Cuba."

"You are still at point-counterpoint, eh, Mr. Singer?"

"Just an observation," I said, moving off down the path. "Sometimes a cigar is a cigar."

"Yes, but not, I believe, when you light it and then try to ram it up someone's ass." He hadn't resumed walking, and when I turned to face him he looked, now, less exploratory than extraterrestrially Bolshevik, with the snow—which was intensifying again—swirling about him. He stood perfectly upright in his carapace, a few feet away, gazing at me austerely, as if I had failed to hold my individual portion of the line against the Nazis outside Leningrad. Off to the side, some schoolboys on an outing tossed a Frisbee back and forth. Dr. Morales picked up some snow, compacted it vigorously, and, encumbered as he was, fired it at the tree I'd aimed at. Bull's-eye.

"I don't think this treatment is getting me anywhere," I said.

"You must give it time, Mr. Singer."

"I want to stop."

"Please do not do that, Mr. Singer."

"I thought this whole process was supposed to be more sympathetic, kinder."

"That is what you want? Someone to be kind to you?"

"Yes," I said, and with that, tears welled up in my eyes. "Yes, that's what I want."

"I'm afraid this is not my function. What I shall try to do, if you will permit me, is to help you learn how to obtain from others what it is that you want."

The tears were now starting from my eyes, as if expelled by some great interior pressure, and even as I wept I smiled in childlike pleasure to feel such sudden lightness across my shoulders, such relief in not being able to govern myself. Dr. Morales walked along the path toward me. Despite what he had said, I expected that *he* might put *his* arm around *my* shoulders or explain that it was for my own good that he remained so aloof and exigent—some gesture of concern. But even in the face of my weeping he didn't let go an inch, and what I got, after a Frisbee player ran between us, his coat flapping and his orange scarf trailing behind him like a pennant, was "I am sorry but our time is up. I must return to my office."

We walked out of the park once again in silence, and Dr. Morales once again struck a lively pace. I hurried along, in order not to lag behind like a kid, which is very much what I felt like as I tried to wipe the snot and tears from my face with the back of a snow-crusted glove. At Fifth Avenue, Dr. Morales gave me a single formal nod of the head and hurried off. He walked against a red light that was about to change, and a gypsy cab trailing the herd of cars that had just passed and driving too fast for the weather looked like it was going to hit him. I thought, My troubles are over, and then, It's all my fault, but the cab swerved away. The street was slick with snow, so the car fishtailed into a parked delivery van with a muffled thump and a treble accompaniment of tinkling glass. The van's driver, dressed in jeans and shirtsleeves, got out and shook his fist and issued an excited bulletin of *chíngate*s and *pendejo*s and *puta*s across the avenue, but Dr. Morales stalked on.

When I got on the westbound crosstown bus, there was the fat woman, occupying two of the seats reserved for the elderly and the handicapped.

HE WORKED OUT—I was sure of it. His striding through the
snow, his dead shot with the snowball, his billowing shoulders
led me to imagine him at a gym, lifting weights and then
putting in half an hour on a NordicTrack. Next to a priest. It
was some kind of special, exclusively Catholic gym that I imagined, serving only the various brands of maniacal, too-bright-a-
gleam-in-the-eye types that that religion appears to breed. The
spirit of the place was martial. The fanatics went there and
hardened their bodies into worthy vessels of the all-consuming
vocations they followed. So we had mafiosi grunting and
sweating alongside philosophy professors, and young, shark-
like politicians holding the ankles of supermarket managers as
they did sit-ups with barbells. Scattered throughout the cavernous facility, whose only ungrotty feature was a south-facing
stained-glass window, were those who had gone the whole hog
and become priests. And there was also a sprinkling of zealots
who had somehow landed in the "helping professions"—tyran-
nical nurse supervisors, militant social workers, and one or two
lunatic analysts like Dr. Morales. Commitment and determination burned like invisible fire in the air around them.

This vision came to me on my way to a session with Dr.
Morales as I walked through the hollow where we stood in the
snow, me crying, Dr. Morales not relenting. It was spring—one
of the few genuine springs I could remember in New York.
After the snow on the back of Johnny Carson's pig melted,
there were soft, cool days and chilly nights, with weeks' worth
of trees fuzzing up with foliage, and none of the usual fore-
tastes of the heat of summer, and no six-day block of rain and
rawness.

I still felt as though in that blizzard I had lost a battle in the
war I waged triweekly with Dr. Morales, but it evidently in-
stilled in me a love of combat, for I went on seeing him, hold-

ing in reserve the ultimate weapon: quitting. Soon after the al-
fresco session, in fact, I had taken to leaving every morning at
exactly the same time and walking across the park, to make
sure I wouldn't be late, feeling a shade less desperate but not
wanting to acknowledge it officially, for fear it wouldn't last,
muttering all the way, revising and rehearsing the devastating
termination remarks that had yet to be delivered. As the
weather turned, I'd been making the trip more and more
quickly, and I thought, that particular spring morning, how the
impending conversation might go if Dr. Morales were to in-
dulge me and himself in a cease-fire:

Me: *Have you noticed that I'm not late anymore? This morning I
was actually ten minutes early.*

Dr. Morales: *Yes, I have noticed. And why do you suppose this is?*

Me: *I think it's just that I'm getting into better shape and doing
the walk faster and haven't adjusted for the difference yet.*

Dr. Morales: *I see. Do you take any other exercise?*

Me: *No. Well, a little scrimmaging with the basketball team.*

Dr. Morales: *It must be that and not the walk that is putting you
in better condition.*

Me: *Well, you ought to know.*

Dr. Morales: *And what does this mean?*

Me: *I just remember when we went to the park in the snow that
day. You seemed to be in very good shape yourself, the way you
strode around and threw that snowball. Walter Johnson. And
you look as though you lift weights or something.*

Dr. Morales: *The Big Train, yes?*

Me: *Yes.*

Dr. Morales: *You are amazed I know this?*

Me: *Yes.*

Dr. Morales: *Yet you know that baseball is if anything more
popular in Cuba than it is here?*

Me: *Yes, I guess so.*

Dr. Morales: *No guesses, Mr. Singer. And you also sound
surprised that I am in shape. You remark on this as though it
defied credibility, like a snake with tits.*

Me: *I'm surprised that you would have the time—that's all.*

Dr. Morales: *Well, as you know, it is not my custom to discuss
details of my personal life, but since you are so interested, I will
tell you that you happen to be right—I do go to the gymnasium.*

Me: *Every day?*

Dr. Morales: *No, this would be impossible with the routine I
follow. At my age the body must rest between these kinds of
workouts. So, then, what do I do? I go every other day. I fool
the body by letting it rest. That is essentially what one must
do—get the body ready for strenuous work and then fool it on a
regular basis. Sometimes, when the body is ready the next day,
I fool it even more completely by taking another day off.*

I couldn't help laughing as I pictured my invented Dr.
Morales resolutely shunning the gym every other day, pulling
the wool over his body's eyes. That image reminded me of his
hirsute face and his stiff smile as he told me the time was up,
and my own smile faded.

This is what happened in my pathetic version of real life:

Me: Have you noticed that I'm not late anymore? This
morning I was ten minutes *early!*

Dr. Morales: Yes, I did notice. You must know that this
would be very disruptive when the buzzer rings in the
middle of someone else's session, and I wonder if you
are not becoming jealous of the time I spend with other
patients.

SPRING GAVE WAY to summer, and the school year was out. I
had made no plans of any kind, "except to guarantee that you

will receive the only reward of which you believe yourself worthy after a hard year of teaching—that is to say, continued anxiety and depression," Dr. Morales predicted. He would have been completely right if a young woman who moved into the apartment below mine hadn't been so pleasant to me in the elevator. It was a rent-stabilized building on West End Avenue, right around the corner from the Coventry School—cheap and spacious, which you could still get back then, especially if you didn't mind living on the fringe of a bad neighborhood. The girl who moved in and exchanged elevator chat with me didn't herself invalidate Dr. Morales's prophecy, though at first I thought she might. She was an ur-American white-blond, white-bread buxom Lutheran farm girl from Minnesota. Her name was Janet. The farm, ten thousand acres, had been in her family for generations, and the family was rich. At seventy, her grandfather still worked the land, and she had disappointed him and her father by becoming a teaching assistant at a school for delinquent boys in St. Paul instead of marrying the handsome young Lutheran from the neighboring ten thousand acres. She was beginning on a master's degree in social work at Columbia starting in September, she told me. Maybe she could do some social work on me—she took such a strong interest in desperate cases.

After a while, my schemes to run into her, based on the kind of surveillance that only social cowards and pathological criminals practice, began to work too often. I had her mailroom and grocery-shopping schedules down pat, and she began to look worried as I kept popping up. In the middle of July Dr. Morales reversed roles and implied that he would terminate the treatment himself if I didn't cease stalking Janet. At least I've told you about it, I said. I've been honest. Either ask this victim of yours out on a real date or leave her alone, he said. I treat neurotics, not bushwhackers.

So I did ask her out, in the mail room, and she said it was

sweet of me, but I just wasn't the right kind of person for her, she didn't think. One last, inadvertent bit of surveillance proved her right and Dr. Morales's summer-neurasthenia forecast a couple of degrees wrong. I was coming back on the D train from a Yankees day game, feeling like the only person left in America for whom baseball was still a literal pastime, when at the 125th Street station, in the heart of Harlem, Janet got on with a very large, very black man in dashiki-hippie attire. He looked like Richie Havens's tough older brother. She didn't see me. I held a scorecard up in front of my face. At Columbus Circle, she and her boyfriend—yes, he was her boyfriend, or at least a boyfriend; holding on to a pole in the middle of the car, they had kissed once, passionately for so public and vehicular a locale, and I peeped at them over the scorecard, while the other passengers made a show of not noticing them at all—they got off and transferred to the uptown IRT, as I did, in order to go home, and I saw them go into a bar on Broadway at Ninety-third Street called Uncle Victor's.

I'd never been in there, never noticed the place particularly. The sign over the plate-glass window had the name of the establishment in brass-looking letters, with a jaunty, canted martini glass with two or three brassy bubbles hovering above it at either end. It was a joint, I'd always figured. Counting forlornly on the good times I'd had in bars during high school and college, I'd tried joints a few times early on in my career as an urban anomic, found the cost-benefit ratio prohibitive, and, luckily, wasn't the kind who tried to close the gap with more drinking. But now that I was feeling better, and because I was curious about the farmer's daughter's dive, a couple of nights later I went into Uncle Victor's, sat down at the bar, and asked the walrus-mustached black bartender for a beer.

It quickly became clear that it was a hookers' place. Five or six pretty young black women sat at the bar, sprinkled among other, more nondescript customers. Every now and then a burly middle-aged guy with a shaven head and wearing a Hawaiian shirt and brown Sansabelts would emerge from the obscurity of the tables in the rear and whisper something to one of the girls and they would leave. The guy, as I soon learned, was Uncle Victor; he was German, philosophical, and, one girl told me, hard-hearted. He took calls in the back from the business's real customers and dispatched its real wares on their sexpeditions. The first night I was there, two uniformed cops came in and sat in the shadows with Uncle Victor for fifteen minutes, the operation was that traditional and that brazen.

As July wore on and the sidewalks turned into griddles and I found myself with little on my hands but time, I spent a lot of it at Uncle Victor's, nursing beers for an hour, talking idly to a denizen or two. The girls favored Stax and Motown on the jukebox—Sam and Dave, Otis Redding, the Supremes, the Four Tops. In my sentimental isolation I decided that this was all inexpressibly sad music at its heart. I thought all music was sad then—even the up-tempo bluegrass stuff I'd kept listening to on the Columbia University radio station after arriving in New York after college, to say nothing of the genuinely sad folkie material warbled by the Baezes and Mitchells and Ian and Sylvias of a few years before, and to say even less of union tearjerkers like "Joe Hill," which just about liquefied me entirely, and which still do.

The bartender at Uncle Victor's, Arthur, pretended oblivion of what the politics of the day would have called the exploitation of his black sisters, gave them their Cokes and 7UPs while they waited for calls, and pressed quarters on the other customers to play the Dorsey and Sinatra records he'd levered in among the R&B classics when the jukebox-service guy made his rounds. I sometimes did some personal paperwork for him—a credit-card application, a license-renewal form—and we whiled away the afternoons and evenings.

The girls talked to me a lot, too—more out of boredom than hope or interest. They told me about their children—they seemed to have exactly one kid apiece—being raised in Pittsburgh or Buffalo or D.C. by Grandma, and showed me pictures of them. Some of the stuff that jumped out from around the edges of this space-filling conversation was harrowing: a boyfriend back home had taken a knife to one of them, leaving a scar like a section of necklace on her throat; another said a state trooper up in Albany had saved her from a kidnapping at gunpoint by a crazy trick who wanted to emancipate her. "That's the word he used," she said. "I was sitting in the front seat of this crazy man's car, with him holding a gun while he drove, and the trooper pulled him over for speeding. He aimed the gun at my head and told me he was going to kill me to save my soul while the trooper was getting out of his car, but he didn't. 'Cause here I am."

It reminded me of a black bar I had gone to a lot with some of the boys I played basketball with in high school, in Rockland, twenty miles north of the city on the Hudson River. Many of them had already started training for adult lives of real trouble, had already seen their family lives surrender to desertion and crime, had seen older brothers father children at seventeen and sisters go on welfare, had themselves already been arrested for stealing, had already used a knife. They didn't have doctors for fathers, as I did—had no fathers around at all, in most cases—and they wouldn't have a couch or a trust fund out of which to pay the man behind it when they grew up and made an effort to sort themselves out. Same with the girls at Uncle Victor's. They didn't have the means to live anything but the lives bequeathed to them by their childhoods.

One of the girls, Terry, was really beautiful—a modest Afro, clear skin, delicate features, as un-lamé'd and unbedizened in her way of dressing as her trade would allow. She's the one I talked to the most, partly because she got fewer whispers from

Uncle Victor, and I thought she liked me. "You don't go with girls for money, do you, Jake?" she once asked sadly over Wilson Pickett's Midnight Hour promises. I told her I didn't, and she said, "That's too bad for me, I guess." She put her hand on the small of my back and added, "You have a nice slender build to you."

That little touch almost changed my answer to Terry's invitation, as I told Dr. Morales the next morning. The heat was already oppressive, and the air conditioner in his office seemed to be returning the hot air it had sucked in from all the blathering patients that had come within its range. "Ah, yes, you want them to make the first movement," he said. "Even when the first movement is, as it so obviously was in this case, strictly business."

"You think she was just giving me a line?"

"And even when they do make the first movement, you are frightened, and you say no. You want to have been fucked in the past pluperfect but not to fuck in the present."

"You think I should have gone with her?"

"It would be more honest than this Olympian distance you maintain."

"I don't feel superior to anyone in that bar."

"A most interesting case of self-flattery through self-insult," Dr. Morales said, as the compressor in his ancient cooler kicked in. "Of course you are superior to them. They are whores, pimps, drunks, drug addicts, I have no doubt of it. Or you would be superior to them if you could untangle the knot of self-defeat into which you have tied your unconscious."

"I'm surprised that you haven't berated me for going to a hooker bar in the first place."

"Which means that you long to be disciplined. You want me to take the first step, as you want your friend Kerry to unzip your fly for you and use her hand like a tugboat to manually escort what she finds there into port. No, this eslumming of yours, for all I have said about it, is at least a beginning, of however a strange sort." As Dr. Morales spoke, his office descended in temperature from Saharan to sub-Saharan, thanks to the wheezing machine in the window. "I feel you are practicing."

A few days after that, I was sitting in Uncle Victor's when Janet came in with her dashiki friend. She smiled at me pleasantly and sat down at the far end of the bar. Arthur served them and got the boyfriend to play a Tony Bennett song on the jukebox. Five minutes later, Uncle Victor came up and whispered something to them both. Janet picked up her purse and left. Whew! Was Dashiki a recruiter for Uncle Victor? Was Janet doing hands-on social-work research? I imagined being her analyst. What tales of depravity she would tell. It would be a way of putting some vicarious spice in my life, to hear the kinds of miscegenation-threesome-bondage reports I imagined she could deliver. Was that the sort of material Morales was waiting for me to come up with? His voice got treacly when he asked me about sex. Was that what all psychoanalysts did, as common wisdom had it—batten on their patients' sexual secrets?

August came and Dr. Morales went. I weathered his absence and the weather in the cool dimness of Uncle Victor's. Terry and I became just good friends. Janet moved out, I realized when the name on her mailbox changed. I thought of Dr. Morales striding up and down on the burgher-sodden beaches of Truro, on Cape Cod, the traditional R&R haunt of New York shrinks, and hankering after the sugar-white sands of the Caribbean.

My father called in the middle of the month to tell me, stiffly, that he, too, was going on vacation—to junket cardiology meetings in England and France for three weeks. He wanted me to know I could reach him anytime through his office, in case anything should happen, without even beginning to suggest what "anything" might be. He asked about my health, and that was that: the longest conversation I'd had with him in more than a year. The bridge wasn't all the way down—a plank remained in place—but just when I was about to offer to drive up to Rockland to see him, he said he had to take an urgent call from the wife of one of his intensive-care patients.

He came home, as he informed me in another ultraterse phone conversation. I don't know what I was expecting—news that he'd gotten engaged to a duchess or a mademoiselle, interest in my version of August—but I got nothing and gave it back. I prepared course outlines for school. I practiced on the old Mexican nylon-string guitar that I'd bought from a college friend of mine. His name was Dave Leonard and we were in the same class at Bristol, the hard but bohemian little Quaker school in southern New Jersey which I'd attended over my father's Columbia-hopeful objections. Dave had an old Communist uncle who owned a house in the Berkshires but went south of the border every winter and hung around with the expatriate Socialist community down there and brought back wares to sell at considerable profit. The old man's house was in New Berkshire, Massachusetts, the nephew told me, and if I thought that guitar profiteering was a strange occupation for a Commie, I should see the house, which was old and beautiful and huge.

"Wildwood Flower," I played in my solo jam sessions. Doc Watson's "Brown's Ferry Blues," or as close as I could come to that nonpareil master of flat-picking. "Frenario," Phil Ochs's broadsides, Blind Reverend Gary Davis's version of "Got to Get to Heaven in Due Time," doing my best to roar it out like the old black minister I'd introduced at Bristol's 1963 Folk Festival—the apogee of the efforts of rootless, in my case literally motherless, young urban Americans to grab hold of the roots of others before turning to protest politics as another item of faith, often in combination with the music, especially union songs. How my neighbors felt about the amateur imitations of the CIO dirges like "Which Side Are You On?" and geriatric blues shouts and high, lonesome bluegrass plaints emanating from my apartment, they were too polite to tell me and I was too self-absorbed to worry about.

SEPTEMBER ARRIVED, and it was a great pleasure to go back into the classroom, despite the continuing dislike bordering on contempt that I felt for Coventry's headmaster, an upper-class Scotsman named W. C. H. Proctor—imported by the board of trustees to battle the adolescent excesses of the late sixties and early seventies—who had old-fashioned rules and athletic competitiveness occupying all the concern that he should have been giving to teaching and learning. And Dr. Morales was back, with, of all things, a tan. The short, bald, muscular, black-bearded Catholic Hispanic tyrant-genius of East Ninety-third Street took up the scourge he called the treatment right where he had left it, and by the time October, with its bitter Halloween memories, was over, I still wasn't sure how much if any improvement I had achieved for myself, but I knew I had made a lot of progress in my analysis of my analyst.

In fact, I could have written a case study about Dr. Morales. About how his habitual throat-clearing got louder as his boredom increased, about how he chronically expressed pity for the rich and famous, about how his voice turned cloyingly sweet when he asked me about sex. About how, as he was charging at my character with lance levelled, I could unhorse him by raising the conversational shield of investments. If I'd mentioned these observations to him, he would have replied, "Ahem! Respectively, your interest in my cough betrays on your part a repressed preoccupation with bodily functions, your envy of celebrities demonstrates a lack of self-respect, the lubricity you hear in my voice tells us more about your inhibitions than about my voyeurism, and you think I am obsessed with money because you earn so little."

On the one-year anniversary of the treatment, I told him that I'd passed up another chance to sleep with a woman, this time a respectable one, a teaching colleague, because she smelled funny. He said, "Now, Mr. Singer, as you should perhaps know by now, this was your own odor that you detected. I do not refer to the odor of your body but to the way in which you transformed your continuing disgust with your sexual appetites into a physical stench and then attributed this stench to this woman." Dr. Morales's accent, thick to begin with, stiffened further as he whipped it with the extra enthusiasm of an interpretation he found especially impressive. It wouldn't have surprised me to see the *r*'s in "refer" roll past the couch I was lying on.

"I didn't say 'stench,' " I said. "I didn't say she smelled bad, just a bit odd."

" 'A bit odd,' 'a bit odd,' " said Dr. Morales. "Why have you not told me this before that you are actually British and not American?"

That skirmish developed into a separate war, over Dr. Morales's assertion that I held his English in contempt. I did not. His English was far superior to that of most of the teachers in the English Department of the Coventry Preparatory School for Boys—to say nothing of that of my students. Superior in clarity, grammar, and economy—to say nothing of forcefulness of expression. Much later in what he called "our work," I was able to say calmly to Dr. Morales that it was his own insecurity that led him to make such an accusation against me, but at this point I was just beginning to learn his tricks, and it was only with agitation that I started to suggest that I wasn't the only one in that office at the rear of the top floor of a brownstone just off Fifth Avenue who was capable, on a Monday, Wednesday, or Friday morning from seven-thirty to eight-twenty, of tarring himself with his own brush.

SAMIRA LAUGHED. I was walking around in my bathrobe, doing an imitation of Dr. Morales touting triple-tax-free municipals—"Eet ees as eef the government were eessuing to you licenses wheech permeet you to rob eet"—and she was lying in bed, now wearing, unbuttoned, the white shirt that, along with slacks and a sports coat, I'd hung over the back of a chair for my appointment with Morales on Monday morning. "Speaking of money, how can you afford to see an analyst three times a week?" Samira asked in her slow, dreamy, quiet voice. "I mean, on a schoolteacher's salary and all. And you paid for dinner with a credit card. Are you rich or something?"

"I can't afford it. Except I can, in a way. This place is rent-controlled, for one thing, and also I've been living like a monk. Well, until tonight, ha-ha. The credit card is left over from when I was on better terms with my father. He got one for me tied to his account, but I hardly ever use it. Also, I do a lot of tutoring in the summers, and I have this small trust fund that I could use that my mother left me when she died. And even though my father and I don't get along, I guess I could always go to him."

"You know, you don't have to be so nervous," Samira said. "Why do you go on seeing this shrink if he's so weird?"

"I don't know. It's as if I have to keep going back to make sure he's real."

"Is he helping you?"

"It's hard to tell."

"I feel like I'm talking to the Invisible Man or something," Samira said. "Come back over here where I can at least see you." She raised herself up on her elbows, and the shirt fell open. Blue-white light from the streetlamp outside my window on West End Avenue fell across her.

"Oh, Jake, please don't look at me," she said, laughing again.

"But you're beautiful," I said.

"But one of my breasts is a little larger than the other."

"Terrible!"

"And they're both too big. You know—the pill and all."

"One outrage after another," I said.

"I really think you can relax now." She got up, took the shirt off, and let it drop to the floor. "By the way, do you have any cake or cookies around here?"

"I'm afraid not," I said.

"Nothing to be afraid of," she said. She sat down on the edge of the bed. "I'll manage."

I went and stood in front of her. She reached up and pushed the robe off my shoulders and turned me around. "Tell him about this," she said.

"AND WHY ARE you smiling so broadly this morning, Mr. Singer?" Dr. Morales asked the next day as I stretched out on the gray leatherette couch with the gray leatherette jelly-roll headrest. He had ushered me in with his customary grin and his ironical-looking demi-bow and had then sat down in the gray leatherette chair, where he started fiddling with his answering machine. There we were, washed up again on those two tiny barren sister atolls, about to cast our lines into the Great Sea of the Unconscious.

"Well, I met someone over the weekend," I said. "She's very nice."

"Good," Dr. Morales said.

Silence.

Then: "Did you fuck her?" The question had the honeyed tone characteristic of his sexual interrogations.

"I beg your pardon?"

"Please take your penis out from under the English bowling hat, Mr. Singer," Dr. Morales said tiredly. He was still fussing with the machine, which suddenly emitted five seconds' worth of backward Chipmunkese. "Did you fuck her?"

"Bowler," I said, "and as a matter of fact I did."

"And did you as a matter of fact enjoy it?"

"Greatly."

"Greatly."

"Is there an echo in here? What's wrong with 'greatly,' for Christ's sake? I enjoyed it a lot."

"Better. How many times did you fuck her?"

"Two or three. I don't know. Don't you even want to know her name? Don't you—"

"All in good time, Mr. Singer. You and I are not on a date at the opera. Here we do not have to comment on how very like a camel is the cloud overhead or raise our pinkie when we drink our tea. Did she have a climax?"

"I don't know. She said she did. Jesus, this is like a high-school locker room."

"Precisely. It is lamentable but true that that is the last time for many people to discuss these important matters. Now, what kinds of noises did she make?"

"*What?*"

"Perhaps you do not know because you have these episodes of deafness."

"Now listen. You can't—"

"No, *you* listen. Mr. Singer. It is *you* who cannot. You cannot bring yourself to acknowledge that you think in such terms and to speak frankly to me about this sexual experience. You are ashamed, and so you force me to interrogate you, so that you can express the shock that you feel toward yourself. Not only do you claim that you do not have to sit down to move your bowels like the rest of us poor mortals, you claim not to move them at all, and then you react with disgust after compelling me to move them for you."

"A neat trick, you must admit. And why are you associating sexuality with defecation, by the way?"

"So now we have swimming into the session the red herring of your alleged humor, followed by a touch of turnaround is fair play. 'Love has pitchèd his mansion in/The place of excrement,' as your esteemed Butler Yeets has reminded us so musically, is it not?"

We sparred a bit longer, and then Dr. Morales resumed his extraction of graphic details. After the most deviant of these specifics, which he received in reverential silence, I added, "And she told me to make sure to tell you about it."

Dr. Morales awoke from his trance with conviction renewed. "You see, you see," he said. "She knows what is important. She and I are on the same frequency." He added, forlornly, "So you have discussed our work with this woman. Later, we shall have to analyze why you have broken our agreement." He was always doing this—adding another waltz to our therapeutic dance card, as if he wanted the music never to end. "Now, would you tell me what positions you used?"

I left the session feeling like a porn potboiler that had been thumbed through by some creep in search of the good parts.

SAMIRA HAD SAT down at a table with me in the cafeteria of the Metropolitan Museum. It was a mild, dreary November Sunday, with wind-driven rain streaming out of the sky over Central Park. The weather had herded thousands into the museum. The hubbub depressed me even more than waiting out the afternoon with the NFL in my apartment would have, and it was a measure of my mood that I didn't notice the small, beautiful olive-skinned girl with a sketch pad sitting nearby until she asked me to pass the sugar.

"Oh, please, don't watch," she said. "I have an awful sweet tooth. I could probably grow crystals in this stuff." Her speech was soft and languid, as if the words themselves were coalescing one at a time.

"Yeah, well," I said. I looked up. "As a matter of fact I have a sweet tooth myself." *The clam opens his shell, eh, Mr. Singer?*

"Small world," she said dreamily, and she gave me a solar smile.

A regular museum pickup, as I recalled such things—except that she started it off, and her conversation's veil of pretense was ultrathin. What did you come to see? she asked me. I don't know—nothing in particular. The Vermeers look good on a day like this—all that sunlight pouring in the windows. I gave a private word of thanks to my art-history professors in college, and a fainter one to my father, who took me on short, regular—almost militarized—visits to the Metropolitan after my mother died. But Vermeer is so calm and buttoned up, don't you think? Samira said. The Baroque stuff here isn't that great, but still at least there's passion and movement. But it's pretty theatrical, I said. *Now you are throwing her out of the bed even before she is in it and feels your chilly feet.*

And so it went. Her name was Samira Khoury. She was born in Lebanon and was brought here when she was six. Her family was Christian in background, but they lived in a Muslim neighborhood in Beirut, and she couldn't say which was worse—the cold, eyes-averted hatred of their adult neighbors or the stones and curses of the children. I wondered later if living through such hostility as a child hadn't helped her become the composed, often nearly detached person she seemed to me in the brief glimpse I had of her. I also imagined that so much early disorder might have steered her toward art. And it was private disorder as well as public. Samira's father, a wealthy doctor in Beirut, anticipated the chaos that was lying in wait for his country and uprooted himself and his family and fled to the United States. But he hadn't anticipated and couldn't handle the despair that lies in wait for all émigrés. He got a job as a lab technician here and stayed in it, and he and Samira's mother lived their lives—demolished lives, I gathered from Samira's tone—in Wayne, New Jersey, in a tract house.

This city. Cuban psychoanalysts, pompous Scottish headmasters, Hungarian superintendents too busy polishing the brass to fix the boiler, fierce-looking mustachioed Afghans running grimy delis on Tenth Avenue, Senegalese street-corner umbrella sellers, British TV-commercial directors, island girls playing sweetly with the children and despising the parents, Sikh cabdrivers short on English, old Yiddishers inching along the streets carrying plastic bags with cut-rate bruised fruit in them. Sexually intrepid Lebanese-born artists.

Samira must have been talented—four years on scholarship at Carnegie-Mellon—but when I asked if I could see her drawings *(Ah, we are back in business, Mr. Singer)*, she said, "Oh, please, don't even ask. I'd be too embarrassed." Very demure she was in her manner, and very alluring in her black skirt and sweater and red tights. She was doing freelance catalogue work for Honeybee, and she lived in Chelsea with another hopeful artist—from Turkey, of all places—and her roommate's boyfriend, a musician from Rio. She was going to take a course at the Art Students League at night, starting in January, if her father could lend her the money.

When she said no about the sketch pad, I said, "Well, then, would you have dinner with me instead?" *Olé, Mr. Singer!*

I never got a chance to tell the real Dr. Morales any of this. He missed his chance to cough through a description of walking back through the park with Samira, or how lively she seemed in the sharp rain and among the fallen leaves and dutiful dog walkers. He lost the opportunity to needle me about my relentlessly self-deprecating dinner conversation when Samira and I met at a restaurant on Broadway in the evening, and about how I tried not to hear her when she said she didn't really want to go back to her place afterward. Didn't I mention that my apartment was on West End?

No building of narrative tension for you, Dr. Morales, from Samira's telling me she found me very attractive. No trembling like a pointer when she adds that I can easily find out *how* attractive, as she is wearing nothing under her cute short tan suede skirt. She said all this as pliantly and informatively as an exotic stewardess offering in-flight services on an excellent Pacific Rim airline.

No, he missed all that, and I never got a chance to fill him in on it. The affair was a short one, and Dr. Morales and I spent the remainder of it shouting at each other like grade-schoolers in a playground. I'm rubber, you're glue. Whatever you say bounces off me and sticks to you.

ON THE TUESDAY after I first met Samira at the museum, I took her to a Coventry football game up at Baker Field at the northern tip of Manhattan. It's Columbia's football field, and they let Coventry use it for weekday games. The rain that had been falling since Sunday let up as we arrived, and a wind not yet cold but promising winter started blowing out of the northwest. Pewter clouds raced along below the leaden sky. I could hear the water coursing through Spuyten Duyvil, and the Henry Hudson Bridge vibrated with heavy traffic to and from the Bronx. Like so many ordinary activities in New York, the football game seemed to me dwarfed, improbable, and precarious, as if the skies might open and a Jehovian hand reach down and pluck all us up, a huge wave might crash in from the river, the bridge fall down.

"Would you look at their *be*hinds!" Samira muttered. We were standing on the sidelines and watching the boys flop around happily in the mud. "They're so beautiful," she sighed. She took my arm and adhered to my side. The question of how fully dressed she might be drove anomie from my mind. "I don't think I could ever be a teacher with kids like that. Or maybe when I was sixty-five." The Coventry student spectators, for their part, kept sidling up to us on one pretext or another, for a closer examination of this chick and a teacher of theirs in the unfamiliar role of human being. I ended up enjoying myself.

On the way back downtown, we stopped at a Middle Eastern grocery. Then Samira went back with me to my apartment and cooked couscous and lamb stew for us. In the kitchen she was careful and neat. I helped her, and we kept on bumping or backing into each other. "Sorry." "Excuse me." The meal was excellent, but we got up from the table in the middle of it, and by the time we might have gone back, the food would have long since been cold.

"Do you want to talk while we're waiting?" Samira asked. She was sitting up and gazing out the window as the dark gathered and the streetlamp on West End waxed full. I lay beside her.

"You're a good cook," I said. "Who does the cooking in your family?"

"My father now. My mother used to, in Beirut, but here he has so much time on his hands."

"He isn't trying to get accredited as a doctor?"

"I think he has given up. It's so sad. I hate to go home at all anymore. Maybe you and I are birds of a feather. It must be hard for you, with no mother and being on such bad terms with your father."

"It is," I said. "Morales must have done it—passed some test or something to be a doctor here—but then he's a maniac."

"Morales, Morales."

"You're right. I won't get started."

"You know, I had to call my father yesterday, because the first payment of the course I wanted to take is due soon. He doesn't have the money and he was ashamed to tell me."

"That's sad. Is this teacher really that good?"

"He's very good, and he also happens to be very attractive. I'm going to seduce him, if I ever take his class."

"Sex, sex."

"Everyone has their own way of changing the subject, I guess. Sometimes I think that painting and sex are all I let myself care about."

"And sweets," I said. "Which reminds me." From under the bed I brought out a package of chocolate cookies.

"Ooh, look," Samira said. "How nice of you."

"You know, I could lend you that money," I said.

"Oh, no. I couldn't accept that. You hardly even know me."

"I know you well enough that I can't see you skipping town exactly," I said. "It's only a loan. I have to go into my trust soon anyway, for Morales. All it will take is a little juggling, and Morales will just have to wait a couple of extra days for his fee. I think he'll understand."

"OF COURSE I understand," Dr. Morales said the next morning when, about fifteen minutes into the session, I told him I had lent Samira some money and wouldn't have his payment until Friday. "I understand that you have finally worked up your courage to sleep with a whore and now you have to pay her."

"Hey, hold on a second. I can't believe—"

"I am on the moon, Mr. Singer. I am on the moon—"

"I'll say," I muttered.

"What?"

"Nothing."

"I am on the moon looking at the earth through my shiny
new telescope. I ezoom in on New York City and then on the
West Side. What do I see? What do I see? I see a man having
sex with a woman. And then in the morning through my telescope I see the man giving the woman a check as she is leaving.
Now, you must tell me what interpretation I am to put on
these events."

"But this is nutty. You're not on the moon. You're here,
in this office with me, and I'm telling you it wasn't like that at
all. There was no arrangement about money or anything like
that."

"Did she know you had any money, Mr. Singer?"

"No. Yes, actually. She asked how I could be a schoolteacher and pay for psychoanalysis at the same time, but—"

"So she established that you had at least some money.
There are all kinds of whores, Mr. Singer, as you have discovered for yourself during the summer—including those who do
not know they are whores."

"Whores don't give back the money they're paid."

"You are so certain that this woman will repay this
money?"

"Of course she will."

"I wish I could share your confidence. Perhaps you would
like to discuss why you are so offended by the suggestion that
you might have paid for sex. It has happened once or twice in
the world before, as you know, without this sort of anger and
shame."

"No, damn it—you are the one who is angry," I said. I
didn't know where the idea had come from, and I wasn't even
sure what I meant.

"And so now you put on the harmor of rage in order to re-sist the—"

"No, *you* are the one who is enraged, and *you* are the one who feels like a whore. I pay you, your patients pay you, for this kind of relationship. Now I come and tell you for the first time in more than a year that I'll be two days late with your goddam fee because I lent the money to someone else, and you get so angry that you construe my relationship with this person—the first nice thing that has happened to me in quite a while, I might add—the same way you secretly construe your patients' relationships with you. Angry and jealous—you are jealous. The money is only the paper on the surface. You know I'm responsible about your fee. You've been *slighted*. Your cus-tomer has put someone else before you."

There was a long silence, after which Dr. Morales, sound-ing distant—sepulchral, as if he'd passed over and were trying to communicate with the living—said, "In my judgment, Mr. Singer, you are projecting your view of me as a prostitute onto me, because you wish to disown it. No, I am sorry. I am lower than a prostitute. For you have paid the prostitute. That is my judgment, which, of course, you have already made sure to dis-miss if not ridicule, this morning and frequently in our work together. But let us assume, for the sake of argument, which is after all what you so often desire to substitute for analysis—let us assume that you are correct, and that it is I who is angry and jealous, that it is I who is trying to disavow his feelings of defilement. Let us assume that you are right. Then my question is: Of what benefit is your interpretive triumph to you? What sort of ground have you gained with this counteroffensive, as you no doubt view it?"

Silence again.

"I shall tell you what you gain by such measures," Dr. Morales went on. "You become impervious to change. If you confront me, you do not have to suffer the pain of confronting yourself. This is *your* analysis, not mine, but your knowledge of your conflicts and your mastery of them will grow by neither an inch nor an ounce if you pursue these tactics. If you busy your mind with a war against me, you will never make peace with yourself."

"Well, then, if I'm incapable of doing analysis, of making any headway here, then maybe—"

"I did not say that, Mr. Singer. Perhaps saddest of all, and most insulting and demeaning to me, is that you refuse to admit the value of what you have managed despite yourself to accomplish here. Your failure to pay my fee on time is one aspect of this denial."

"And your rigidity about the money shows a pretty shaky sense of self-respect," I said. "Am I catching on? Listen. I'll cash in one of the CDs after school today and pay you on Friday. I'm sorry I missed the payment, but I really don't see that it's—"

"And the last thing you will admit is that this new sexual liaison of yours, whatever its nature, would have been out of the question for you when we started our work."

"You're taking the credit?"

"How did it come about?"

"You were too preoccupied with the endocrinology of it to find out."

"Please try not to be a smart alex, Mr. Singer. How did it come about?"

"Aleck. I met her in the museum on Sunday and asked her out to dinner."

"Would you have asked her out to dinner under the same circumstances a year ago? You do not see that— Why must you cash a CD? You will lose some of the interest." Dr. Morales's voice had suddenly lost its otherworldliness.

"The trust fund is in CDs. Five of them, ten thousand dollars each."

"And what other instruments do you have?"

"Instruments? Investments? None. I've told you before. It's all in CDs."

"Surely you are joking! For how many years has it been this way?"

"Ten—since I turned twenty-one. I just roll them over."

"Now, really, Mr. Singer, you must diversify. Do you have any idea how much money you have already lost? Perhaps we may talk about this in the next session. Our time is up for today."

And a good thing, too. I might have got up and hit him if it had gone on a second longer. Next session, next life, I said to myself as I walked out.

I ASKED SAMIRA if she had ever been with women. Yes, she said with a drowsy laugh. Why did I want to know? A man and a woman? I asked. Yes, but they hadn't done much more than fool around. Older men? Yes, she said—you. She turned over to face me. I guess she thought I was taking a straightforward midnight sexual history, as new lovers often do. But in fact the sordidness of the session with Morales in the morning had been working within me like slow-acting venom.

"Have you ever been with two men?" I asked.

"One time."

"Did you ever have sex in front of other people?"

"Yes, once, when I was seventeen. But, really, we were just kids."

I went on for a few more minutes. The intimacy in Samira's voice gave way to puzzlement and then anxiety. I began to feel as Morales must when he roasts his patients on the spit of his own prurience. Finally Samira had enough. "I don't do those things anymore," she said. "And I don't want to talk about them anymore. This is mean."

In my mind, I said, *No, of course you do not wish to continue our discussion of the way you have chosen this unbridled sexual behavior to punish your father for his failure.* The idea made me feel brilliant, and horribly lonely.

After a tense silence, Samira asked me, as if in contrition, whether we could spend the weekend together. She seemed now not even faintly a gift from sex heaven or a member of some serene rescue squad or exactly what I'd been waiting for, but thoroughly and alarmingly human. I said I was going to have a lot of papers to grade, and I would call her. I didn't get to sleep until just before dawn. I'd have been surprised if Samira got any sleep at all.

When the alarm went off, I heard Samira moving around in the kitchen. I went to the closet and put on my bathrobe, and when I turned around she was standing there, dressed, holding her yellow parka. "That was too weird last night," she said. "What happened?"

"I'm not awake yet," I said. "I don't know what to say."

"That's exactly right," Samira said, with tears in her eyes. "And when you figure it out it will probably be too late. You could be so nice, you know?" She turned and left, and the small sounds of the apartment—the ticking of a clock, the frigid wind sighing at the windows, the hiss of the radiators, a siren from the street—came back as if they'd been switched on.

I stumbled into the kitchen. On the counter next to the stove, on top of a paper napkin with doodles on it, I found the check I'd given her, ripped to small pieces. I threw the scraps away and noticed that the doodles on the napkin were not doodles but a drawing. A drawing of me—almost but not quite a caricature. It showed a rail-thin young man with coarse straight black hair like a shoe brush, a big straight nose, big circles under his eyes, standing in front of a blackboard and gesturing expansively, almost frantically, with both hands. In the foreground was a row of ovals—the backs of kids' heads in a classroom, like eggs in a carton except for a cowlick here and there and one oval leaning over at a seventy-degree angle: asleep. It was a wonderful piece of work for something so offhand. Every line showed energy and discipline and wit. It was affectionate, in contrast to the figure it depicted, who looked as if he couldn't care about much more than the sound of his own words.

With dismay, I found myself rehearsing what I might say to Morales about the rejected check: *See? So much for your commercial theory.* Or did it paradoxically prove him right? And the drawing. I held it in my hands and imagined myself showing it to him. *See? See?* And so, I realized, I would be going back to him after all. I was still practicing, as he put it when he told me he had no objection to my fraternizing with real whores. The rehearsal with Samira as an unfortunate walk-on had been a disaster, a flop before the production even got to town. What a shame! She was terrific. But evidently, for me it was still Dr. Morales or nobody.

WHEN I WAS in high school in Rockland, I got myself into a certain amount of trouble. I hung around with a bunch of kids mostly from working-class families, and we stole some records and knocked over garbage cans at night and crashed parties and drove too fast and boasted about all of it. I also got into some pretty serious fights. First I lost them. Then I learned to start them by surprise when they seemed inevitable, and won more than I lost. Then I learned they were hardly ever inevitable, and I learned how to avoid them without looking like the coward that, strangely enough, I wasn't. But not before I lost an adult incisor to a runt named Jimmy Evans, who surprised me with a left hook before I could surprise him with anything, and two weeks later had two ribs broken by a black-Irish kid named Gallagher from Clarkstown in a bar across the state line from New Jersey after a basketball game.

My father had decided to send me to the pretty tough public school in Rockland because he didn't want me to have things too easy, so maybe to return the favor, and to get his full attention, I was trying to make it tough for him, too. Anyway, I spent a certain amount of time in Rockland police headquarters, waiting for my father to come and get me and listening as the officer who had caught me uprooting mailboxes or just staggering down the street singing Dion songs expressed surprise that a kid from my background would be involved in this sort of thing. My father, who had to raise me alone, didn't need the grief I was giving him, the cop said, and he warned that the next time charges might be brought against me.

This period of my life has risen and fallen in my memory like a tide. When I was thirty-two it reached flood stage, because there I was, back among adolescent boys—this time as a teacher—and because I was seeing Dr. Morales, which forced me to return to such autobiographical nexuses like a police dog being repeatedly led back to a particular, suspicious-looking suitcase. When I mentioned this analogy to Dr. Morales, he said, "Mr. Singer, I am disappointed that after one year of our work together you are still capable of feeling so subservient to me. Now you are a dog and I am leading you around on a lish."

"Leash," I said. "And you sound more gratified than disappointed."

"And after one year you are also still trying to turn over the table," Dr. Morales said.

Once, near the end of my wild adolescent career, the Rockland police chief grabbed me by the collar and dragged me from the broken-down bench where I was sitting and into his dishevelled office and yelled at me for almost half an hour using language so foul that it actually shocked me. He looked electrified with anger, with his short red hair bristling up like a brush, his face red-hot, spit flying. Throughout this horribly exciting castigation, I kept my eyes on a small photograph on the captain's desk, of him and two small red-haired boys, all grinning as if they were plugged in. I wondered whether his wife was red-haired also, and why she wasn't in the picture.

("You were thinking maybe she was dead, too, like *your* mother," Dr. Morales said.)

The police captain was genuinely angry, but I think he was also trying to shake me up and scare me—to inoculate me against real trouble by giving me a dose of what it would be like. When I hazarded this speculation to Dr. Morales, I sensed a great golden glow of agreement emanating from him toward the back of my poor screwed-up head. The glow intensified when I went on to say that by messing around I was trying to shake up and scare my father—to shake him loose from the effects of my mother's death, ten years earlier, a tragedy that I was sure had frozen her into a tyranny of virtue and beauty in my father's mind. The Morales Effect nearly sizzled when I concluded that I pushed my father for my sake more than his. So that the clock in the front hall would tick less loudly for me as well as for him, I added, to myself. So that he and I might have had conversations instead of transactions, so that our fishing trips and museum outings and family visits might have been jolted from duty into comfort. Maybe even so that he might have found someone to confide in and thereby find his way back to me.

("You know," Dr. Morales said, sounding for a moment more like Emerson than Batista, "duty is not an ignoble motive.")

It hadn't worked. My father would ask me why I'd done what I'd done and I'd say I didn't know and wait for him to get angry, and I'd feel my isolation grow even greater as weariness rather than rage crossed his face. He would lecture me, perhaps take away my driving privileges or tear up a pair of tickets to a baseball or football game, and that would be that. We'd resume our diplomatic relations. I came to see that my misbehavior and his reaction to it were a distant early warning of the estrangement between us, which deepened when I didn't follow in his footsteps through Columbia, when I went out with girls he considered in one way or another unsuitable, when I refused to apply to medical school, when I dodged the Vietnam draft by becoming a teacher, first in a Quaker boarding school in Bucks County and then at Coventry.

And I have to admit that I messed around at least partly just because it was fun, by that hormonally deranged adolescent-boy definition of fun. I remember that I loved to cruise slowly down Blauvelt Avenue all by myself at three in the morning, half gone on Schaefer beer, and challenge myself to close my eyes for ten seconds. I'd try it. It was exhilarating, it was like being a ghost—it was, in my drunken state, the most fragile, thrilling bliss. I always opened my eyes well before the ten seconds were up. I always stopped short of the disaster I was courting. I never had an accident. And I never got into serious crimes or misdemeanors.

("Coming to me was like opening your eyes," Dr. Morales once said. "In both cases, whether you knew it or not, you were about to kill yourself.")

Only one or two of my friends sank into grave irresponsibility or outright crime—most went on to be roofers or truck drivers or whatnot, got married young, incurred a family to complain about and to keep them in line. They were smarter than I was—they knew they needed something.

Those were the white boys. I was eighth man on a twelve-man varsity basketball team that consisted of nine black kids and three white kids, and I saw firsthand that most of the black kids were truly desperate men in the making—men who were counterparts of the ladies plying their trade at Uncle Victor's. All but one were over eighteen, one of them had a chronic ulcer, two were arrested and sent to jail for auto theft, one was expelled in the middle of his senior year for hitting a teacher over the head with a chair, another had had Bell's palsy from the age of fourteen from a knife wound to the face, another told me one night, through streaming tears, when we were drinking in a black bar called Chick 'n' Charlie's, that his father was his uncle: not his mother's husband's brother but his mother's. These kids' insubordination and anarchy were a given in the school—something you could count on—but they all had great respect for our coach, Frank Hayes, an old guy from South Carolina with a thatch of red hair going gray who shuffled around scratching his crotch and spoke very quietly. His wife was in a wheelchair.

("This is why he scratched his genitals," Dr. Morales said. "Prostatitis or urethritis.")

He was going nowhere and had nothing to lose, but he loved the game and he liked the boys and they knew it, and he was philosophical about them.

The start of basketball practice in my fourth year at Coventry got me talking to Dr. Morales about Coach Hayes for the first time—about how kind he was, how pleased when we won, how sympathetic when we lost or screwed up. "We wanted to do well for him," I said. "Even the black kids, who didn't care about anything else." I concluded, "I wish all authority figures were like that."

"No, you do not," Dr. Morales said.

"Of course not," I said. "Please forgive me—I should have known better."

"You have told me more than once how exciting was that policeman's rage, how you hoped for your father's wrath. You wish authority figures to be like the captain, to be like me, to be like this: *Spare me your sarcasm, Mr. Singer!*" Then, resuming his usual oleaginous, insinuating tone, he said, "I am so sorry, but our time for the session is up. I shall see you on Monday."

IT'S FUNNY WHAT happens when you're in psychoanalysis—there are periods when your life takes on the eerie, overdetermined quality of an analytical session, or of the dream you recount in that session. It's as though someone were pulling all the ragged threads of your days into a tight, dark pattern. Conversations echo other conversations, gestures in the present parody gestures from the past, you meet five hairy accountants the same day, you develop a toothache while watching a movie about a dentist. Your life turns into something like fiction as you bounce from the couch to the allegedly real world and back again, trying to interpret the earliest chapters of your childhood and your work in progress in a way that will lead the later chapters, the ones yet to be written, toward a happier ending than they might have had without such relentless exegeses of the psyche. For me the two weeks following my recollections of Coach Hayes and Chick 'n' Charlie's took on the aspect of a precocious, callow writers'-workshop short story—so loaded and worked with resonating themes and images that I'd never have cared about it or even believed it if I'd been reading it in a book.

The evening after Dr. Morales's outburst, Coventry played its first basketball game of the season, against Collegiate. On defense, a big Hispanic kid playing center for their team filled the lane like concrete. He could move and jump, too. He was the best high-school basketball player I'd ever seen. At the half, Junior—that's what the other Collegiate players called him—had blocked seven of our shots and had scored twenty-three points. I scrimmaged with the Coventry varsity sometimes, and during games I sat at the end of the bench; from there I always had a good view of the headmaster, W. C. H. Proctor, a few rows back in the stands. And in that game I could see jealousy strike a green spark in his usually dull eyes. Only sports and challenges to his authority—in other words, competition, of one kind or another—livened Proctor's expression, and never pleasantly. Well, he could also brim over in the presence of any sort of sacrifice for the school—grimaces of pain from a quarterback hobbling off a muddy football field, a notable contribution to the alumni fund.

Our own ace ghetto scholarship ringer, Walter Cooper, was getting pissed off about Junior. I could see it in *his* expression, which generally showed nothing but distrust or dissociation. I could tell he was getting angry by the look of amusement he wore—I'd noticed it when I stole the ball from him in practice or faked him out, and it often preceded an "accidental" trip by him, or an overaggressive screen. And I could also tell because I knew what a basketball game felt like when there was trouble coming. I'd learned some of my best fighting lessons—especially Anticipation 101 and Being Elsewhere 102—on a basketball court. It wasn't a good sign that Walter continued to wear his expression of faint amusement as Jim Galgano, the coach, harangued the team at halftime, stupidly singling him out for not driving to the basket—as if he could drive, with Junior blocking up the middle.

A few minutes into the third quarter, still wearing that quizzical expression, Walter dribbled the ball into the key, turned and backed into Junior, and wheeled around to shoot, literally under Junior's nose. Another blocked shot, but this time Junior paid for it. Walter's left elbow flew up and hit the other boy very hard beneath the jaw. Something came out of his mouth as he landed, and he sank to his knees with his hands over his face and blood welling through his fingers. What had fallen to the floor turned out to be the front third of Junior's tongue.

In those days, a gung-ho Coventry-alumnus doctor attended our games, and he rushed out onto the court, where Junior remained in an attitude of prayer, and took over. He

got the boy over to Mount Sinai, and I heard later from
Hiram Soto, who was in one of my English classes and lived
near Junior in Spanish Harlem, that they sewed the tongue
back on but that part of it became necrotic—"One side rotted
out," Hiram said—leaving Junior unimpeded in English but a
post-traumatic Castilian in Spanish. I don't know how that
could be.

When I arrived at the Coventry School, Proctor had been
headmaster for five years. Those who oversaw the school in the
mid-sixties, watching in fear and envy as the boys' hair grew
longer, their nights later, their ties louder, their test scores
lower, and, with increasing frequency, their pupils as wide as
pineapple slices, must have liked what they saw in this Scottish
autocrat. Tall, solid, straight as a post, always dressed in a
blazer, white shirt, striped tie, and gray slacks. Bald but with a
fringe of close-cropped iron-gray hair. Regular features, ruddy
complexion, aristocratic British idiom and accent, with the
faintest hint of a burr. Water Closet Head, the boys called him,
and there *was* something functional about the way he oper-
ated, reflexively snatching baseball caps off the heads of those
he caught wearing them indoors, speaking in clipped apho-
risms, prescribing fresh air for everything from acne to the
death of a parent, taking low-comic roles in school plays as if it
were a brand-new hilarity every time.

Proctor put me on the Scholarship Committee because I
could play basketball. It was OK with me. My depression may
have been less abysmal and my anxiety less high, but still, after
the liaison with Samira which I had ruined, and after three
years of teaching and going on two years of emotional vivisec-
tion on the slablike couch of Dr. Morales, I had very little in
my life besides him and the school. So I threw myself into
teaching like someone who chronically travels in order to
avoid being at home. The winter of my second year, I had
started going up to Harlem and East Harlem and the South

Bronx with Galgano to scout the boys who had applied for scholarships. Proctor, like nearly every headmaster in New York of that era, spoke only of moral obligation and democracy as he searched the bare Pine Sol'ed halls and mean gyms of the understaffed, broken-desk intermediate and high schools up there for kids who would bring his school athletic glory—black and Dominican and Puerto Rican kids who had earned glowing testimonials from their coaches while managing to compile what looked like decent academic records. We'd hunt them up, lure them downtown, grade them easy, and cheer them loudly, and then send them on to college, only to hear, all too often, that they'd dropped or flunked out.

"NATURALLY, WE ARE all concerned about what happened on Saturday night at the game," Proctor said at the next meeting of the Scholarship Committee, the following Tuesday after school. The five of us sat around his baronial mahogany desk, which matched the wainscoting he'd had installed in his huge office. The office was on the top floor and had views north to the George Washington Bridge and west over the Hudson—the whitecaps on this crisp January day looked like sparkling white trim on a vast blue uniform—and to me it all seemed foolishly majestic for a headmaster. "We must give Walter the benefit of the doubt, I think," Proctor continued, "and conclude that the injury was inflicted unintentionally."

"He threw the elbow on purpose, there's no doubt about it," I said.

"We can't know that," Proctor said sharply. His face went red.

"I know it," I said. "He sent two kids into the hospital last year, when he was only in the ninth grade."

"They were trying to rob him," someone else said. "It was in the principal's letter."

"His family is all broken apart, his mother is an addict and so is his brother, and he's angry," I said. "That was in his file, too. I think he's a time bomb. He's almost two years older than anyone else in his class—he shouldn't be here."

There was silence for a full thirty seconds. I'd been such a quiet creature for so long—frightened and nervous, except in class, which was the only place I could relax.

"What do you know about it?" Mac Preston finally said. He was a math teacher with a trust fund of his own—far bigger than mine and of more patrician provenance—but he had a yearning to be rough and proletarian. This was the early seventies, so the kids loved him even more than they ordinarily would have for his denunciations of their privileged lives.

"I know a lot," I said. "I went to school with kids like Walter, and I played basketball with them."

"Is that right?" Mac said.

"And I scrimmage with the team and I guard Walter a lot and he guards me, and I know an elbow like that from him is no accident. Plus he's in my class. And the interview with him last winter—we were all here. If he said six words besides yes and no, I didn't hear them."

"Well, of course, I had some reservations about Walter myself," Proctor said.

"But don't you remember?" I blurted out. "After the interview you said he was a fine, composed young man and we could offer him an opportunity to rise above his circumstances."

Silence again, this time even louder. Proctor's eyes were blazing. "I did not know I was speaking before the FBI," he said. "Do you fancy yourself some sort of tape recorder, Singer? I said at the time and I say again now that we must watch this boy. In any case, we can't prove malice in what he did in the game, so there's an end to it. Now let us review the applications we've received for admission next fall."

When the meeting was over, Proctor followed me out into

the hall. "A word, Mr. Singer," he said, his face still bruised by anger. "I'll thank you not to contradict me in future. I hope you realize you've only made a fool of yourself." He turned on his heel and went back into his palace.

WEDNESDAY MORNING WAS brilliant and frigid and very windy. I walked across Central Park over the crackling grass for my appointment with Dr. Morales. Nobody was out but me and a couple of mounted cops, but in my high indignation at Proctor I felt less lonely than I usually did in that lonely place at that lonely time, and I was less mindful than usual of the noise of the traffic circumscribing the park, less weighted by the memory of the empty quiet of my apartment when I woke up, all the books listing in the shelves, the half-empty closets, the chairs for nobody, the dead gray of the television screen waiting to put in its three hours of bright, useless service that night, the old Mexican nylon-string guitar that I'd bought at Bristol from Dave Leonard leaning against the wall like an orphan.

Morales's office looked like steerage in comparison with Proctor's pin-neat captain's quarters. Dust clouded the face of the nurturing mother in the Käthe Kollwitz print that hung on one wall in the waiting room, and dust rendered the streets and buildings in the Utrillo reproduction on another wall even more noncommittal than the artist had managed to make them in the first place. The African mask hung off-center, the magazines were messed on the nominal coffee table, the philo-dendron that had replaced the dead cactus on the sill of the gloomy window looked pale and parched. I was a few minutes early, so I went back and forth from the grimy little bathroom with a Dixie cup and, hissed all the while by the white-noise machine, I watered the plant.

The door from the inner office to the hall opened and closed. The woman who went before me snuffed and blew her nose, as usual, all the way to the coat closet. Was it an allergy, or did she produce tears every time? She had to be really rich. She saw Morales five days a week—as I knew from having my own sessions rescheduled from time to time—at seven o'clock, and I often thought I heard her crying.

As I lifted the philodendron's lower leaves and poured in another cupful of water, the door to the waiting room opened and there was Dr. Morales. His usual lunatic grin of salutation evaporated immediately, and he said, "What are you doing, Mr. Singer?" He stood up straight out of his half bow. His shiny bald head caught a stray piece of light, his thick black beard glistened, his weight lifter's shoulders bulged out of his pin-striped vest as if inflated.

"Just this," I said. "Just watering this plant. It really needed it."

"I see," Dr. Morales said.

I went into the inner office, with its stalagmites of books and journals, rudimentary bookshelves, a desk covered with papers, and the dull brass crucifix on the wall behind Dr. Morales's chair, and I lay down on the couch. Dr. Morales came over and sat down, still looking—the last glimpse I had of him—taken aback. Jesus! Water a plant and cause an earthquake!

I told him in detail about the Scholarship Committee meeting—he already knew about Junior's tongue, because I'd described what had happened in the game during our Monday session. "What a hypocrite!" I concluded, about Proctor. "He took this kid for his shooting percentage and made believe it was for his sake, and now he's claiming that he knew it was a high risk all along and said so. And then he gets furious at me for telling the truth."

"It's outrageous," Dr. Morales said, his accent lending the *e* in that word a prominence it seldom enjoys. "I do not understand—"

"He's a bully—that's all. He doesn't have an ounce of self-awareness."

"You are in great style this morning, Mr. Singer," Dr. Morales said. "Your phrases are so exact and perfect—filled with measurements, eh? High risks, shooting percentages, ounces of awareness."

"Well, I guess I'm just trying to be emphatic—I guess I'm still angry."

"It is quantitative analysis with regard to the character of the headmaster, but you have once again only guesswork to offer about yourself. How many times must I tell you—*no guesses!*"

"What are *you* so pissed off about—that I watered your plant? You looked like the sky was falling when you opened the door."

"Now it makes sense to me, however. After your history lesson to the headmaster yesterday, you are correcting my horticulture today."

"But you agreed with me that the way he acted was outrageous."

"No."

"No?"

"No. I was about to say that I do not understand how *you* could behave in so outrageous a fashion and expect anything but fury in return."

"Me?"

"But I am so glad that your further adventures in arithmetic kept me from saying this lie, because I do actually understand."

"I was outrageous?"

"It amazes me that you were not fired on the spot. I would have fired you without hesitation."

"Consider me fired," I said, getting up from the couch. I turned to face him. "Why is it that every time I think I'm getting somewhere you have to pull the rug out from under me?"

"Because that is the way you insist upon seeing the help I am trying to give you," Dr. Morales replied.

"You are a sadist," I said.

Dr. Morales rose out of his chair. His notebook fell to the floor, and I saw his fists clench at his sides as he leaned toward me, and I suddenly had a vision of myself walking down a hallway as long as my life, going from office to office, provoking and then enduring the wrath of one non-native martinet after another. I took a step backward.

Dr. Morales straightened up and plastered his grin back on. "Do not get your hopes up," he said. "I am not going to satisfy your great wish for me to hit you." Then he shouted: "For the good Christ's sake, Mr. Singer, do you need so badly to hear me say that I love you?"

"That you *love* me?"

"I do of course love you, Mr. Singer," Dr. Morales said, lowering his voice into weariness. He sat down in his chair as if depleted. "Now will you be still and listen?"

I lay back down on the couch.

"Baboons," said Dr. Morales.

"Baboons?"

"Yes, baboons. Humans in any enterprise have practical business to accomplish, it is true. The household must function, the company's business must go forward, the book must be published, the rocket ship must be lownched—"

"Launched."

"*Lawn*ched. In the case of your school, the children must be taught, the sports played, et cetera." Four very separate syllables. "But this whole time we are primates, with hierarchies and the rituals of behavior, the metaphorical grooming and aggression, et cetera. Only in true intimacy may we abandon these forms and conventions. Very important is the mounting behavior. You see it most, um—how does one say it?—flamboyantly in baboons. The dominant males may—indeed, they must—mount not only the females but the lower males. The lower males must proffer their colorful buttocks or risk a drubbing and perhaps even becoming a pariah. So in our organizations we have a figurative mounting behavior like this. If a lower male wishes to challenge for leadership, he must do it with cunning and patience, not with direct defiance, unless the leader has become so decrepit that he cannot establish physical dominance."

"Asses, apes, and dogs," I said.

"So the headmaster's convenient memory and his reprimand of you are mounting behavior, Mr. Singer. He is fucking you in the ass, and you must, as it were, stand still for it. In the English public schools, the masters would cane the nowty boy and the nowty boy would have to say, 'Thank you, sir, may I please have some more?' is it not? But in this meeting, just as the headmaster has gotten astride you, you turn around and punch him in the face."

"Yes, but what about the truth? I mean, we're not baboons, and Proctor did say—"

"We are coming to the end of our time, Mr. Singer. We shall continue our conversation on Friday. It is bad technique but I tell you now anyway that (a) in such situations, establishing what you so comfortably call the truth will serve no purpose that I know of beneath the sun, and (b) your anger at this man is, like your chronic anger at me, acting out old conflicts. This we have discussed before. You should be at this point mastering these conflicts, instead of continuing to seek shelter in them from the professional success you might so easily attain and an emotional life in the now and here."

"You believe I could easily—"

"I shall see you on Friday, Mr. Singer."

I DIDN'T SEE Dr. Morales on Friday. Or the following Monday, or Wednesday. I was at Mount Sinai myself, recovering from a knife wound in my side and a nicked kidney. Hospitalization—finally an excuse so pure that even Dr. Morales will have to accept it at face value, I tried to tell myself for a second or two after waking up in severe pain and realizing where I was. Only then did it occur to me to remember what had happened.

We had lost our fourth basketball game of the New Year, to Trinity, 76–75. Walter Cooper played extremely well, scoring twenty-two points, with eight assists and eight rebounds, but the Trinity team had a balance that we lacked. Walter put us ahead 75–74 with a strong drive with fifteen seconds to go, but Trinity came back with another basket just before time ran out. Galgano started screaming at Walter before the buzzer stopped sounding. "Ten more seconds!" he yelled. "You hold the ball for ten more seconds, like I told you, and they don't get it back."

I got up from my end of the bench and tried to quiet Jim down. "Come on, we might not have gotten a decent shot if he'd waited that long."

"It's called following orders, Cooper," Galgano said. "It's called playing as part of a team."

"Hey, he had eight or nine assists, Jim, and—"

"I wanted that clock down to five seconds or less, like I told you."

So it went—off the court, across the hall, into the locker

room, all the way through Walter's shower. Even after that, Galgano couldn't leave him alone, and kept circling back around to him as he was getting dressed.

Facing his locker, with his back turned toward the coach, Walter took a knife out of his jeans front pocket and opened it. Galgano couldn't see it. It had a small hilt, like an old-fashioned dagger.

I rushed over and stepped between them. "OK, Walter," I said. "He doesn't know what he's talking about."

"Who the hell asked you, Singer, you skinny fuck?" Galgano said. "I thought I was the coach here."

Walter turned around and faced me, wearing that look of mild amusement.

"Walter, he does this all the time," I said. "You don't have to pay any attention."

"You're good," Walter said. He stepped forward and pushed the knife at me. I tried to dodge down and away from it, but he caught me in the side and I was hung up on the knife for a couple of seconds. Where the knife went in, my body felt strange or even dead to me—like something that *should* be cut, like insulation, or bread, or a sack of grain.

Walter pulled the knife out and I fell to the floor. I looked up and saw Galgano with his mouth finally shut—well, open but with no words coming out. Walter put the knife down on the bench beside him and walked out of the locker room. He never went home, Proctor told me when he came to visit me in the hospital. He was never arrested, never even found.

I lay there trying to hold my side together, my hands greasy with blood, realizing that when it came to my own physical welfare, the old antennae for danger I'd grown as a kid had failed me. Shock descended on me like a chilly mist. Luckily, the gung-ho medical alumnus was in the locker room, as he usually was, trying to relive his high-school years, or just—it occurred to me a few seconds before I passed out—being gay.

· · ·

PROCTOR ARRIVED ON Saturday evening, forty-eight hours after I was admitted and just a half hour after my first visitor, Mac Preston, who had evidently been impressed by the hint of hard knocks in my youth, left. Between the two visitors came a phone call from my father, whose voice I hadn't heard since the summer, when he announced his travel plans to me and more or less hung up. The school had gotten the number of his office at Nyack Hospital and told him what had happened to me. He hadn't come to see me right away because as always he had medical crises to deal with, and the person who called from the school assured him I would be all right, he said. Only he didn't say "the school," he said "Collegiate" instead of "Coventry." He didn't even know where his skewered, stitched son worked. Would I excuse him for not rushing into town? And now he was at the hospital on Saturday for an emergency, and since I would be released on Sunday, there wasn't really time for a visit. But I should be sure to tell him if anything further went wrong. Sometimes a doctor in the family can be very useful, he said.

Proctor's outfit made a single concession to the weekend— no tie—and he stood stiffly near my bed for the quarter of an hour he was there. He started off calling me Jacob, which was a first for him, and then outdid himself and called me Jake— incessantly. "That was a brave thing you did, Jake," he said, after telling me that no trace of Walter had been found.

"Thanks," I said. I shifted in bed and felt a jolt of pain where the wound was. "There must have been a better way to handle it." I had already begun to anticipate Morales's dissection of my motives. "I should have just shouted a warning or something."

"I have always had some questions about Mr. Galgano's demeanor with the players."

"But you've always said he was so— Most of the kids know how to just put up with him."

"I've been meaning to say, Jake, that the incident in the committee meeting last week was most unfortunate. I hope that these unpleasant incidents won't affect your work. I suspect that you don't quite realize how much the boys admire you. But now you must see about getting well. Fresh air will help, Jake—as soon as you're up to getting around a bit."

"Yes, thanks," I said. "The doctors say I'll be fine. If you have a chance, would you tell my senior section they should finish reading *Billy Budd* next week?"

"Of course, of course," Proctor said, paying not the slightest attention. I looked at him and saw that his eyes were moist with tears. My God—he loved me, too. To my horror, my eyes also misted over. Proctor put his hand on my shoulder and said, "Jake, what you did was probably impulsive, but I also maintain that you were very courageous." There was an extra burr in those last three words, like the faint skirl of the bagpipes wafting over the heather or across the lough.

"WHY ARE YOU so scornful of someone who is praising you?" Morales asked when I mentioned the thickening of Proctor's accent under the weight of sentimentality. "Perhaps it is because he appears to be more astute about your character than you might wish to acknowledge."

"Praise," I said.

"If you feel that your wownd will excuse you from answering that question, maybe you would address this one: Did you believe when you interposed yourself in this situation that you were Ruby Goldstein?"

God, he knows boxing, too, I said to myself. "No," I said aloud, "I didn't think I was Ruby Goldstein. I thought that

Walter and I understood each other and that I'd get him to put the knife down. That's all."

"I'm sad to say that it is never all, Mr. Singer. I am also sorry about your injury and I know these questions are hard for you to answer at this time, but I must ask you what you believed the blood that you were so eager to shed would purchase for you."

"Well, I hardly planned it, but it seemed to earn me Proctor's affection, at least until the next time I cross him."

"You will not cross him again."

"Is that a prediction or an order?"

Dr. Morales was silent. I rolled onto my side and looked at him. "Is that a guess or an order or a prediction or a hope?" I said. "And by the way, you did want to hit me last week. You almost did. Your fists were clenched."

"My fists were not clenched, Mr. Singer."

I turned again onto my back. "Your fists were clenched, and that's that," I said. Why did this item of truth suddenly seem crucial? There was a silence, and then I went on: "When Walter stabbed me, he said, 'You're good.' And just before I passed out I was thinking how weird it was."

"Even in extremis," Dr. Morales said, "you were intellectualizing."

Silence again.

"Well?" Dr. Morales said.

"Well what?"

"What do you think he meant?"

"He was about three inches away from me," I said. "It seemed so—I don't know—confidential, or intimate. It reminds me of something that happened to me when I was in high school, but I'm not sure why."

"Perhaps when you have completed this prehahmble we might discover the answer together."

"Preamble. Give me a second, will you? I'm trying to re-member this specific thing. The rest of it we've been over before."

The rest of it was this: In the middle of my senior year, a couple of months after the police captain yelled at me, I quit fooling around. It wasn't fun anymore, I told myself, and it didn't give me whatever else it was that I hoped to gain from it. Near the beginning of this reformation there was a basketball game against Bronxville High in which I got a lot of playing time and did extremely well—better than ever before or after. I was put in at the end of the first quarter to give a rest to Marvin White, one of our guards, and I stayed in the game until the end and scored twenty-four points and blocked some shots and had a lot of assists. And I scored the winning basket, with less than ten seconds left on the clock. I played out of my mind, actually. I scored on a fifteen-foot left-handed hook shot. I scored while I was falling on my ass five feet beyond the key after some hatchet man had given me a vicious elbow to the ribs. I out-rebounded guys a foot taller than me. I was eight for eight from the line.

"Here's the part I'm just now remembering," I said to Dr. Morales. "We won by two points at the last minute against the rich kids, so the locker room was sort of delirious when the game was over. Everyone was joking around in the shower. The guard I'd replaced, Marvin, had come back in at the other guard position in the second quarter, and in the shower he came up to me and put his hand on my shoulder and said, 'Jake, man, see what you can do when we decide to help a white boy out?' I said something like 'I just brought you guys up to my level for once, that's all,' and he said, 'No, Jake, you're good, now that we have taught you how to play this game.' I told him I just hadn't wanted to show him—"

"Excuse me, Mr. Singer, but you do realize that this boy used the same words as Walters—'You're good,' no?"

"No. I mean yes. I mean I didn't realize it."

"When you were in the shower these many years ago, your teammate was saying, 'You are all right—you can be in this disreputable athletic club, at least temporarily,' yes?"

"Yes, but—"

"And Walters was initiating you into the other club, as it were. To him you were, if I may use your phrase, an authority figure, whether you want to be one or not, whether you want to act like one or not. By the way, both incidents contain latent homosexual elements, of course, but we shall save that—"

"Oh, please."

"Have you not said how intimate you felt just before Walters stabbed you? And this other boy has put his hand on you in the shower, yes?"

"Yes, but—"

"You should apply for a patent on those two syllables, Mr. Singer. We shall save this homosexual—and miscegenation—material for another time. If you will permit me now to continue: You see, you are reaching the stage in your life when you must decide how you are going to act, whether you are going to conduct yourself in a mature fashion, with all the compromises this entails, or turn into an anachronism, an angry teenager in the clothing of an adult—for example, offended by, rather than sad about, your mother's death. Because, you see, if you insist upon reenacting these habitual conflicts and reacting to those in positions of maturity and authority with defiance and rage, this immaturity will inhibit you from . . ."

Usually Dr. Morales's language flowed with such strong currents of zeal and fanaticism and hostility that I found myself tossed along on them like a cork, but sometimes even he subsided into tedium. This was one of those times. I stopped listening and started daydreaming. In this fantasy, my father, dressed in hospital greens, stood in front of the high mahogany doors of a private mansion. On the lintel above these doors were polished-brass letters spelling out "Sceptre." The *S* was askew. Battalions of fleecy clouds floated in the sky, sunbeams like long ingots of light shone down, and the air was filled with the sound of a symphony orchestra playing major triads. Up the flagstone walk leading to the mansion, flanked by formal French gardens and straight rows of palm trees, strode Dr. Morales, dressed in a white suit and smoking a Havana. My father and he gave each other the club handshake and grinned at each other like little boys with a secret, and then the doors swung open and Dr. Morales entered the mansion. Proctor came up next, in a kilt, playing the "Skye Boat Song" on a set of pipes. He walked in the slow, stately gait of the military piper. He said "Fresh air" to my father, and my father opened the door for him. Next came the Yonkers police captain, wearing his dress uniform and trying to suck in his sizable portico. He flashed his badge and was shown in. Coaches Hayes and Galgano were next. They did a pick-and-roll around my father and went on in, too. And here I came up the walk, dragging my feet. My father turned away from me with an unhappy, uncertain expression. Dr. Morales came back out of the mansion and cheerfully waved me forward. I wanted to run away, because I knew that if I joined this club, whatever its benefits might be, it was a life membership, with heavy dues, and with no resigning allowed. The episodic, picaresque narrative I'd tried to break my life up into, so as to avoid more tragedy, would surely give way to some thick, dark Tolstoyan tale whose webbed plot I would never be able to escape. I'd have to grow up, as King Ernesto kept on finding new and more boring ways of saying on his throne there behind my back. Neurasthenia seemed a small price to pay to avoid such a fate.

"What are you thinking about, Mr. Singer?"

"*Our* club," I said. "I wonder what happened to Marvin and those other guys I played basketball with in high school."

"Of course. You have begun to make strides in your profession, you have remembered with the Lebanese estrumpet that you have fully formed adult genitahlia to deal with, and so your emotions run backward to sentimentality, to homosexual miscegenation in the shower room, to a time of no mature responsibilities."

"And Walter Cooper."

"What about him?"

"Well, is anyone going to help him?"

"Who cares?" Dr. Morales said.

THE EMPHATICALLY RICH New York represented by the great majority of Coventry's student body was a New York I didn't see at close range until the following spring. I knew it only through the exquisite Paul Stuart wardrobe of the occasional senior trying to resist the seventies fads of bell-bottoms and as much bohemian shabbiness as could be laid over Proctor's rigid jacket-and-tie rule, and through squibs in the papers about society events. These notices reproduced what I imagined such things must have been like: a background blur out of which emerged one rich or famous mug after another. The pictures that floated out of the inky blackness above these name blurts always made the people look abnormal—prognathous, narcoleptic, Tourettic, or as vacant as unlaid storm-drain pipes. This was strange, because when some of these same people drove in their limos or 190 SLs over to the West Side to drop their sons off at the Coventry School, they were handsome and cheerful, the dads in slim business suits, the moms in pricey jeans and burgundy or wintergreen sweaters or sweatshirts. Every head of hair with a suave streak or swath of gray; good skin, with crinkles instead of wrinkles; amphitheatrically perfect white teeth. Maybe the combination of dusk and engraved invitations threw them into a gargoyle phase.

After what Proctor continued to insist on seeing as my locker-room heroics, he put me on more committees and asked me to speak on behalf of the school to parents and prospective parents and groups of alumni, which pushed me nearer to their checkbooks but didn't propel me into their bosom. I found it uncomfortable under Proctor's wing, but I also began to feel more present in my life, at least my professional life, as if some psychic clutch had finally engaged and the neurasthenic idling—

Now, really, Mr. Singer—it is most embarrassing to listen to this narrative masturbation. I know that you had a good rhythm going as you flipped through the pages of your dictionary to find all your impressive words, and I'm so sorry to interrupt, but you are beginning to mix up metaphors, with your wings and bosoms, and, more important, perhaps you could try a little harder to get to the point!

This is the voice of Dr. Morales, of course. By the time the spring that brought me face-to-face with real affluence rolled around, I had internalized Dr. Morales's accent and speech patterns and the machete-like sarcasm that he wielded in the slash-and-burn process he tried to pass off as "interpretation," and I guess such internalization is part of the point of analysis. It's true that life improved for me as I went to him, but whether if I could do it all over again I would actually choose to have the homunculus of an insane, bodybuilding, black-bearded Cuban Catholic Freudian shouting at me from inside my own head, I am not sure.

Dr. M. *(clearing his throat, his audible for boredom): Please let me know when you* are *sure of something, Mr. Singer.*
Me: *Sorry.*

Dr. M.: *I'm surprised that you didn't say that you* guessed *you were sorry.*

Me: *Sorry.*

Dr. M.: (Silence.)

Me: *What's wrong now, for Christ's sake? I said I was getting better—you should take it as a compliment.*

Dr. M.: *So you ask me to kiss your ass in gratitude as you waste my time with this interminable prehahmble? Even an analyst's patience has—*

Me: *Preamble—I told you before: it's preamble.*

Dr. M.: *Pree-ahmble. Even an analyst's patience has some limit, Mr. Singer.*

Me: *OK, OK.*

So anyway, at school, things were going well. I gave these talks to groups of parents who were considering Coventry for their boys, and I seemed to be convincing a lot of them. Of course, I'd be so nervous I'd spend a half hour on the shitter beforehand, but—

Dr. M.: *Ah, honesty. It is always so refreshing, like a breeze through the palmettos in Havana. It is a pity we are still ninety miles off the shore of your subject.*

Anyway, there was a day in the middle of April when the air in New York was as cool and clear as—

Dr. M.: *And now we have the weather report! Isn't the news supposed to come first, Mr. Singer?*

—as a day in October, while—

Dr. M.: *What about the rich and famous people?*

Me: *I'm getting there. I'm just setting this up, trying to give the whole picture.*

Dr. M.: *This giving of the entire picture, as you say, is your characteristic way of putting painful matters on the shelf for a while longer, preferably until they are stale and unappetizing. I would wager that you wish to speak of the problems that brought you to me in the first place—your rage at your mother for dying, the fact that months and months had elapsèd when no woman even so much as glimpsèd your penis, the estrangement between you and your father, the compromises involved in your profession. Here they all are, these many years later, still preying on your mind as if they were the eagle at the livers of Prometheus, no? This is what happens when a patient terminates the treatment before he should.*

Me: *But—*

Dr. M.: *But most of all, once again you wish to avoid the recognition of the crucial role I played in your life. You cling still to the belief—no, the delusion—that one can be his own man, create himself, and as it were have no parent of any sort.*

Me: *But that's what this is about. If you'd just give me a chance to get started, you'd—*

Dr. M.: *Mr. Singer, you would put off the sunrise if you were not quite ready for breakfast.*

Me: *But—*

Dr. M.: *But if we could not make progress in this area in our real work together, what chance is there, I ask you, of our getting anywhere in this absurd imaginary dialogue of yours? So proceed with your meteorology, if you feel that you must, but you must also forgive me if I catch forty whinks while you do.*

There was a Sunday in the middle of April when the air in New York was as cool and clear as it is in late October. The trees in Central Park had gone blurry with buds, the Great Lawn had begun to lose the look of an old blanket thrown down to protect the earth, and the water in the Reservoir had a fine chop, like a miniature sea. A few people—the avant-garde of the jogging movement—beetled around the gravel path. It was all down there and I was up here, many stories above Fifth Avenue, on the terrace of an apartment that occupied the top two floors of a magnificent Deco building between Eighty-third and Eighty-fourth streets. To my left, in his usual blue blazer and gray slacks, stood Proctor, nautical in appearance and demeanor.

"Ah, fresh air, Jake," he said, putting his hand on my shoulder. "There's nothing like it, even in New York City."

To my right stood Allegra Marshall, the hostess of this Coventry fund-raising lunch. Luncheon. My first point-blank encounter with the Manhattan of serious money and glamour. Five round tables of eight in a huge dining room with wainscoting and a *Close Encounters* chandelier. White maids in black uniforms and white, lace-edged aprons. Cutlery, linen, chased silver. Not a bell-bottom in sight, no ankhs, no zoris, no peasant blouses. It could have been the fifties. It could have been now.

Before I escaped to the terrace, one sleek fellow, the grandfather of a student of mine, asked me where I was going over spring break, and I said, "Nowhere," and he said, "Well, what a good idea!" He and I then discussed the Yankees' prospects for the coming season, and he pointed out a relative of Jacob Ruppert's across the vast living room or parlor or whatever it was. "This is a man who won't touch a drop of anything," the sleek fellow said. "I've heard that he's ashamed of his fortune." My other conversation was with the mother of one of my advanced-placement seniors who simply could not get *over* how wonderfully *detailed* my comments were on her son's papers. She herself got a terrible *rash* all over her *torso* whenever she concentrated too long on *anything* written, even *books*.

When Proctor and I arrived, Mrs. Marshall gave me an

automatic smile but a firm handshake—the kind that a girl's affluent, manly dad or independent-minded mom tries to install at an early age. She was wearing a short black dress and a black wristband. Her husband—Coventry '59—had died, of cancer, on New Year's Day, leaving her with a six-year-old son—in first grade at the school—an infant daughter, and his millions to add to hers. The apartment was beautiful and tasteful to the point of hilarity, and its mistress, with her tall, willowy stature, pale complexion, bright-blue eyes, and long, dark, ironed-looking hair, and her aristocratic imperfection of feature—a real nose with a real bump in it, one very white front tooth slightly overlapping the other—also seemed comically perfect for her role of young society personage gamely pressing on. Now, out on the terrace, in the presence of Proctor and his bromides, she seemed sad, and her perfection looked frayed at the edges, and after a fellow blazer-and-gray-flannelsman hailed the headmaster back inside, I thought I saw her roll her eyes.

"Sometimes I think he'd make a better admiral than a headmaster," I said. "Do you ever see any muggings down there?"

"You're Mr. Springer?" she asked.

"Singer. Jake Singer."

"You're the one who is going to do the sales pitch."

"Yes. I've done something like this three or four times now, but I keep getting stage fright. Especially here. I mean, I feel sort of out of place."

"Proctor says you do it very well. When we set this thing up, he told me the applications pour in after you talk."

"You know, a year ago he was barely speaking to me."

"Why?"

"Oh, I was always arguing with him, always mouthing off. Nothing better to do, I guess."

"What do you mean?"

"You know, just trouble with authority."

"But he certainly likes you now."

"I just calmed down, I suppose."

"Just like that?"

"No, it probably has something to do with being in analysis, though I'm not supposed to talk about it and I don't like to give my lunatic analyst any credit."

"I'm seeing someone, too, so you're safe."

"But you have a real reason, not just the vapors, like me. Anyway, one thing I am sure of is that it isn't Proctor who changed. He'd prescribe fresh air for you if your husband had died." Good work, Jake. "Oh, Mrs. Marshall, I'm so sorry. What an idiot I am."

"It's all right. I've discovered it's like having two heads. But when you collect yourself I hope you'll call me Allegra. And by the way, these things make me as uncomfortable as they make you." She went back inside, leaving me alone with my clumsy self.

At lunch, Proctor and I sat on either side of our hostess, and I said how delicious the consommé was. "Actually, it's turtle soup," she said. It was difficult to eat the rest of the meal, with my foot so far in my mouth and the butterflies in my stomach. But I nodded and smiled and chewed as best I could, and I made what seemed to me an English teacher's joke—something feeble about cashing in Mr. Chips. Mrs. Marshall's frozen smile thawed into a real laugh—very musical—and I felt as if I'd done her a small turn. "Great chicken," I said when the veal chop was served, and she looked at me uncomfortably until I shrugged, whereupon she got it and smiled a real smile again. Before dessert and after a trip to the bathroom, I made my speech: To afford the kind of diversity in our student body. All the way from catcher's mitts to calculators. Provide the brand of leadership that seems so sorely lacking in our nation.

Instill a sense of values, stem the rising tide of drugs. To defray the cost of mandatory haircuts and install narrower and quieter ties. *(Polite laughter.)* To pay for the polish Proctor uses for his brass blazer buttons and his bald bean.

THIS LAST I said to Dr. Morales in his cold, cluttered office the next morning as I lay on the slab-flat couch with the cervically inimical jelly-roll headrest. It was a chilly, drizzly day, the bad side of spring. I had already told him about Allegra Marshall and my high anxiety and various faux pas. "You did not really say this about the polish, Mr. Singer," he said.

"No—it's a joke."

"I have asked you to tell me what you said in your speech and first you drone like an old priest and then you become sarcastic—sarcastic and rude, if I may say, since I, too, am bald. Why do you suppose you cry in fear before the hand?"

"Beforehand. Who said anything about crying?"

"These attacks of cramps and diarrhea—you are weeping like a frightened child, but since you are a man you must do it through your asshole. And I shall ask the questions here. Why are you so frightened of something so boring and contemptible, Mr. Singer?"

"If I don't know the drill here by now, I really should be ashamed of myself. It's *not* boring and stupid. I act that way only because I care about it so much and want so badly to do well, to appease the spirit of my dead mother, whom I magically think I must have killed, and to earn the respect of my father, who believes I'm a failure and wishes I had been a doctor like him, and to please you. Always to please you, of course."

"Again this same sequence—dull recitation with following it the scorn. Ho-hum and fuck you, is it not?"

"Well, I mean a few years of—"

"No, it is thirty-two meenoose six years, Mr. Singer—twenty-six years of preventing yourself from genuine involvement in your feelings and your life. I swear to Christ that if Marilyn Monroe came to you with no clothes on and a wet pussy, you would not know what to do with her. Now please listen to me. If you joke, I shall kill you and spare you the effort of this slow suicide. Is this school of yours a good school?"

"Yes. It could be—"

"*Is it a good school?*"

"Yes."

"Do your students respect you?"

"Yes." Satisfaction, as surprising as a twenty-dollar bill on the sidewalk, came to me with this answer.

"Tell me one important thing you have done for the school besides the teaching."

"Well—"

"It is dry, Mr. Singer."

"I'm helping to get scholarships for poor kids," I said, more proudly than I meant to.

"Good, there is feeling in your words at last. Anything else?"

"I'm convincing more people to apply, and now I'm helping to raise money. As of yesterday."

"Ah, your voice has fallen here. Why?"

"I don't know—the whole idea of raising money, being with rich people, glad-handing and putting on a show."

"*It is a good school!*" thundered Dr. Morales. "You are trying to make it better according to your convictions! Making a speech is not selling eslaves or torturing cute lambs! A President of the United Estates has attended this school, three or four *Nobelistas,* many professors and doctors, the director of the Peace Corps, I believe, the head of Sloan-Kettering, the man who designed—"

"How do you know all this?" I asked.

"I have looked it up. I should not have revealed this, perhaps—it is bad technique—but just maybe you will take a leaf from my tree, Mr. Singer. I am *interested* in my work. You are my work. I am *interested* in you. And one more thing—if there are rich people in the world, why should you not be among them? You yourself are hardly from the road of tobacco. Your father is a physician, he has no doubt paid the mortgage off on his house in Rockleigh, he is a widower, you are an only child. Someday, if you will mend the fence with him and stop sitting astride it as if it were the horse's ass you are making of yourself, you may inherit this estate. So if there is—"

"Will you be my investment adviser?"

"So if there is, Mr. Wisenheemer, a rich young widow making gooey eyes at you, why should you not fuck her, I ask you. Why should you not marry her, when I come to think of it. Why didn't you mention how she looked when you were speaking of her?"

"Less Marilyn Monroe than Ali MacGraw," I said. "But beautiful enough. Quite beautiful, in fact."

"In fact? I did not think it was in fiction. I do not know who is this Alice MacGraw."

"She's the one in the movie of *Love Story*—the girl who dies."

"Ah, yes. This is interesting. We must stop now, Mr. Singer, but have you by any chance happened to notice the corpses that have littered our conversation this morning like a battlefield, as if it were? Your mother, the husband of the hostess, the character of this movie."

"Marilyn Monroe."

"Very good, Mr. Singer. You are quite right, I have joined in this necrophilia. But it is *spring*, Mr. Singer. Time for the new beginnings, for the birds to tweeter and among the twigs to build their nests."

Dr. Morales's crude incitement concerning Allegra Marshall at the end of the session had not come out of nowhere. Near the beginning, when I mentioned her widowhood and the opulence of her apartment, I could feel him coming to attention like a setter behind me. I was surprised and annoyed to feel myself coming to attention the following week, when I was in the nurse's office at school, getting a Band-Aid for a wound inflicted by the staples that had interfered with my reading of "Hester Prynne: Hawthorn's Revolutionery Heroin." A little kid was lying on the cot looking green around the gills, and the nurse, a clinical type with a neurosurgeon's hauteur and the name Gladys Knight, of all things, was on the phone saying, "You and the baby-sitter probably have the same organism that George has, Mrs. Marshall, with the nausea and the vertigo. I'd bring him over for you myself, but George is the fourth incidence today, so I really should stay here."

I asked if it was Allegra Marshall she was talking to, and she covered the phone and scowled at me. "This is important, Mr. Singer, if you don't mind," she said. "This child *and* his mother *and* the baby-sitter have all come down with gastroenteritis, and we're trying to figure out how to get him home."

"I met Mrs. Marshall last week. I'd be glad to take him home—I've got two free periods. Tell Mrs. Marshall it's me."

In another five minutes, George Marshall and I went out into the April sunshine and hailed a cab on West End Avenue, after a parting advisory from Miss Knight: "One of the other children had projectile vomiting." As we drove across the park, yellow with forsythia and daffodils, George sat still and regarded me. He was small for his age but built solidly, with blond hair and a turned-up nose with a few freckles sprinkled over it—he looked nothing like his mother. "My dad died," he said when we stopped for a red light at Ninety-sixth Street and Fifth Avenue. "I know," I said. "It's very sad for you and your family." "My sister doesn't realize it," he said. "She's too little. Are you a teacher in the upper school?" I told him I was. "I thought I saw you," he said.

The taxi started up again, and George faced forward, looking sick and unhappy. His feet didn't quite reach the floor. Even though I'd never met this boy before, I knew for a fact that he believed that he had done something to cause what had happened to his family, and I wanted to reach over with both hands and shake the innocent truth into him before the guilt worked itself too deep into his heart.

George said he could go up in the elevator by himself, but the doorman said that Mrs. Marshall had asked me to take him upstairs, if it wasn't too much trouble. So up in the elaborately scrolled and panelled elevator we went. When the door opened onto the apartment's foyer, Mrs. Marshall was standing there looking very sick and forlorn herself, plain and ashen and lank-haired, so that the elegant dark-blue Chinesey housecoat she had on seemed as beside the point as the Aubusson on the floor and the modest Corot drawing on the wall behind her. "I'm tired, Mom," George said, and he tottered away down the long hallway. "I'm going to lie down for a while."

"I'll be right there," Mrs. Marshall said.

"I hope your daughter's all right," I said. "The nurse told me your baby-sitter is sick, too."

"Emily is fine. And George's mother will be here in half an hour. She lives just over on Park. We'll be OK."

"George's mother?"

"My husband's mother. My late husband's mother. Georgie is George Junior."

"Oh."

"It was nice of you to bring him home. Thank you."

"It was nothing. He's a sweet kid."

"Let me pay you for the taxi."

"Oh, no. That's all right." I looked over her shoulder at the living room, glowing with perfection in the morning light. "I know this is silly," I said, "but I wish there was something else I could do for you."

"Why is that silly?"

"I mean, I've only met you once, and—"

"Is it silly because I'm rich?"

"Yes."

"Ah—honesty. But it shows what you know." Tears were in her eyes now, and her nose looked more broken than distinguished, and she seemed skinny rather than slender and pathetic rather than tragic; and I felt ridiculous instead of gallant, and furious at Dr. Morales for his careless manipulations, and for regarding this woman so lubriciously and so lightly, like a personal ad, like a sitting duck. "I'm sorry if I've upset you," I said. "Don't worry about it," she said, pushing the elevator button.

"AND I THINK you should be ashamed of yourself," I said to Dr. Morales the next morning, after telling him as calmly as I could what had happened with George Marshall and his mother the day before.

"I am," Dr. Morales replied. "I am truly ashamed." He rattled some papers around and cleared his throat a few times.

I sat up and put my feet on the floor and looked at him. He had a tax form over the yellow pad he used for taking what I assumed were scathing notes about me and his other victims.

"Filing late?" I said. "I hope you applied for the automatic two-month extension."

"This is against the rules, Mr. Singer."

"You mean the New York Psychoanalytic Society has an actual rule against doing your taxes during sessions with your patients? Why, that's positively draconian."

"I shall not explain myself to you, Mr. Singer. This is as forbidden to me as sitting up is to you. But God and Freud will pardon me, I feel certain, for occupying myself with other matters when a patient enters my office in an inappropriate rage, insults me further by thinking to disguise it, and then has the amazing condescension to tell me that I should be ashamed of myself, as if I were a four-year-old child who has deliberately belchèd during Communion."

"I would never have made such a fool of myself if you hadn't—"

"Had not what, Mr. Singer? Had not held a pistol to your head to force you to volunteer to take the boy home? Had not squeezèd your heart in the taxi to make you recognize his psychological situation and sympathize with him? Had not transformed you into Sharlie McCarthy and then like Edgar Burgeon thrown my voice into you standing there in front of the mother and to diminish her humanity on account of her wealth? By the way, Mr. Singer, will you please lie down."

"You want it both ways," I said. "You want me to behave the way you think I should, and then when I try and then fail, you disavow any part in the matter. 'My advice is to jump, Mr. Singer, but if you break your neck, don't blame me.' "

"Had not, in general, as I was saying, miraculously reached into your soul and poured into it the poison that you are convinced is so powerful as to threaten also anyone whom you might love. Like your mother, your father, like a woman. Like me. You are not Shiva, Mr. Singer, nor Attila nor Hitler, nor even Sharles Starkweather. You are not so lethal as you wish to believe. Now please lie down."

"No. I don't feel well. I'm going home."

"You know, I truly *am* ashamed that after this much of our work together you can still busy your mind with any amount of anger at yourself and at me to ignore what is really going on in your life—for example, the possibility that from the start this woman has taken some interest in you, and that this was why I tried gently and humorously to encourage your interest in her."

"*Gently?*"

"Why else would a person divulge within five minutes of meeting someone the highly intimate knowledge that she was in analysis, as you divulgèd it to her also—why else would she say this if she did not feel immediate trust and confidentiality? And why else would she have asked you to accompany her son in the elevator if not because she wished to see you again, and being in a very unattractive and weakened condition, what is more. Now please do lie down and try to address these matters."

"No, I really do feel ill," I said. "I'm leaving."

"So now the regression and withdrawal will be complete."

I CALLED IN SICK and spent the rest of the day in or very near the bathroom in my apartment. From time to time I hazarded a walk into the living room to watch TV. I would doze on the couch, wake up to a soap opera or a game show, whose gaudiness the flu rendered almost hallucinatory, get up, and turn it off. And before stumbling toiletward again, I once or twice looked around my place and took stock. In January, as my responsibilities grew at school, I had through an effort of will upgraded my domestic situation. I had discarded the bricks and boards and sofa *trouvé* and card table, and the bottom half of a bunk bed sold to me by the building's gaunt Croatian super for thirty-five dollars, and the dieseling vintage refrigerator, which I called the Serf of Ice Cream—another English teacher's joke—and replaced them with Door Store merchandise and new appliances. A captain's bed, a blond wall unit or two, a big, round, tan hooked rug in the living room, an oak table with a chrome base, even a Zurbarán print and a Magritte poster—that kind of thing. All in all, it had become a decent middle-class bachelor's place on the eleventh floor of a nice building on West End Avenue—plenty of light and a nice breeze in the spring and summer. But so what? It was still a pocket of isolation—especially in illness, when you'd like to be able to call on someone—and I felt like a penny in the pocket. Whatever progress I'd made seemed to have been in baby steps, or in a marionette's hinged gait, with Dr. Morales pulling the strings. I felt far less desperate than I had a few years earlier, but the absence of desperation is not life.

The flu subsided. I took a longer, deeper nap, looked in listlessly as Thurman Munson and his teammates braved chilly April conditions at Yankee Stadium, ate some chicken soup, drank a lot of water, stayed on my feet, barely, in the shower, and collapsed onto my bed and into an even deeper sleep, which lasted the night.

I FELT MUCH better in the morning but couldn't face the red-letter discussion looming in my advanced-placement class or the concluding negotiations over *A Separate Peace* in my regular junior courses, to say nothing of playing pepper with the base-ball team in Riverside Park after school, so I called in sick again and read and dozed on the sofa. I was brought out of a semi-dream, in which Dr. Morales lobbied the halls of Congress on behalf of a particular brand of very large Cuban stogie, by the ringing of the doorbell. It hadn't rung in so long that I'd for-gotten when the last time was. I opened it without using the burglar scope or asking who was there. What can anyone do to me, after all? I said to myself in the self-pitying aftermath of my stocktaking and influenza.

It was Allegra Marshall, well beyond influenza and its aftermath—looking very beautiful once again, in fact, if nervous.

"I'm sorry, I should have called," she said. "I know you're sick, but you live so close to the school that I thought I would just stop by. And then the doorman said he didn't need to announce me or anything."

"It's the super," I said. "My friend the super."

"So here I am. I hope I'm not disturbing you."

"I'm much better," I said. "It's OK. Is George all right?"

"I took him back to school yesterday, and I asked for you and they told me you were out sick. And when they told me you were out again today, I felt even more guilty. You probably got this from George, or maybe even from me."

"Oh, it's going around."

"But that isn't why I was looking for you at school in the first place," she said. "I wanted to apologize for being so rude to you the other morning. Here you had done me this kindness."

"I was rude first—worse than rude," I said. "You caught me out. I asked for it."

"Well, I'm sorry anyway. Now I really should leave you alone."

She turned away and started back toward the elevator, and as she did I heard that insinuating voice, which had already installed itself in my mind, say, *Now, Mr. Singer, I ask you—what do you wish this woman to do, take out a full-page advertisement in the* New York Times? I drew a deep breath and said, just as she was about to push the "Down" button, "Wait, um, Allegra, as long as we're apologizing." She turned again, to face me. "I wasn't really doing you a kindness. I offered to take George home so I could see you. It was just an excuse. And my analyst sort of put me up to the whole thing anyway."

"You mean you *didn't* really want to see me?"

"No, I did, I probably did, or I would have, but this doctor of mine gets himself in the middle of everything, so it's hard to tell. He egged me on. He said *you* were interested in *me*."

"He was right."

"What?"

"He was right."

"He was right?"

"He was right."

THEY WANTED TO have children right away, but she didn't get pregnant. The specialist she saw couldn't find anything wrong. Still, she and her husband had sex by the chart, she took hormones, they went on tense "relaxed" vacations. None of it worked. At length her husband said maybe he was the one with the problem—she had to give him credit for that. The specialist he saw, who wore a bright-red toupee, said "Whee" when he looked through the microscope at the semen sample, and the subsequent, more scientific assay found nothing wrong. Now they had both no one and each other to blame. It was an open field. It's like a poison in a well that you're both drinking from, Allegra told me. They kept trying to conceive a child but meanwhile adopted a baby boy through one of the most reputable private agencies in the city. They gave up on biology, and on sex, a couple of years later, and a few years after that, in the midst of growing strain and louder silence between them, which they managed to hide from the agency's social worker, they applied to adopt another baby—a girl this time—in the hope that this would somehow solve their problems. Three months after that, when Emily had been with them for only a week, her husband was diagnosed with pancreatic cancer, and three months after that, he died. A social worker from the Packard-Weekes agency came to visit. She said they would normally move to finalize the baby girl's placement at six months, and they were sure everything would work out, but they wanted to put off the court procedure for a while, until Allegra got over the shock of her husband's death.

Allegra's and her husband's parents were friends. She had known him all her life, through Brearley for her and Coventry for him, Radcliffe for her and Yale and Wharton for him, summers at Sag Harbor, winters skiing out West. They went out with other people from time to time—she even slept with a few other men—but nothing came of that. They thought they were comfortable with each other. They got married when she was twenty-three and he was twenty-five. The comfort seemed to evaporate overnight. Even without all the reproductive trouble, there would have been trouble, she was sure. She should have learned something from the way the dark skinny boys with the scraggly beards and the banjos and their protest songs à la Phil Ochs attracted her in Cambridge. She should have gone to graduate school in English at Berkeley and thrown herself into the free-speech upheaval out there. She should have done a lot of things. Until her husband died, she felt as though her life had been written down before she was born, in a novel so boring and predictable that even the writer realized it and put the manuscript in some drawer and left it there.

Now she had despair to add to the tedium. No one would come near her in her grief. Or maybe she pushed them away. And she *was* grieving—you can miss someone you don't much like, she had discovered. This was depressing all by itself. Men stayed away, out of propriety, and just as well, in most cases. Her family and her husband's family seemed afraid of her. She loved her son and daughter so much and so feared what would happen to them if she couldn't give them what they needed that she felt it almost guaranteed that she wouldn't be able to. She sometimes had nightmares about having them taken away, taken back by their biological parents. Her husband had been a good father—she had to give him credit for that, too. As good as his long hours at Thomson & McKinnon, Auchincloss permitted. He hadn't had to work but he did, and that was really the only other thing she would give him credit for. Though she realized it was not a bad list and he was not a bad guy. Just the wrong guy. And she had found herself wondering, out there on the terrace when we first spoke, whether—dark and thin as I was and scraggly as my beard might be if I grew one—I played the banjo.

"Now I should leave you alone," she had said in the doorway after saying that Dr. Morales was right. "I wanted to get another look at you—that's why I asked you to come up with George when you took him home. I could have just written you a note, after all."

"Well, would you like to come in?" I had said.

"Are you really feeling all right?"

"Yes."

"Then yes, I'll come in for a little while."

And that was when she sat down on my Door Store sofa and told me about herself. And then she asked me about myself. "And I don't play the banjo, but I do play the guitar," I concluded, pointing over to the old Mexican model I used to resort to from time to time to try to cheer myself up.

It got to be eleven-thirty, and I found I was hungry, for the first time in a couple of days, so, still short on social awareness, I excused myself and went to the kitchen and wolfed down a bowl of cereal. When I went back, Allegra stood up and said, "I thought that talking to someone new or doing something different might help me out of this trap I feel I'm in."

"I'm flattered that you think of me as new and different. I feel more or less like the same old thing."

"I really should go now," she said, pulling at one of her cuticles.

"You don't have to."

"Then would you please kiss me?"

I went over to her and put my arms around her and kissed her. She tilted her head back and looked at me. She was so tall: eye-to-eye with me. Face-to-face.

"Cheerios," she said. "Would you please really kiss me?"

I did my best.

"Good," she said. "Give me your hand." She took my hand and put it on her breast. She tilted her head back and looked me in the eye again, as if she were measuring something. "That feels very good," she said. "You don't know how long it has been."

"Yes, I do," I said. "But I think I can take it from here. I'm getting tired of people telling me what to do."

IT TURNED OUT that she wasn't really directorial about sex but, as in that firm handshake when we met, just well mannered. "May I suck your cock?" she asked, with that unnerving look in the eye, and when I said "Sure," she said "Thank you." "Would you mind if we stopped for a second so that I can get on my hands and knees?" "Could you please hold my shoulders down?" "Would you put your finger in my ass?" She sprinkled these courtesies among other, much more preverbal utterances, and the whole effect was wonderfully, almost overwhelmingly lewd. After a while, she didn't really have to ask but I let her every now and then anyway, for the pleasure of hearing her.

"Socialite widow Allegra Marshall, after copulating with prep-school pedagogue Jake Singer," I said, while we rested.

"What?"

"You know—those society-party pictures in the papers. I've probably seen you in them and had no idea who you were.

And now here you are. And you turn out to be a regular human being. So regular that you probably came over to the West Side just to use me. But if you did, I must say that I can't understand why women are always objecting to being used."

"After we fuck a few more times and then I tell you I don't care about you, you'll find out," Allegra said.

"Is that likely to happen?"

"The fucking? Oh, yes, I hope so. Right now, in fact, if you can, please. But I'll have to be discreet. I am a widow, you know. As for the rest, I have no idea. Maybe your analyst does. He seems very smart. All mine says is 'Why is that, do you think?' and 'What does this bring to mind?' "

"That sounds good to me. I think I have to wait a few more minutes here."

"Play something for me on the guitar, then."

"Oh, no—I'd be too embarrassed."

"Please."

"All right, but I won't sing."

I got the guitar and, sitting naked on the edge of the bed, I played "Lulu Walls," with the best approximation of Pa Carter style my rusty fingers could muster.

"I've never seen a guitar decorated that way," Allegra said when I was finished.

"I got this guitar from a kid named Dave Leonard at Bristol. His uncle Sol bought them seven or eight at a time in Mexico. It was weird—Dave looked and acted so much like me that it was almost embarrassing, so we weren't good friends. We just played and sang folk songs together." I put the guitar down on the floor.

"You're really good," she said.

"I'm OK, I guess. I mean, thanks. You sound surprised."

"I am, a little. You don't seem exactly a down-home type, which is what that music sounded like. What song was that?"

"It's called 'Lulu Walls,' " I said. "It's by a group called the

Carter Family. You know, speaking of being surprised, I don't know why you need analysis—you're so direct."

"The closer I am to people, the more distant I feel, it turns out. And don't you think it's strange for someone to tell all her secrets to someone she has had maybe fifteen minutes of conversation with before? And then beg for sex?"

"You didn't exactly beg," I said. "And anyway I don't think it's strange."

"Well, you should."

THREE WEEKS LATER, after coaching third base in the varsity's last game, against Trinity, I went down to Tiffany's and bought Allegra a silver-and-onyx bracelet for Mother's Day. She had discreetly come to my place again a week after the first time. And I discreetly had supper once at her apartment, late one night. She cooked some kind of chicken and I made some salad. Her kids were asleep. I dried the dishes afterward—I could hardly bear to use the dish towel, it was so exquisitely folded. I left just as the sun was hitting the tops of the buildings on Central Park West. Proctor told me I looked tired when he stopped by my classroom to ask if I would say a few words at graduation. He suggested I get some fresh air after school. Luckily, all I had to do that day was give final exams.

"Mother's Day is Sunday," I said to Dr. Morales when I lay down on the couch the morning after the trip to Tiffany's. "Too bad I don't have one."

"It is indeed too bad, Mr. Singer. It is not funny."

"Well, at least I don't have to buy a present or anything," I said. "So, do you think Nixon will be impeached or not?"

"For permitting you to employ him as a smoke escreen, do you mean?"

"For abusing his power," I said, as pointedly as I could.

"I don't know, Mr. Singer. Can we return to Mother's Day? I know you were just being humorous, but here so sadly, as you know, there are no jokes."

"Why should we talk about it? What's the point? I remember making a card for my mother when I was in first grade in Rockland, and she loved it. And then she died. Now I don't believe in it—it's just commercial. I think that's probably because my mother is dead. Just bitter, I suppose."

"Remove the 'probably' and 'suppose.'"

"Well, so there you are."

"What about your new lover? She has children."

"So? I'm not one of them."

"I shall tell you what, Mr. Singer. I shall make a bargain with you, not because I am feeling magnanimous toward you, the good Christ knows, but because my heart goes out to this woman, this poor woman who cannot have children naturally, this woman whose husband has died, this woman who is trying to fight her way out of depression and make changes in her life, this woman who would be cut to the quicks if she could hear you speak so coldly and callously about her, this woman who has what suddenly appears to be the further misfortune of taking you into her bed. The bargain is this, Mr. Singer: Take the fee for this session and get your narrow and self-absorbèd ass off my couch and go to Tiffany's and with the money buy this woman something beautiful. And then give it to her. And do not come back here until you do."

"Free advice—a first for you," I said. "Well, even the analyst can have a breakthrough, I guess." I reached down to my briefcase, which was on the floor next to the backbuster, and took out the little blue box tied with a white ribbon and held it up over my head.

Dr. Morales was silent for a full minute. Then he said, "Why did you feel the need to tease me in this way, Mr. Singer? Could you not bear the idea that I have helped you to take such a step for once without having to get in the back of you and push?"

"I think you hit the nail on the head," I said. "When I went to buy this, I wouldn't have been surprised to find you driving the No. 4 bus down Fifth Avenue, and when I went into the store I could hear you whispering, 'Now, don't be a cheap-skates, Mr. Singer,' and the only thing that almost kept me from going ahead was knowing how much satisfaction this whole thing would bring you." In the middle of this I had started crying, though my voice didn't break. Tears just ran out of my eyes as if from a spillway.

"Think instead of the person who will receive this gift and how pleased she will be."

"We even came up with the exact same store. You know, I could accept help from you a lot more easily if you were less constantly critical of me, less sarcastic about it all, and if I didn't suspect that you were getting some kind of perverted kick from disparaging me and trying to run my life."

"I think this is the *only* way you can accept help, Mr. Singer. I think I am doing what is right. I do have my own life, you may be certain of that. I am not living through you or my other patients, much as you wish to believe it so."

"Are you sure?" I said, tears still flowing down my face. "Was there a gram too much protest in there somewhere?"

I WALKED BACK to the West Side through Central Park, try-ing to calm down. The morning was soft and warm, flowers were everywhere, but I was still arguing with Dr. Morales—so self-regarding that I ignored the funny feeling at the nape of my neck and the subliminal sound of running footsteps from behind me. Before I knew what had happened, I was flat on my face and someone was running away with my briefcase. The next thing I knew, I was running after him and then catching up with him and knocking him flat on his face and taking my briefcase back. He got up and ran away. He was just a kid, a druggie in jeans and a black T-shirt, with a peace symbol hanging from a thin chain on his narrow, sallow chest.

"HE PICKED THE wrong guy," I told Allegra, late on Sunday night. We were in her kitchen again, eating leftovers from the sumptuous meal the cook had prepared for her and her parents and in-laws that afternoon. She had a cook. How much cooking could the cook cook for this little family? Allegra paid me the compliment of saying that getting through the day had been much easier because she could look forward to seeing me at night. "If you ever meet my mother, you'll know what I mean," she said. " 'Aren't you worried that Georgie will break that? Shouldn't this be a little more to the left?' " She shuddered, and then, as if to cheer herself up, she put on the bracelet I had just given her. It was kind of her to be so enthusiastic about my present, I thought, when she probably owned enough jewelry to sink a yacht.

I went on bragging. "That guy in the park couldn't have known about my blazing speed or all-around athleticism, I guess."

"I did," she said. "Proctor told me when he told me about you before the dinner last month. Did you know that the white-haired man you were talking to, Alex Something—I forget his last name—gave the school a hundred thousand dollars the next week?"

"Yes, Proctor told me. How did you hear about it?"

"In the thank-you letter Proctor sent me. He said wasn't the school lucky to have you as a spokesman, and he thinks you have a brilliant future in education."

"What would he know about education?" I said. I ate a forkful of potatoes as perfect as pearls. "You have a *cook*."

"You know, I can see where you could be scary."

"But you like me," I said.

"*And* I like you," Allegra said, standing up and taking my hand. "Will you come with me now?"

"Shouldn't we clean up first?"

"Leave it for the maid this time. I really can't wait."

"You have a *maid*."

Her bedroom was huge and looked like a chamber in an English country house, with a frayed but magnificent tapestry on the wall, a washstand in front of it, a vast mahogany wardrobe against the opposite wall, and a quiet Oriental rug the size of the Caspian Sea. The bed itself seemed a Yankee interloper; a thin and complex patchwork quilt covered it, and underneath was an off-white down comforter and pillows as yielding as fresh snow. I, too, felt like an intruder there, for all of Dr. Morales's reassurances. I folded my clothes into small dimensions à la the dish towel and put them in a little pile on a wing chair with flowered upholstery. Then I put my wallet and keys and change in a tiny pile on top of the self-effacing clothes pile. I turned off the marble-based lamp that sat on a delicate table next to the bed.

When Allegra came out of the bathroom, I could see by the moonlight pouring in the tall window from over Central Park that she had nothing on. She stood in front of me and turned the lamp back on and said, "Do you like me, too?" She was thin, but her breasts were full and her hips curved just widely enough to escape boyishness. It occurred to me that there is something to be said for motherhood without childbearing, and the luxury of my immediate material and sexual circumstances came home to me and seemed less like a stroke than an assault of luck.

"Yes, I like you," I said.

. . .

"IF IT'S OK, I'd like to get astride you," Allegra said.

"All right."

After this rearrangement, she leaned over and turned the light back on again. "Would you mind talking for a few minutes while we're like this?" she asked.

"Fine with me. You are like an erotic dream come true, you know."

"I swear I've never acted like this before. I wish you could stay with me until the morning."

"I wish I could, too," I said. "But there's your children, and the baby-sitter. And the cook. The maid. And my classes start at eight-thirty."

"I don't even know what a job is like. Is that awful?"

"Teaching is wonderful when it goes well."

"But you have to do it even when you don't want to."

"That's one of the good things about a job."

"That sounds puritanical."

"I think it's just middle class."

"I don't have to do anything I don't want to do."

"Of course you do," I said. "You have to take care of sick children even when you're sick yourself."

"That's love—it's different. Speaking of love . . ." she said.

"So this is love," I said when she was still again. To keep myself from coming, I had been trying to think about how it would feel not to have to work. This beat my dusty old delaying tactic of mowing an imaginary lawn, even though in the middle of my reverie of wealth I felt Dr. Morales's influence seep into the room like swamp gas. *Mr. Singer, I suspect and fear that you are about to open this gifted horse's mouth and inspect its teeth, is it not?* I could hear him say. *Can you not resist your impulse to piss on your good fortune?*

"It might be," Allegra said. "I feel as though we would always get along well."

"But you don't know me at all," I was about to say, before

Dr. Morales whinnied mockingly in my head to warn me away from that kind of honesty. "Would you mind if we turned the tables here again?" I said instead. "Because if it's all right with you I'd like to finish this off as if I were in control, pretty please."

Allegra laughed. "You're making fun of me," she said.

"Yes, but I really would like to do that."

"All right, turn me over now, and we can come at the same time. Let's watch each other, OK?"

"Sure," I said. "It would be a pleasure." And like an eight-year-old boy who has succumbed to wearing a tie for the first time, I silently added to the Dr. Morales inside my head, You win. I'll try to throw my lot in with this rich and interesting woman—who happens also to be a staggering piece of ass—and her wainscoted world. What would that world make of me, a neurotic schoolteaching secular atheist Jew without a Corot, Herreshoff, or nine iron to his name, I wondered—if it ever got to that point. Oh, well, I went on, I have nothing to lose. And I might have told myself that lie and forgotten about it and everything else for a little while if Allegra, holding me in her direct and at that point hectic gaze, hadn't said "Jake, Jake, not yet, please" and I hadn't believed, for a split second, that she was begging me to cancel the calculating decision I'd just made. I did have something to lose, I realized then, as I tried to oblige Allegra—whether more for fun or strategy I was suddenly no longer sure. In fact, some part of myself had just gone out the window and was hurtling down to the sidewalk below, although I couldn't put a name to it. "Now, Jake," Allegra said, and just before ardor obliterated any further thought, I heard my indwelling Dr. Morales say, *Mr. Singer, you may now begin your adult personal life at least a foot or two outside the Eden of anxiety. I promise you it will be interesting. What I am saying is that it is your innocence—your virtue, as if it were—that you have lost, and for that it is a high time.*

PART TWO

The Great Imponderables

I TELL THE STUDENTS in the one English class I still teach that people usually don't think about the accidents that do so much to determine the course of their lives—accidents starting with conception itself, a shot in the dark if ever there was one. Leading or knowing about lives into which chance intrudes unignorably, with an untimely death or oil under the backyard or finding her phone number in your wallet when you thought you'd lost it or a bullet bouncing off a dog tag, helps you to understand where at least some of the impulse to make things up—to give form and meaning to what lies beyond our control—comes from. Our brains seem to require us to try to account for everything, to transmute the brute happenstance of our lives into logical, explanatory narratives.

Small fabrications serve oneself narrowly, selfishly, though they, too, issue from the desire for control—over one's own character and actions. I finished third in my class. I came to a full stop. You told me to. He hit me first. We didn't even kiss. When it's the general human condition of powerlessness and incomprehension that is under attack by the mind's fabricational forces, and when talent and discipline come to its aid, and when everyone including the producer knows that the result is cock-and-bull at its core, a concoction, then instead of dishonesty you get art. Fiction, most obviously, but all the rest of it—architecture, music, painting, sculpture, dance, the whole bag of meaning-hungry tricks—as well. All a grand con, I've come to think after so many years of teaching, but at its best grand indeed, by the measure of anything else we know, and poignant in its aspirations in each instance, and comforting overall in the lovely illusions it creates and in the way those illusions help to keep the huge black sea of what we don't know and can't control from drowning us and in the paradoxical power of those same illusions to give us a bearable inkling of that dark sea's depth and to take us to its shore and make us laugh in wonder and amazement or weep in dismay as the mighty waves of contingency sweep in and break around us in wild confusion.

Speaking of laughs, the kids in my class laugh at the shot-in-the-dark line about conception every year when I talk about some of the reasons for fiction. Those few brainiacs and melancholics who have already caught a whiff of the cosmic arbitrariness I'm talking about and those other few who have already suffered from it, with a leukemic sister, say, or a violation, or schizophrenia in the family, laugh ruefully. But, without rue, the rest laugh, too, even though in the full bloom of adolescent solipsism they don't want to acknowledge that a real or even feigned headache might have obviated their existence. They feel unshakably secure in fate's saddle, and so they laugh only because their headmaster is talking about sex.

Victims of flagrant bad luck or as yet unscathed bystanders, they think I'm blathering just about the books we're reading. None of them realize, I hope, how directly from the heart I am speaking of the real lives I know—lives like my father's and Allegra's. Lives, I guess, like mine. OK, Dr. Fidel of the Right: Lives like mine. I know—very well, now—a woman who was once

pregnant with a child whose father died in an accident the odds
against which must be a jillion to one. The father and mother
were about to get married. The accident almost destroyed her,
too. But, thanks partly to her own native resilience, she has recovered, and without worrying too much about what what she
has been through means. Like most of the kids I teach, like
most people in the world, no doubt, she doesn't sit around
brooding about the great imponderables. I and my type brood
for her. And I suppose because of the brain's insistence on
stitching the scraps and tatters of what happens to people into
some sort of whole cloth, I find myself conflating what I do
know about her with what I don't know. Oh, maybe I'm also
trying to Walter Mitty myself into one of the Twains, Melvilles,
and Hawthornes I've been teaching for so many years, or one
of the Munros, Roths, or Updikes I read. Dream on, Jake.

AN OLD GRAY Ford Escort was parked close to the door of
Jonesy's sub shop. Paul Sullivan pulled his pickup in behind
and at right angles to it, leaving enough room for the Ford to
maneuver out pretty easily, and left the motor running. It was
Sunday, but he was going to be working, as usual. There was a
big job of pruning lilacs up on William's Lake Road, before the
real spring arrived, for an old man who ran his big old farmhouse like some kind of hotel. Paul had meant to start in the
morning, just after breakfast, but first it was too comfortable
to sit in his small house and read the Berkshire *Eagle* about Indian Hill's prospects for the coming baseball season—Paul had
played baseball himself in high school and felt that sports had
helped to get him through growing up—and then he decided to
go across the street, to his mother's house, to see her during the
couple of hours in the day when she wasn't drinking. It wasn't
much worse than a duty for him now. He had stopped trying to

get her to get help, stopped talking to doctors about her. His father had moved out when he was nine years old, to do his own drinking alone. Paul sometimes saw him up in Lee, clearing brush from the roadsides for the Highway Department. He had nothing to do with him anymore. Paul remembered going fishing with him a couple of times when he was very young, and there was never any actual fighting or beating. But it was a desperate, dirty household with no ladder to climb out of it unless Paul built it himself. He had no idea how unusual his escape made him. He knew now that he couldn't do anything for his mother—mumbling and staggering through her yard and through her house every day—if she didn't want anything done. She even refused to let him paint or fix the house for her in anything more than a temporary way. So all he could do was see her a few times a week and try to keep an eye on her. He was just going in to Jonesy's to buy a can of Coke, the one indulgence he allowed himself—living across Mills Road, as he did, from the shambles that alcohol had made of his mother's house and his mother herself. No beer, no tobacco, not even coffee. A Coke or two every day, that was it. He didn't feel moral about it; he just believed that he had pulled his life together, out of the mess it had started in, and he didn't want to take any chances. As he went up the six outside stairs in two bounds, a slight, pretty woman around twenty-eight or twenty-nine came out of the door to the shop holding a little boy's hand. Paul noticed the delicateness of the woman's wrist, the wisp of light-brown hair that fell across the fine features of her face, the tired but careful and loving way she gathered the little boy up with one arm and rested him on her hip when he started to cough before they went down the steps.

At the cash register, Ernie Jones asked Paul what luck he'd had in trying to find new homes for all the squirrels that were evicted when Paul cut down the trees they lived in. Paul and

Ernie were good friends. They went hunting in the fall, but they didn't make a big deal of it. Ernie sometimes had to laugh at Paul, because he was so careful about the hunting. Ernie himself basically didn't give that much of a shit about it. It was just something they did, as far as he was concerned, and he knew that Paul, even though he was so cautious, felt the same way about it—not like some of the bozos who went nuts with these fucking elephant guns and crashed through the woods drunk, thinking they were the Last of the Mohicans. They had gone to Indian Hill High School together—class of '64—and Paul stayed the serious, highly kiddable person he'd been back then. You think it's funny, Ernie, he said now, but as a matter of fact I do feel bad about the birds. The squirrels I don't care about—rats with fuzzy tails, the way I look at them, and you know what they can do inside the walls of a house. But when I'm working in the spring, like now, and I see those nests. You know. Gosh, Paulie, Ernie said. You're breaking my heart here. Woody Woodpecker out there on his own, all the little pecker eggs broke open on the ground, like Humpty-Dumpty. Heckle and Jeckle with no roof over their heads. All the little Peckles flapping around on the ground with no feathers in the wind and the rain. I don't know why I hang around with you, Ernie, Paul said. You are such a sarcastic guy. Prick, Ernie said. Face it—I'm a prick. I hang around with you because you're so good. I just keep on not believing that someone can be as straight an arrow as you are. Any minute now you're going to freak out and go nuts, and I want to be there when you do. God, Paul, I think I love you, and if I wasn't married to Linda I'd propose to you. You're so cute—all that nice blond hair, and you're so strong from wrestling with the trees. Not fat like me, from all the provolone and the mozzarella. Nah, said Paul—I'm not all that good, Ernie. I have my moments. Yeah, said Ernie, you do like a good stiff Coca-Cola every now and then, I have to admit it, and didn't you hold hands with that MacKenzie girl last year after the football—

A dull metallic thump followed by the tinkling of glass came to them through the glass door, and Paul looked outside and saw that the woman with the kid had backed the Ford into his truck. The running board was pushed in and the door on the driver's side was a little folded over. He and Ernie went outside. It was a clear, windy March day with some of winter lying on the air like cold, wet sheets. In the silence after the junior collision, the traffic noise from Route 6 outside seemed loud and threatening. The woman got out of the car and went around to the back of it. The little boy stayed in the front seat. She stood with both hands on her hips, shaking her head. She turned around and looked up at Paul, squinting in the watery sun. The way she was looking up at him made Paul feel like an older person—even though he was probably a few years younger—who would decide her fate. I'm really sorry, she said. Don't know how I could have been so dumb. I saw the truck when I came out, and then when I was backing up . . . She turned around and looked at the truck and the back of her car. Paul saw her shoulders start shaking. Shit, shit, shit, she said, through her tears. Crying like a damn woman. What am I going to do now? The insurance. The little boy got out of the car on the driver's side. The woman had left the door open. He went to her and watched her cry. He, too, looked around at Paul and Ernie. Paul went down the stairs and over to where the woman stood. She turned to him and, smiling through the tears streaming down her face, she said, All I need. Probably all you need, too. The little boy said, You're crying, Mommy. She said, I'm just upset, honey. Had a little accident. Don't worry—it will be OK. The light's broke, the boy said. The man's door looks funny. Nobody got hurt, though, the woman said. You're OK, aren't you, Robby? I'm OK, the boy said. Now that Paul was standing next to the woman, he recognized her. She was a

waitress just down the road at Friendly's. He had noticed her
because she was pretty, and she usually had a fed-up look on
her face but also a pleasant or funny word to say. She looked
even prettier in the jeans and old gray sweatshirt she had on
now. She picked up her son and rested him on her hip again.
My husband is going to go crazy when he hears about this, she
said. This is his car. His car? Paul said. She said, We got divorced in the winter. Ex-husband. Got to learn to say that. It's
his car—he still owns it. Paul said, Well, don't tell him. She
said, But we have to call the insurance people and fill out the
forms and everything. I can't afford to just get this fixed. She
began to cry again. Paul said, Forget about it. My friend Bruno
Paone will do the body work for me at cost. I'll take care of that
part. He owes me a favor or two. It's not like I can't get to my
job today. I'll just use the other door. Bruno will give you a
break on your car, too, if I ask him. You're being too nice, she
said. You have to look out for yourself. You don't have to do
this. Paul said, It's all right. The little boy said, Why is he going
to break your car, Mommy? She said, What, Robby? He said,
It's already broken.

Sarah Gibson lived with her boy in a small but handsome
house, built in 1875, in New Berkshire, on the road between
Deerwood and Wheaton. She had taken her maiden name
again after she was divorced, and that's what it said—"S. Gibson"—in handsome hand lettering on the wooden mailbox that
she had made herself and painted green and hammered onto a
locust post, the posthole for which she had dug herself. Downstairs, the house was one big room with a kitchen behind it big
enough to eat in. The man who built it and lived in it for forty-
five years worked as a salesman in a feed store in Millbridge,
and he must have liked nature, Sarah thought, because an
oversize window in the kitchen looked out behind the house
on a stream called the Potakonk and the windows everywhere
else in the house were larger than the kind that most builders

were putting into houses at that time, out of respect for the frigid Berkshire winter. Upstairs were two small bedrooms made, this century, out of the one large one that the original homesteader had designed, and a bathroom, over the kitchen. In the ceiling of the nominal hall between the bedroom and the bathroom was a hatch door that opened up into an A-shaped attic. After the feed-store salesman died, the house went through three or four owners, tradesmen from the town, but the people who sold it to Sarah and her husband, for close to a song, were from New York, summer people, the husband a young rabbi, his wife a social worker. They had restored the house with their own hands but had then found out they couldn't have children and so passed the place along with sad generosity to this other couple who came to see it one day but couldn't afford even the reasonable price they were asking. They needed a house so badly, with a child on the way. The rabbi and his wife went back to the city to try to come to terms with the death of their only real dream.

Sarah's sister lived in Wheaton and took care of Robby when Sarah was working. The sister's husband was a carpenter. Sarah did the eight-to-four shift at Friendly's and wouldn't do the evening except as a favor to another waitress and if her sister didn't mind. She was good enough—efficient and cheerful—so that she could control her own schedule, even though she'd been doing the job for only six months, since her husband left her, in October. She thought of it as marking time while she looked for accounting or clerical work, which she'd done before she got married. Still, she took a real interest in the truckers and the retirees and the families that packed into the place for breakfast and then hamburgers and grilled-cheese sandwiches. The winter had been hard, with a lot of snow and the Ford breaking down twice, but she had kept up the hope that her situation would somehow improve. Because she had grown up on a farm, over in Columbia County, in New York State, and because she'd had to help around the place from the time she was just a little kid, Sarah was handy and matter-of-fact. When Robby got sick, she didn't hover over him or worry herself to death but treated him like a sick animal, which, after all, was what he was—giving him his medicine on time, staying calmly close by, resting through the all-night coughing fits he had. She gave the car its tune-ups, buying the spark plugs, the oil, and the filters herself. She had taken accounting courses in high school and was a good bookkeeper, not that she had much to keep track of. She could hang a door, reglaze a broken window, fix a toilet's flush mechanism, rewire a lamp, flip an egg in a frying pan. So she wasn't easily discouraged; but when, in the middle of March, her husband told her he would probably have to sell the house she and Robby were living in and Robby came down with his third pneumonia of the year and was diagnosed with asthma, her hope and confidence began to fail her. She had backed into the pickup at Jonesy's the next week, just after the boy had started coughing again in the shop. The minute she heard the tiny, high-pitched squeal in his breathing after the coughing, she saw herself up with him all night or taking him to the hospital for oxygen and then trying to get in to work the next day and getting orders mixed up, and she looked at the field of such days in front of her stretching out like clay. Her parents still owned and worked the farm over in Columbia County. They were nice to her after her husband left—they had disapproved of him because he was a musician without steady work, and Sarah and he'd had to get married—but they couldn't help her with money. She hardly ever cried, and she felt embarrassed about crying there in the parking lot, and then ashamed when the big kid with straw-colored hair who owned the pickup made his generous offer. But he seemed to take it as just a routine thing, not a big deal, and that eased her mind.

When she went to pay the auto-body man over in

Ridgefield for fixing the Ford the following week, he said that
Paul Sullivan had said that he would take care of it, that the bill
should be sent to him. She found his name under "Sullivan's
Landscaping" in the phone book and called him to tell him
that she couldn't accept the money and he said he would appreciate it if she would. She said she was sending him a check
and did so, even though she had other bills to pay, as always.
He came into Friendly's a few days later, already tan despite
the chilly spring days, and sat in her section, and after a few
awkward words about nothing much, he got up and left. She
found the check she had sent him torn up into little pieces
under his empty Coke glass. She decided to send another
check to the auto-body man and insist that he take it and re-
fund Paul's money, but that same day, a Sunday, Paul stopped
in his pickup in front of her house when he caught sight of her
out on the patch of brown lawn with her son picking up fallen
twigs and larger branches form an ash tree that the winter had
damaged. This is where you live, I guess, Paul said. Yes, Sarah
said. About this money, Sarah said. I'm getting a little ticked
off– Listen, Paul said. I'm having a good spring. I'm on my
way over to Tyringham right now to start a big job on this family compound over there. I'm contracting for a backhoe to dig
up a spring and rechannel it. And they have an old orchard
they want me to try to restore. Sarah said, The last time I saw
you was a Sunday. On your way to a job then, too. You work
every day? Just about, Paul said. I don't want to turn jobs away,
not when I'm so close to hiring a few men to help me. My business is growing pretty good. The summer people have some
money to spend and one customer tells another. It's getting to
the point where it's beyond me. I never get to the account
books. Oh, said Sarah, I'm good at that. I took courses. If you
can believe it. A lot more subtraction than addition right now,
though. That's what I'm saying, Paul said. Sarah said, I'll keep

your books for you for three months. In exchange for the work on the car. Hey—that saw at the end of the long stick in the back of your truck there. Do you think that limb from the ash tree over the house . . . ? Could I just borrow that saw for a second before you go? Let me do it for you, Paul said. Thanks, but it's OK, Sarah said. I can do it.

Paul was tireless and considerate. He was considerate enough to wait until she did his bookkeeping for him for a little while so that their making love had no contact with the transaction about the accident and the car, even though she knew he knew that he wouldn't have had to wait, the way she began to look at him, the way they bumped into each other and he brushed by her when he came to the little house with checks and bills in a file folder. He helped her down through the trapdoor from the small attic the second time he stopped by—she'd been putting in new insulation—and even though she was a few years older, she felt like a child in his hands and went weak when her feet touched the floor. Not much experience, except for the back of a car at the Canaan Drive-in with his girlfriend in senior year in high school, and then there was a girl on the swimming team he went out with before he had to drop out of Springfield when he was a sophomore because the scholarship money just wasn't enough, especially since his mother kept getting into bad situations. Sarah had to tell him to enjoy himself more and not be so much like it was a job. Get more out of it yourself, she whispered to him one day when he was with her in her bedroom while Robby napped in the even smaller room next door. He began to let himself go, and then he took over, and Sarah was glad to let him. He would turn her this way and that and look at her, sometimes almost clinically, as if he were studying her—it was always broad daylight, at first. One time he looked up between her legs to try to see her diaphragm inside her. She felt he was trying to figure out what women were like. What they were. Then he would cover her with himself and take her so forcefully she sometimes thought he was angry. Though he remained kind and sometimes boring, he began to dominate her physically, sometimes even ignoring her when she asked him to stop the thrusting that practically drove her off the bed when he was behind her. When he did ignore her this way was when she had the most intense climaxes and thought for a few seconds that she cared about nothing else and couldn't really have anything else in her mind. She would also look at him when he wasn't aware of it—he was lean and strong and had a kind of golden glow around his body. They began to go out—her sister would take Robby, and Paul and she would go to a restaurant or to the Egremont Country Club with Ernie Jones and his wife to dance to the good local rock band that played there. As the spring went on, the boy's breathing got easier. Because I'm happier? Sarah wondered. Sarah's ex-husband got work managing a music store in Hillsdale, and this eased the urgency about selling the house. She felt she was returning to herself, to the more easygoing and practical person she'd been before she'd gotten married to the wrong man. She had to admit it to herself a few years into her marriage, when her husband stopped getting work as a musician and started paying less and less attention to Robby: Her parents were right. She had tried to live her life responsibly and carefully since the marriage began falling apart, but there hadn't been much more than duty and too little money to it until Paul came along. She knew she would probably always feel at some distance from him if they stayed together, but maybe that wasn't such a bad thing.

One warm April night after he took her to the Old Mill in Egremont, he put his hand under her skirt while he was driving and then pulled the pickup off onto the deserted dirt road that went into the Pinewood ski basin and had her standing up against the truck because he couldn't wait, even though she didn't have her diaphragm in. Then he apologized, and she said, No, it's exciting. He told her then for the first time that he loved her and said he was worried that what he did to her and the way he treated her "in sex" was dirty. He used to hear his father grunting over his mother, he said. She said, Do you think I'm dirty? and he said no, and she said, Well, I like it, too, so it's not dirty. Really like it. He got back into the truck, and she was about to go around to the other side when she decided instead to open the driver's-side door. She unbuttoned the fly of Paul's jeans and took him into her mouth. He wanted to have her again, but she said, No, I want you to come this way. After he did, she said, I was married. This part . . . It doesn't last very long. Not usually. So don't spoil it for me by worrying about . . . anything. He said, Your husband and you— We . . . , she started. Don't worry about that, either. Nothing like with you, I swear. I think about you sometimes and my legs begin to open without my even realizing it. Getting wet right now all over again. Let's go home and you can do me again."

Early the next morning, on his way to William's Lake Road to do some more work for Sol Leonard, Paul stopped at Sarah's house and got out of the truck holding a rifle. Sarah was using a paint scraper to free a stuck window in the living room when she looked up toward the driveway and laughed—the first full laugh she could remember in a long time. Of course he's going to kill us, she said to herself. Things were going too good. He had cracked. Paul was at the door, and she was just about to go to the tiny kitchen and get a knife and order Robby to go upstairs and get in the closet when she saw that Paul had put the rifle down and was knocking on the door. If they're going to kill you they probably don't knock first, Sarah said to herself. She opened the door—why not?—and Paul said, Here, I want

you to have this. I don't like you living out here with Robby by
yourselves. It's just a twenty-two, but it's some protection.
Sarah looked at the rifle resting against the clapboards. It had
an old wooden stock—it was very handsome, she thought. It
looked like it was from the Revolution, or something like that—
an antique. I'll teach you how to use it, Paul said. I know how
to use a rifle, Sarah said. My father taught me. But I don't
think I should have a gun in the house with Robby. Nothing
will happen if you're careful, he said. Keep it.

This is so old-fashioned, Sarah said to herself. She picked
up the rifle—it felt wonderful to hold a rifle again. Always point
it down, Paul said. I remember, Sarah said. But what if I want
to shoot you? She put the gun down and opened the bathrobe
she had on and embraced him. You don't know what can happen, he said. People go crazy sometimes.

SHE WAS PREGNANT, and they were going to get married in
May. She still feared his serious virtue a little, but as she
learned more about the circumstances it grew out of, she began
to see it as something close to amazing. And Robby ran to
him when he visited, and Paul treated him gently and firmly.
She was realistic enough to know better than to screw up this
good second chance. One week before the small wedding they
were going to hold at her sister's house, Paul was driving south
on the Massachusetts Turnpike when a hundred yards ahead
a large crate of machine parts fell off a flatbed coming north
at seventy-five miles an hour and the crate burst open on
the road and the parts went up from it like shrapnel. Paul
tried to steer the pickup out of the way, but the gears and cogs
had spread out to fly over all three southbound lanes. Two
heavy steel gears exploded the glass in his windshield, one hit
his forehead and stunned him, and the pickup went off the

road and crashed into the abutment of an overpass. Paul died instantly. Gone like a movie that gets stuck in the projector and burns through, Sarah thought after she learned what had happened. They couldn't pull him up out of the truck cab by his legs until they'd unpleated the accordion the impact had made of the metal.

Ernie Jones arranged for a service for Paul at the Lutheran church. Some people who knew him through his landscaping work came—like Mr. Leonard—and a lot of Paul's friends from high school and of course Sarah and Robby and Sarah's sister and brother-in-law, and her parents. Ernie wept throughout the service and at the graveside in the cemetery near his shop on Route 6.

Still in shock, sure she would never come out of it, Sarah called the man who had been her pediatrician in Claverack. She had always loved Dr. Mandel when she was little because he would play with words while he examined her or when he gave her a shot. "Let us tintinnabulate your knee here for just a moment," he would say, and, "This may stingify your armature a tiny bit." He was close to seventy now but still in practice. She could not even consider an abortion, she told him, but she also could not take care of another child.

He started the arrangements for her with the adoption agency in New York City—it was called Packard-Weekes, and was one of the most respected in the country, Dr. Mandel assured Sarah—and then they treated her so well that to her surprise, insofar as anything could surprise her in her shock, she went through with it. She listened politely as the social worker explained the papers she had to sign, and she understood what she was saying and appreciated the respect and courtesy she was shown, and there was no question in her mind that she was doing not only what she had to do but the right thing, but she couldn't make sense of what had happened to Paul and to her.

She left her job when waiting on tables became too difficult—Robby was still young enough to believe that she was just getting fat—and they stayed with her parents for the last few weeks. It's amazing how a tragedy will soften anyone's heart, she told herself as the days went by and the rolling Columbia County hills turned orange and gold. Her parents treated Robby like royalty, as they never had before. They were about to let go of another grandchild, after all.

Sarah didn't miss Paul himself as much as she missed the idea of him and the new turn her life had taken—missed that promise of change in a way that had her feeling beaten up, or beaten down, like something left out in vicious weather. She didn't understand what kind of point or learning could possibly come from what had happened. She would stare out the window for hours at a time wondering if some plan in all this would ever be revealed. Before Paul's death she would have laughed at such vague questioning. She found the hippies and their mystical ideas ridiculous. Her troubles had been real and practical. Now they still were, but this other, heavy and arbitrary blow, just when she thought things would be getting better for her, had made them and her seem puny, as if she were just something underfoot.

The adoption agency paid all her medical costs and living expenses. The baby was born in the hospital in Hudson, New York, and Sarah never saw her—did not even know the baby was a girl but was sure it was—as she went out at the mercy of the world. The social worker for Packard-Weekes took her right away to the foster home she would stay in for three weeks before she went down to the city, where her second parents would receive her and take her home. The parents were George and Allegra Marshall and the home was their apartment on Fifth Avenue overlooking Central Park, and George already had cancer, though he didn't know it—and of course Sarah knew nothing about the destiny she had given to her daughter.

In that way she was like every other woman who has ever given birth.

She had barely enough will left to pull herself together for her son's sake. She returned to the little house as winter again closed in on the Berkshires, and her ex-husband, who had somehow gotten enough money together to buy the music store he had been managing, took pity on her and gave her both the house and the car outright, in exchange for an end to child-support obligations after one year had elapsed. She accepted these short-term gifts with gratitude where once they would have broken against her pride. A personnel man at the First Agricultural Bank, a cousin of Ernie Jones who knew what had happened to her, took a chance and hired Sarah as a teller. She did all right, though she often felt she was walking through her life now as if through a waking sleep filled with dreams made crazier than real dreams by their realness. Her quietness and the look of resignation in her eyes transformed her slender prettiness into beauty.

A lawyer who came into the bank often, a short, intense young man named Paul Winship, from an old Lenox family, asked Sarah out to lunch one day a few months after she started at the bank. He was a year younger than she but very forceful and intense. His father was a lawyer, too, and his mother was the head of the board of the Edith Wharton estate and one of the directors at Tanglewood. His own practice was thriving, because he worked so hard and was so conscientious. But he was also in the midst of a bitter divorce and he accepted Sarah's quietness as sympathy. The woman he had married came from the same kind of family as his and he had known her since he was a kid, but it turned out that she had no responsibility, he told Sarah. He said that his wife lost things all the time and never paid attention to obligations and started projects and never finished them. The vegetable garden dried out every July, bills went unpaid, gifts went unacknowledged, she would run out of gas in the middle of nowhere. Two days before his parents' fortieth-anniversary party at their house, she realized she had told the caterers the wrong date. Paul courted Sarah correctly and respectfully, and was so mannerly and determined that she found herself giving way to him. He had no children with his first wife, but Robby was no obstacle to him—even though the little boy gave him the cold shoulder—and neither, evidently, was any part of Sarah's history. The part she told him about, anyway. She didn't say anything about her second child, who was now God knew where. He wasn't quite a stranger to bad luck himself, though it seemed to have done nothing more than make him angry. He went at things so straight ahead that he began to bring her along with him, passively accepting his attention.

He introduced her to his parents at lunch at the Red Lion Inn in Stockbridge. His father and mother liked her in spite of her ordinary background because she was so beautiful and seemingly serene. Parents generally go for that kind of woman for their sons, as long as she is not weird or painfully shy—they can admire her beauty and easily assume that she shares their attitude not only toward their son but toward everything else. Sarah saw that Paul's father, who was even shorter than his son, tried to make up for his height with a strutting gait, a no-nonsense way of talking, and prejudice about black people and the Poles, who had settled in Berkshire County half a century earlier, and, particularly, New York Jews, who, he said, were going to ruin everything good about the county, like Tanglewood, which was already turning into Coney Island right in front of their eyes. Didn't his wife agree? There was nothing they could do. It wasn't like a country club, where you could keep whole groups of people out, if you chose to. Paul said, Well, no one has to sell their land and houses to them, but they tend to have the money. Sarah hardly knew what a Jew was, except for the kind, sad couple who had sold her and her husband their house and the old man on William's Lake Road that the first Paul had worked for. She wondered if Jews from anywhere but New York were OK, but she kept quiet. She almost always kept quiet. Paul's father regarded his son the way a coach regards an athlete, it seemed, and she herself felt like a prize that Paul wanted to win and wouldn't be denied. It made her uncomfortable at first, but she began to get used to it.

This Paul drank—two drinks a night. He threw himself into whatever he did as if precision and the will to enjoy himself equalled enjoyment. This looked silliest when he went bowling one night with Sarah at Al's Alleys, opposite Jonesy's sub shop. He was uncomfortable, for once, and couldn't seem to come to terms with the kind of slatternly fun that surrounded him and that Sarah enjoyed—the catch-as-catch-can, low-rent, overweight fun. He had a run-in with a heavyset off-duty cop named Ed Andruss who was bowling a little drunkenly in the next lane and half fell into Paul at the ball-return carousel. Watch where you're going, Paul said sharply. Relax, pal, Andruss had said. This ain't a courtroom.

Paul kept making advances, like a well-trained army on maneuvers, and Sarah rejected them. Paul had been a wrestler in high school and college, winning championships here and there in the lightweight division, but he never treated Sarah roughly. It might have been better if he had, she sometimes thought—if he'd lost some of his control. Even her rejections seemed like part of his plan. When she did finally sleep with him, he took for granted that she was satisfied with him, and that was a relief. In fact, she had felt almost nothing but a sort of disembodied physical intercourse. He never struck her or even came close, and he let her do what she wanted even when it conflicted with something he wanted. But it was always clear that he was letting her. He asked her to marry him two years almost to the day after the first Paul's death, and she said to herself that she could think of no reason to say no, though she more than ever looked at her life and everyone else's, even this new Paul's, as shreds of chance carried randomly here and there on the wind. Actually, that didn't conflict with her decision to accept his proposal. It seemed to support it. Paul appeared to believe that he happened to things instead of things happening to him—he opened the car windows just so far, he arrived on time, he changed lightbulbs right away, he had his shoes resoled before the soles wore through, he made coffee that always came out exactly the same strength, he was an expert marksman with a pistol and kept the one with which he had won first place in the national collegiate championship in a display case in his study at home—and Sarah found it funny and sometimes almost sweet to watch him operate his various systems. She wondered if this big difference between them was what held them together and, if it was, wondered if it would last.

The only time exempt from her nearly Arabic resignation was the time she spent with Robby—it alone seemed within her power to direct, because even though she usually let him choose what games they played and what they had for dinner and what books she read to him, it was her decision to let him. His health was good, he was growing up, so far, without evident harm from the shocks and losses his mother had suffered. Paul affected hearty normality with Robby, and as the boy's diffidence continued, so did the heartiness. But Robby, unlike Sarah, could still hope for what he wanted and hope to avoid what he didn't want.

She did have dreams about the baby she had given away— often idyllic ones in an orchard or in a garden or in a field— which broke her heart when she awoke. Sometimes grief would creep into the dreams themselves as they ended, so that she would start to understand, as she pushed the little girl in a swing made of silver or walked with her in an unboundaried field covered by silk in colors brighter than any the sun had ever shone on, that the child's very presence meant her absence. And she also often dreamed of some kind of unplanned and forced departure from her daughter. She was on a boat as it pulled away from the dock, leaving the little girl behind. A thug in a crowd hauled her away and was too strong for mother and daughter to hold on to each other's hands. The girl walked off from her in a fairy-tale woods in a manner that she found unstoppable. And worst of all, the occasional geometrical nightmare, in which her daughter changed in front of her eyes from a human being to an abstract construction of lines and shapes, with its fleshly content draining away like blood from a carcass, and then the stick-and-air construction that remained dwindled in size to a pinpoint, which disappeared into nothing.

She didn't tell Paul about the baby until the day before she married him. She hadn't been trying to keep it from him—she thought that despite the dreams and the heartbreak, this was the past—that it would stay there and she would deal with it—and in some basic way it was none of his business. Not that she put it like that to him. He took in the information as if it were to be processed. The day after they were married, they set out for Niagara Falls, with Robby in the backseat, because Paul didn't mind. He didn't mind even when outside Albany Robby wanted Paul to let Sarah drive and, when he wouldn't, had a small tantrum, shouting, She's a gooder driver, again and again, trying to provoke Paul to anger and shouting louder and louder when Paul stayed cool, until finally Sarah lost her temper at Robby and he made do with that. Paul had enough money to get adjoining rooms at the hotel and pay for baby-sitting, and this pleased the little boy, and in some disembodied way Sarah didn't have a bad time. The steep walls of water illustrated her sense of heedlessness in the way things happened. When they got back to Paul's big old colonial house on Berkshire Hills Road in Millbridge, he told her that he had been thinking about it and he couldn't stand the idea of there being a part of her that was closed off to him. They were standing on the porch that looked over the town, while Robby chased fireflies on the lawn below them. Paul sounded so reasonable and calm that Sarah had a hard time at first taking in exactly what he was saying, what he was driving at. Only her awareness of her unease about being permanently on his home ground, as if in his grasp, registered with her. She dismissed it as a normal stage of becoming a married couple. Then she found herself thinking, with some shame, that he seemed to her pretty small, physically, to be talking about such a large matter—whatever it was. She still wasn't quite hearing him, and then she understood that that was because she couldn't believe what he was saying and therefore didn't *want* to hear it. And that was when his words finally began getting across to her. He was saying that the poverty that obtained previously no longer obtained. She had a husband who loved her and her son, now, and a stable life. They had even kept the little house in Deerwood, because Robby was so attached to it. Of course—it's mine, Sarah said to herself. And she wondered why he had put the idea of keeping it that way—that "they" had decided to. She had been suffering from shock and grief when she made her decision, Paul went on. And then he said that he thought they should try to get the little girl back. Sarah replied that she couldn't even think about it, and Paul asked if she knew where the baby was. She said she thought New York City, but she really didn't want to discuss it. He said that he understood how she could feel that way but wanted her to reconsider. Robby came up to the porch with a firefly cupped in his small hands. He showed it to Sarah, and when Paul asked to see it, he opened his hands and fanned his captive back at large.

ALLEGRA AND I went on seeing each other clandestinely for six months. It suited her because she wanted to preserve at least the public appearance of mourning. It suited me because cold feet don't always warm up when you tell them to. It suited Dr. Morales, I think, because it meant he could observe how we did in the captivity of discretion before releasing us to the wild of real life. And all three of us seemed to enjoy the tinge of illicitness conferred upon the liaison by its secrecy. Dr. Morales sounded particularly pleased about it as he led me through an impromptu security check on a brilliant Friday morning in the second week of June, when I was lying on the couch secretly wishing my annual wish that he would shut up and shut down the shop until September, as school just had.

"Surely your lover will not be staying in the city for the entire summer," he said, having just reminded me that once again my failure to make plans for the vacation had put "a mat of welcome down for depression. This has happened to you for the last three summers since you have started the treatment," he added. "It is as if by doing nothing and making no plans you believe you can preserve yourself in hamber and cheat death and change in a single stroke."

"Amber," I said. "And it's four summers, not three."

"Mr. Singer, you are like the humpire, never losing track of balls and strikes, and it fascinates me that awareness of time occupies such large quarters in the mind of one who has just demonstrated that he is simultaneously trying to evict it. By the way, the doormen in your lover's building—do they recognize you?"

"One of them, maybe," I said. "They must change shifts at midnight, because whoever is on in the evening isn't there when I leave. And I think they rotate shifts, too."

"I did not request a work schedule, Mr. Singer. Do they announce your arrival to her each time?"

"So far."

"Do you estate your business?"

"What?"

"The purpose of your visit."

"Oh, that—of course. I say, 'I'm here to fuck the lady on the fourteenth floor.' No—they don't ask me that."

"Do you use your real name?"

"I say I'm Judge Crater—what do you think?"

"You are very antagonistic today, Mr. Singer."

"I learned from the master. I just don't want to be here—that's all. I'm supposed to be on vacation."

"Can you please remind me of the time when it was that you did want to be here? You may be on vacation, but I am not, so you will excuse me if I continue. Did you see your lover when she took her child from the school in the afternoon?"

"Occasionally."

"Occasionally."

"Sometimes."

"Better. Did you greet each other?"

"Not until there was a big crowd of kids gathered. Then I would pull up her blouse and fondle her breasts."

"Mr. Singer, you are so funny this morning that I have forgotten how to laugh."

"I just don't see why you're so interested in all these details. I've told you a million times that we're being very careful."

"I ask again, Did you say hello at the school when you saw her?"

"We smiled at each other, usually from pretty far away."

"Did you enjoy that?"

"Yes. It was wonderful to have this secret between us. In a way she seemed closer to me then than when we were together.

She looked at me so boldly. You would not believe how direct her eyes are. It was very sexy."

"It must have been," Dr. Morales said. Then he hurriedly went on, "You see, I am merely expressing the hope that you and your lover have not unconsciously betrayed this private matter, as so many people do in such circumstances, before the time has ripenèd to make it public."

"Before I have your official permission, you mean."

"I would not put it that way, but, yes, you have agreed from the beginning of our work together to discuss with me any major decision in your life."

" 'Do nothing till you hear from me,' " I said.

"I beg your pardon."

"Some old lyric that my father occasionally sang when he got off the phone with one of his anxious patients in the evening. Sometimes sang, I mean. Sometimes. I remember it clearly because it was one of the few times that I ever saw him unbend even half an inch. It was spontaneous, of all things."

"Ah, and why do you suppose your father comes into your mind at this moment?"

"You know, you tried to scurry away from it a minute ago or so, but you sounded pretty wistful when I said how sexy it was to see Allegra at school."

"It is obvious to me that you are missing your father at this time, Mr. Singer. You have met a woman, we have been discussing just now the possibility of important changes in your life, and then you attempt to turn turvy-topsy your desire for counsel from your father—who is also a doctor—by trying to become *my* doctor, as if it were, and by projecting onto me your own wish to replace the cat back into the hat. *You* are the anxious patient whom you have just mentioned. *You* are the one who is scurrying away from your feelings."

"Back into the bag. Or it has to be a rabbit. Or it could be a horse back into the barn."

"I do not care if it is putting a kanjaroo back into the pouch or cramming a blackbird back into a pie or even up the rectum of the king. Wordplay cannot make emotions disappear, Mr. Singer."

"Like Judge Crater," I said.

"*Very* good, Mr. Singer. I would wager that your father occasionally referred to this man who vanished and—"

"Sometimes referred."

"—and that you learned about this story from him. In any case, your new relationship stirs many questions and feelings about your family, I am sure. Perhaps it is time to consider resuming communications with your father. This is something we should think about."

As usual when Dr. Morales added or reentered items onto my psychoanalytical grocery list, I saw myself condemned to wander the obscure and jumbled aisles of my own soul forever, never to make it to the checkout counter. "*He* can always resume communications with *me*," I said.

THE STRAWBERRY MARK on his throat, which when I was a young child embarrassed me but which as a teenager I found distinctive, turned out to be lying atop an aneurysm in his carotid artery. In the middle of May, over coffee in the cafeteria, one of his colleagues at Mount Sinai, a plastic surgeon, asked him if he'd ever thought of having cosmetic work done on the birthmark, which had a shape like that of the Crimean Sea—appropriately enough, as his father and mother had both been born into and fled Orthodox Jewish families in Odessa at the turn of the century for a life of utopian radicalism. The surgeon reached across the table to touch the mark and felt some kind of anomaly in the pulse there. Even in the face of real danger, and even though an angiogram to diagnose the problem should be straightforward, my father refused to have it done until another colleague, a vascular maestro named Waxler, came back at the end of the month from a sabbatical. Waxler left his brain on sabbatical or he was just one of those medical prima donnas, because over the young attending nurse's objections he omitted the standard test for allergic reaction to the dye used in the angiogram and barrelled ahead with it, joking with my father about wishing he'd brought along some of the garden hoses he'd been experimenting with as artificial blood vessels. Shortly after the dye was injected, my father began to cough. Thirty seconds later, his blood pressure dropped and he vomited and then his throat swelled until he could barely breathe and his face swelled until his eyes narrowed to slits. In less than three minutes he had gone from banter to anaphylactic shock and the edge of death. Waxler ordered the substitution of epinephrine for the dye as soon as he realized what was happening, but my father's condition didn't improve as rapidly as it should have, and it was at this point—as my father was being wheeled down the hall toward the intensive-care unit—that the nurse who had tried to get Waxler to run the test and who later apologized to me for the way both he and my father had ignored her and what happened as a result went to the waiting room and, when she found no one there, called Admissions and asked whose name and telephone number my father had written under "In case of emergency notify" and then called me.

The call came when I was struggling to get up out of bed and subject myself to Dr. Morales's summer boot camp yet again. It was eight in the morning of the Monday following his ambassadorial suggestion about my father. Such hints of psychoanalytic intuition seemed always to occur when my belief and hope in the treatment had run to an ebb even lower than usual. At these moments I thought that the Terror of Havana and the theory he represented might actually be on to something. Well after the moment, in this case, because all I could think about right then was how not to faint and Charles Dickens. "I'm really sorry to have to tell you this, but your father is very sick," the nurse said, after establishing my identity and telling me hers. I went cold and light-headed and lay down on the floor as she talked. Nothing got through to me except the persistent tone of apology in her voice and its youthful breathiness and trace of Brooklynese. And what a good time Dickens would have had with the character of a Cockney nurse who struggles to hide her accent while blaming herself for everything, and how I would teach kids about her by apologizing for making them read that part of the book and for being such a boring teacher and so on, until they caught on, and how maybe taking on the personality of a character in a book or getting the kids to do that would be a good way to teach fiction in general—all this as if I were seventy miles away from my body. "Is he going to die?" I was surprised to hear myself ask.

"Well, I'm afraid he's very sick," the nurse said. "We don't really know what's going to happen. Can you come to the hospital?"

"Yes," I said with much more assurance than I felt. "Where should I go?"

"The intensive-care unit on the fourth floor of the Kantrowitz-Hertzberg Pavilion. I'll do my best to wait there for you if I can, but I may have to leave. I'm sorry. But you can page me if you want. But I don't want to intrude. Do you remember my name?"

My mind floated back down toward my skull during this apologia, and I sat up. "You're not intruding—you've been very nice," I said. "Paretti, was it?"

"Parietti," she said. "Francesca. Or Fran is OK."

I don't know if I can do this.
But you must do it, Mr. Singer.

I haven't seen anyone in a hospital once since my mother died—
twenty-seven years.

So you have been very lucky.

Some luck.

You know, it is absolutely amazing, but you have never once told
me the specifics about how your mother died.

You're right, it is amazing—that you don't remember. I told you
during the very first consultation I had with you, three years
ago, when you told me that the treatment would take two
years.

This is a fantasy, Mr. Singer.

Which? That you told me two years or that I told you how my
mother died?

Both.

Bullshit. I can't do this.

But look—you have put on your trousers and shirt. I recall that
she died of a stroke, is it not?

Yes.

How old was she?

Thirty-five.

How awful this is!

Yes.

Was she in the hospital?

Yes—Nyack Hospital.

Did you see her there before she died?

Yes—once. She must have been in a coma. My father told me she
was sleeping. It was Mischief Night, the night before
Halloween.

When did she have the stroke?

At dinner the night before I saw her in the hospital.

You saw it?

Yes.

And?

*She was talking about my new bicycle—asking me why I hadn't
ridden it that day. She was annoyed. She reminded me that she
had had to nag my father to lower the bandlehars the day
before—Sunday. That's what she said—bandlehars. She put her
right hand on her forehead and then looked at the fork in her
left hand. Then she dropped the fork on the floor and slumped
down. My father got up and his chair fell backward on the
floor. He was white. He went to her and took her arm and told
me to go into the living room. She was drooling. I was very
frightened. As I went through the kitchen, I thought for the first
time that the print of* The Peaceable Kingdom *that hung on
the wall there might make sense. I mean, that the lion actually
might be able to lie down with the lamb somehow. Until then it
had seemed ridiculous. A prelude to carnage. I heard my father
on the telephone in the hall calling for an ambulance. Then he
was talking to our neighbors. Their name was Seward. The
husband was an osteopathic whatever-it-is. His office was right
there in his house. He didn't do any work in the hospital, as my
father did. My father had no use for osteopaths, as you might
guess, but the Sewards were very good neighbors. My mother
had even less use for osteopaths, and my father kept reminding
her how lucky we were that such pleasant and responsible people
lived next door. Mrs. Seward came over a few minutes after my
father called, and she stayed with me after the ambulance came
and my father followed it in his car to the hospital. Mrs.
Seward was a little, round woman with round hair. After they
left, she asked me if I wanted to pray with her. For what? I
asked her. Then I said I didn't know how to pray. She got tears
in her eyes and nearly smothered me with a hug. You poor
thing, she said. But I didn't mind, because I was so relieved.*

Relievèd?

*Relieved because I had thought that Mrs. Seward was going to go
to the hospital with my mother and that I would be left alone
with my father.*

Why would you fear this?

*You know. Because I always felt uncomfortable alone in the house
    with him because he seemed so uncomfortable with me. If we
    were going somewhere or doing something, it was all right.
    And because I thought I had made my mother sick because she
    was annoyed with me about the bicycle. And because I thought
    I would have to take care of my father if my mother died, and I
    didn't know how.*

*And so now when this telephone call comes you are afraid that
    you have not taken care of your father and so you have made
    him go to the hospital this time and you may be alone with him
    not in the movie or at the bitch. And the last time you have
    been in such a place was upon the day before your mother died.
    It is no wonder that you feel you cannot fulfill this
    responsibility. But you must. Now that you understand what
    it is that you fear, you are less afraid, no?*

No.

But here you are, getting into the cab.

Yes.

You realize that you must behave responsibly.

Yes.

*But—and I hope you will pardon me for mentioning this at this
    difficult time—you have not called me.*

Why should I?

To cancel your appointment.

It was four years since I had last seen my father. It was in
June, after my final semester of graduate school in English at
Yale. I'd gotten my master's and had had enough. I went up to
Rockland, to the big silent house on the Hudson, a monument
to suspended animation, to tell my father that I had gotten a
teaching job at Coventry and an apartment around the corner
from the school and that I was sure I didn't want to become a
doctor. "I see," he said. But he didn't. I never told him how de-

pressed and anxious I had been feeling ever since I'd graduated from college. He wouldn't have understood. He was a practical, formal, hardheaded person trying to live down his parents' radical legacy by observing convention and to rid himself of the tragedy he had suffered by holding it under.

We were sitting in Adirondack chairs on the brick patio in back of the house. My mother had asked for the patio as a condition for moving into that house and out of New York, and my father, who wanted to accept Nyack Hospital's appointment as head of cardiology, had complied. Beyond the patio my mother's garden grew in a kind of tended perfection that she never attempted, at least according to my dim memory, and wouldn't have liked. It was kept that way by some local landscaper. I had never before been so conscious of how strongly I resembled my father physically—looking at him was like looking through a window into my own future. His hair was curly and shot with gray and mine was straight and black, but we were the same height and weight, we both had brown eyes and long straight noses and long faces, and we used the same gestures. I had also never before been so conscious of the chasm of estrangement that yawned between us.

I had last visited him six months before, at a final, desultory observance of the secular Christmastime that my mother and he had begun observing after they were married. I took the bus up to Rockland on Christmas Eve. My father gave me a very good wallet. I gave him a pretty good wallet. An older couple who lived nearby—a retired NYU law professor and his stringy, shawl-draped wife, Professor and Mrs. Wasserman—came by for dinner on Christmas Eve, and the husband complained for much of the evening about one undesirable "element" or another and about rising sewer taxes, while his wife invited me to join her in deploring the obscurities of modern poetry. The Negative Wassermans, I called them to myself.

Who *were* these people, I wondered, and how had my father, so correct and laconic, taken up with them socially?—but thank God for the company anyway, because without it the meal would have been like eating Christmas ham in a tomb.

My father entertained the querulous couple courteously and noncommittally while he cooked, and the food was as usual plain but perfectly prepared. I had grown up on the ordinary, mistake-free cuisine that my father taught himself and administered to our tiny, stricken household after my mother's death. When dinner was over, I did the dishes and the prof and his wife left, a raft loaded with denunciations of Wallace Stevens and of a rowdy local bar called Jackie's floating in their wake, and my father and I sat in the living room and listened to a Christmas-carol record by the Choristers of the Cathedral School of St. John the Divine, as we had every year since I was born, and he tried to convince me once again that I should at least *apply* to medical school. He appeared as deeply oblivious of my unhappy and self-absorbed anxiety as I was mired in it. The halfhearted efforts we made at less contentious conversation went up in cold smoke between us. When the Choristers' ethereally triumphant exhortation to heav'n and nature concluded, I asked my father if I could take his car and go for a drive to look at the outdoor Christmas lights in the town, and that's what I did, for all of six blocks, to Jackie's, which I had been patronizing with some of my local friends ever since I got my junior-year ring in high school and learned the trick of turning it around on my finger to try to make it look like a wedding band. I'm sure that this ploy didn't fool the landlord—a short, peppery Goldwater Republican Irishman named Paul O'Donnell, who had bought the place from Jackie when he retired into a life of teetotality—but he appreciated the effort behind the charade and had been serving me and my pals, illegally and then legally, ever since. It was from Jackie's that I would drive home and tempt fate by closing my eyes. The next morning my father and I had our cowhide exchange and a silent and embarrassed breakfast of tangerines and coffee cake, and I was on my way.

In the perfunctory post-master's-degree visit in June, as the lovely Dr. Van Fleet roses nodded their approval—even the roses were doctors—my father issued his last injunction to me to get hold of myself and do something practical, law school if not medical school, and said that if I didn't I should be prepared to get along completely on my own, and I took this, in the context of our twenty years' worth of increasing distance and tension, as an invitation to make myself scarce, and aside from a clipped phone call from time to time—when he decided to take three months off to do some research in Arizona, when I was in the hospital after suffering my heroic knife wound—we had had no contact with each other except, on my end, for the shadowboxing I'd done against him with Dr. Morales as my corner man.

The very last glimpse I'd had of my father was at the top of his driveway. He stood there drenched in sunshine but as stern and stony as a statue. And now here he was—somewhere in the sterile, hushed bunker I was forcing myself to enter with knees as weak as gimp—laid out flat and helpless and near death. Six beds, alternately full and empty, radiated like petals from the corolla of the nurses' station in the middle of the room. He loves me, he loves me not. I tried to discover my father within the traffic and paraphernalia that surrounded every other bed. The overhead lights were low, but brighter ones blinked and burned and wavered on scopes and monitors like votive candles, and an incense of isopropyl alcohol sliced through the air.

Just as my body began to back me away from this sanctum and its priests and acolytes, a young blond nurse with a wide face and blond hair in a brittle-looking ponytail turned and glanced at me and then detached herself from the cohort at one of the occupied beds and came over to the doorway. "Excuse me, but are you Mr. Singer?" she asked, leaning forward, as if trying to keep the rest of her ample self out of my way. I said I was. "Your father is just over here," she said. "I'm Fran Parietti. I hope you haven't been waiting for a long time."

"No—I just arrived," I said. "I'd like to stand here for a minute or two until my eyes get used to the light. It's a very bright day outside. I mean, unless he's close . . . Unless . . ."

"No, I know, it's OK. Your dad seems pretty stable right now."

"Can you tell me what happened again? I think I was in shock or something when you called."

At the end of her explanation she said, "This is my third month of real floor duty. If I had more experience, I don't think it would have happened. I could have insisted. I probably shouldn't even be telling you. But it would probably come out anyway."

"Is Dr. Waxler here?"

"No, he had surgery scheduled."

"Another victim."

"No, you know, he's very good, and he's a friend of your dad's. It was just careless. And your dad went along with it. Dr. Waxler looked really shaken up."

"I should hope so."

"He said he was coming back as soon as he finished with this other case. If you want to wait, I mean. It might be about two hours."

"I should go over there now, I guess," I said.

"Less edema, BP's up," said another nurse as we approached my father's bed, and this argot bulletin made Nurse Parietti beam and relax.

"I would have said that I thought he was going to be OK right when you first came in, but I wasn't really sure," she said to me. "Now it sounds like he really is out of danger, thank God. I'm sorry we put you through all this."

I felt my knees give again, this time with relief, and I had to steady myself by holding on to the metal bar at the foot of the bed. My father's legs were elevated, and his body looked as if it had been hauled halfway out of some accident, or as if the top half of his body were missing. I peered over his feet and saw that the fine features of his face had swollen into a pink melon. His curly hair had gone almost totally white. He looked like an afflicted politician, the victim of an assassination attempt. "Falling asleep," the terse nurse said, and she glided away to another litter and another temple task.

"Father?" I said. "Pa? It's Jake."

"Jake?"

"Jacob. Your son."

"Jake, why are you here?"

"The nurse called me and told me what happened. I was worried, but now they say you're going to be all right."

"Thank you. You don't need to stay. I'm very tired."

"I want to stay. I want to make sure."

"All right. How are you, Jake?"

"Better than I was a while ago. I'm so relieved you're going to be OK. We'll talk more when you wake up. I'm seeing some-one—a woman, I mean."

"How are you?"

"He's pretty groggy," Miss Parietti whispered to me. "We gave him a very strong sedative."

"I'm fine. Pa, why didn't you insist on having the allergy test done first?"

"This is the hospital, Jacob. What do you think of it? It was all right before, but you can't come in now." Tears squeezed out of his barely open eyes, and his shoulders began to heave.

"Don't be upset, Pa. Just go to sleep."

"It's too far," he said. He was calming down as suddenly as he had broken down. "Never mind." His eyes closed.

"He's just confused and exhausted," Miss Parietti said. She looked at one of the monitors. "He'll be much better when he wakes up, I promise."

"Why is he so upset? Is it bad for him for me to be here?"

"He was very frightened when he went into shock. He was scared to death. I'm sorry. He wasn't helping himself at all, and we had to give him something to stop the anxiety. And so now he's pretty heavily sedated and doesn't know what he's saying. I'm sure he wants you here."

"It didn't sound like that to me."

"Maybe he's embarrassed because he's so helpless. As a doctor he's very sure of himself—not as an insult. He's professional. Maybe he just feels ashamed or something."

"We haven't seen each other in a long time," I said. "We've had a lot of difficulties together."

"That's too bad. He seems like a fine man."

Not only are there no accidents and no jokes, Mr. Singer, but there are not many questions, as well, in one way of thinking about it. Oh, perhaps in the physics laboratory or in the police interview with the eyewitness to a crime there are real questions. But many questions are wolves hiding in the pants of a sheep, especially in family situations that are stressful. Think about it for a moment if you will. A man is watching the football game in the bedroom on Monday night, is it not? Howard Cosell, Franklin Gifford, and Pat Summerhaul. I enjoy them very much, by the way, especially Howard. The man's wife, let us call her Barbara, and the man's name will be Frederick—Barbara chooses this time to begin to clean out the closet of the bedroom and to rearrange the furniture there, not in the closet of course but in the room itself. "Does this chair look better upon the rug or just off it like this, dear?" she asks

Frederick. "Do you think the dresser should be closer to the door or to the bed?" "Why are you asking me?" Frederick replies. "Do I resemble a faggot interior decorator to you?" Frederick goes to the refrigerator during the cuddle or let us say during a measurement for first down and says, loudly, "Where is the beer, Barbara?" She says, "Isn't it right there?" He shouts, "Would I be asking you if indeed it was right here? What have you been doing, spending the afternoon drinking all my Budweiser and gassing with Betsy and Monica in the kitchen?" She says, "What if I was doing that?" Frederick walks back into the bedroom and finds that Barbara has unplugged the television and is putting it somewhere different. "Why are you doing this now?" he says. "Is there not another time you could do this?" She says, "Exactly when do you have in mind?" He says, "But haven't you seen that I was watching the game?" And she says, "How can you stand such violent nonsense, anyway?"

You see, everything they say sounds like a question but is in fact a howitzer. "Why didn't you have the allergy test done first, Papa?" is also another howitzer as well. You have every right to fire it, because your father has tried to commit suicide by a medical omission, as it were. As a cardiologist, he knows the vascular catastrophe that can accompany this kind of allergic reaction and the anaphylactoid shock that can follow it—it is "anaphylactoid" and not "anaphylactic," by the way—and he consented to ignore the risk. Why the other man wanted to kill him is another question and is for his own analyst to answer, if he has an analyst, which I can assure you he does not, if he is a vascular surgeon of such great renown and believes that he is a god who can abrogate the medical rules at his whim because he has just come back from his sabbatical and his wife has given him a blow job the night before and so he is feeling not only like a god but also lazy and pleased with himself. She probably swallowed his semen and thanked him afterward for the favor he has done for her. Be that as it may be, you have every right to accuse your father of attempting suicide, as you have done, along with expressing your rage and fear in the same question which is, as I have said is so often the case, not a question at all. We may experience the rage and, as it is in this case, the fear and acknowledge them, and then we must assign to ourselves the hardest task of all, to master these feelings, if there is some other prize that we may be seeking which would have cold water thrown on it by the heat of the anger. Fortunately, your father was so sick and out of his head that he did not really hear your question and will not remember it. You yourself may not remember it that before you askèd it of him you told him of the woman you have met. You wish him to know of this new beginning in your life, as we have been discussing. And then you understand that just at this moment when you need him he has threatened you with the same kind of abandonment that your other parent has inflicted upon you.

But I—I am different. You see, unlike this Dr. Woxler or whatever his name might be, I shall not put you in peril by being derelict in my duty. I shall not accept your complicity in ignoring the nose on the front of your face or by cutting it off for you or by allowing you to cut it off in despite of your face. And yes, yes, I know it is asking a great deal to suggest that you forgo the expression of your anger. But is it really what you wish to obtain, the continuation of this bad blood with your father, this perpetuation of a tragedy that promises to make both of your lives proceed, or perhaps even end before they should, in such rancor? This is your father, for the good Christ's sake—this is the man who made you in an act of love with your mother. Perhaps he is a rigid and limited man, but he is not Savonarola, I think. Please try to imagine how keenly the sadness and regret will cut through your soul when you are older if now because you do not try to overcome your own limitations you lose him forever.

FOR MANY WEEKS after Sarah told Paul about her daughter and he said what he said about reclaiming her, neither of them raised the subject again. But Sarah felt that the idea of the little girl, a form without substance, had moved in with them, had simply walked into her waking life the moment Paul gave his opinion on the matter, as if that were the occupancy permit she'd been waiting for, and set up shop. This child, though no more real than the child in Sarah's heartbreaking dreams, had a much more practical, a much more quotidian existence than the one that occasionally enchanted and haunted her nights. The heat of August saturated the valley town of Millbridge and the hills around it, making the leaves on the trees droop and turn their annually terminal dark matte green, and the little girl fussed in her crib in the middle of nowhere at nap time. The single maple on 32 just before Pinewood Mountain which turned orange in the middle of the month as if reconnoitering for autumn drew cries of admiration from the child out of the thin air in the backseat as Sarah drove Robby to day camp at North Wind on William's Lake—at whose shore the other child loved to stamp her incorporeal feet in the water that was so blue it made her soundlessly laugh. In September, when Robby started kindergarten, Sarah went back to work at the bank—partly because she felt she would betray the former, durable part of herself if she didn't and partly because she couldn't imagine spending the day at home alone, in a house where she continued to feel uncomfortable, with the shade of her daughter playing happily away, always in another room, or moping in boredom somewhere just out of sight. The main body of the fall's fire-throwing troops arrived at the beginning of October, igniting their chilly sun-drenched citrus-hued conflagration so vividly that Sarah sometimes closed her eyes against it, only to have its afterimage glow on before her and remind her of her daughter's unreal reality. On the weekends, Sarah would hear the leaves rustle down and around in the yard and imagine the little girl as the wind playing among them.

She went unmentioned and unacknowledged except by Robby, who appeared to know that there was something in the air and mixed it in with his general attitude toward his stepfather and the dislocation of starting school and began wheezing again, and putting on strange little shows at home—eating sugar from the sugar bowl, hiding the car keys from Sarah, telling the other kids in the neighborhood that he and his mother were going to move back to Deerwood. All of this with no mischief but a scary kind of seriousness. He needed to check the front and the back doors two or even three times before he went to bed to make sure they were locked. Once or twice a week, in the middle of the night he would climb into Sarah's side of the bed, saying, "Don't tell him." He was like a weathervane obeying an ill wind before it actually starts blowing. But he was tough, for all that, and he managed, so Sarah continued to take each day as it came.

FAR, FAR OUT in the ocean, two whales breached and then plunged back into the water in unison, then surfaced again and blew out twin clouds of ghostly spray, as white as the whitecaps whipped up by the brisk wind that my father and I were sheltered from by the dunes behind us. The whales were so far away as to appear almost abstract, like animated silhouettes, but they moved with too much grace and spontaneity to be anything but alive. My father saw only remote dark shapes in motion against the ocean's blue. "You must have excellent vision, Jake," he said. "Like your mother."

Instantly I was five years old and my mother had just taken my hand. We were standing on the end of the spit of land that extends halfway into the Hudson from the town of Piermont, ten miles south of our town, Rockland, and the wind coming down the river topped all the waves with white. It must have been autumn, because the trees that lined the road out to land's end seemed to a young boy to be on fire with orange and gold. "Soldiers got onto ships here and sailed far, far away across the ocean to fight against Hitler and the Nazis," my mother said. We stood and looked at the water and the elephant's-anvil moorings, then we turned and started back along the road. A hundred yards ahead, a flock of birds burst from the trees. "What are the red places for on those birds' wings?" I said to my mother. "You can see that from here?" she asked. "Your eyes are as sharp as mine. Consider it a present from me to you." I looked up into her face. "Thank you," I said, and she laughed, and though it baffled me, I felt as though I had given her a present, too. "Why did the soldiers have to fight the Hitzis?" I said, and it must have been another present, because she leaned over and gave me the kind of embrace that children hate and love with equal vehemence.

"I should change this bandage," my father said, while I stood there at the railing of the gray-boarded porch, watching these whales that seemed to me like jokes, they were so miraculous—and realizing, now, that this was the fourth or fifth time that keeping company with my father, which I'd been doing ever since his brush with death, had ignited vivid and exact memories of my mother, for the first time since I was a teenager. My father and I were enjoying a post-traumatic amnesty, and nothing much more intense and intimate than that, at least on the surface. Below our diplomatic exchanges, I could sense the grudging satisfaction he took from the knowledge that I was making my way in the professional world I'd chosen—however he might condescend to its economics—and the clandestine, Morales-like interest he took in Allegra's evident wealth.

"Didn't you change the bandage this morning?" I asked, turning to face him. He was sitting stiffly in a weather-beaten chair. The dressing at the side of his throat was as pristine as new snow. He wore a polo shirt and khakis and deck shoes, all of them brand-new. He regarded our trip from Rockland as a risky undertaking, like a safari, and he had outfitted himself as carefully as he could, given his weakness after surgery, at the men's clothing store on Main Street in Rockland. An arterial resection was what he was going to do, a completely unapologetic Dr. Waxler had told me after the second, routine angiogram, using a different contrasting agent, and he described how he would slenderize my father's carotid artery. And then he did it.

"You were right, Jake," my father said, apparently forgetting about the dressing and gesturing toward the rough but handsome cottage behind us. "My recovery is going well here. It was kind of your friend to offer it to us and kind of you to come with me."

"Well, Allegra hasn't used this place very much since her husband died."

"Still, she is giving it up for us."

"Actually, she isn't going to bring her children here at all this summer. They're all at her parents' house in Sag Harbor. Her husband's parents have a place there, too."

"To be with the family," my father said. "It's important to stay together under these circumstances. It's sad that she is a widow at such a young age. I know what I'm talking about. But at least she doesn't have to worry about money, judging from what you have told me. If this is a serious relationship, Jake, I would look forward to meeting her, of course. Now that you and I are friends again."

"If things get to that point, I'm sure she would like to meet you," I said. "For now she wants to keep everything private, and I think privacy is a good idea, too. She's pretty fragile. Listen, Pa, I'll be honest with you. The only reason we've been seeing each other at all is that she hadn't gotten along well with her husband for years. She bought this place to have somewhere to go to get away, before the children were born. It wasn't like Allegra lost the love of her life when he died—she'd been feeling lonely for a long time. I mean, in case you're wondering why she's having anything to do with anybody so soon after."

"What kind of cancer did you say he had?"

"Pancreatic," I said.

"I would not wish that on the worst villain," my father said, and he shook his head. "At least it's not thought to be inheritable."

"It wouldn't matter anyway," I said. "I mean, if you're thinking about Allegra's children."

"Why not?"

"Because they're adopted."

My father's face lost its envoy's demeanor, and he turned his head and looked out at the water. The whales had vanished. "I see," he said. "In my experience, adoption doesn't work."

"What do you mean?"

"It's not a good idea. It's . . . makeshift."

"But she loves those kids very much. And her husband's dying—I mean, that has nothing to do with adoption."

"No, of course not. As a physician, I just believe that blood ties are of the greatest importance. Have you considered this about her?"

"What do you mean?"

"About how you would feel about this . . . factor."

"No, I haven't given it much thought. It's too soon, and anyway I don't think that the idea bothers me in the least. I know the son a little. He seems like a nice kid. What more would I need to know?"

"Jake, I am a doctor."

"That I already knew."

"What?"

"Never mind. I asked what more I would need to know and you told me you were a doctor. Never mind. It was a stupid joke."

"I see. What I meant to say was that if nothing else the medical history of a family is very important. And you don't know what kinds of behavioral tendencies a child may be carrying."

"You never know that," I said. "You're a doctor, but don't forget that I'm a teacher."

"I still believe it is essential to know where one came from."

"No one can ever really know that either. It doesn't make much sense even in our own family. Your parents and Ma's parents both rejected everything about where they came from—their parents, their religion, their country. They all threw it all away to start in a new place as new people. We might be the last people who should think blood ties are so important. What did they know about their medical history? What do you really know about yours? We can't hold all the cards. At some point we just have to play the hand we're dealt."

"Jacob, would you have wanted to be brought up by strangers?"

Ah-ah, Mr. Singer—restrain yourself. Count until ten, or fifteen, if it is necessary. Remember the lesson your father has applied to your lover and her children and their grandparents just a moment ago—the importance for a family of staying together under tragic circumstances. And do not think that I am taking his side in this discussion of adoption. If the family was created by drawing straws or playing eeno-meanie-meeno-moe, it is nevertheless the family. Those who oppose the general idea of adoption. Or they grandiosely believe that they know God's mind and that God doesn't like adoption. What a rich one that is! God's own Son was adopted by his earthly father, for the good Christ's sake, and in fact the Apocrypha tell us that Joseph was jealous over the impregnation of his wife. Your father put your name down upon the hospital-notification form, do not forget, and if that same name is not prominent in his will, it should be.

Oh, have I offended you now? Was it crass of me to mention the financial element of your situation with your father? I am so sorry to raise an issue that would concern most ordinary mortals, that estiffens the spines of more than half of the novels you teach to your students. All right, then—instead ask yourself what you hope to gain from renewing the Thirty Years War with this old, so sadly limited man who may, unless you help him, have lost whatever chance he had for happiness and joy when his wife died. Mr. Singer, I keep telling you that you must understand and forgive your father. It is not fair, you will tell me, that you must try to understand yourself and those around you when they refuse to or are unable to make the same kind of effort. You are correct. It is not fair. It is the treatment's curse that you must do this hard work while others relax in the indolent embrace of denial and repression and hypocrisy and ignorance and fear. But it is also the treatment's blessing. Because as I told you in the snow one day, if I remember that occasion correctly, it will ultimately bring to you more of what we all want—love, wisdom, sex of the most hot and juicy variety, satisfaction in work, wealth if you desire it. Have I offended you again as I try to put on my coat and leave the room?

Well, then, Mr. Singer, count to a thousand first. Look at the handsome and rugged Jip in which you drove here, and to which the bitch sand is as comfortable as a superhighway, especially because she has not changèd the snow tires off because her husband has died and she does not know about such matters. Gaze away toward the pretty bridge that you and your father crossed three

days ago, as you are trying now to cross the bridge that separates
you—look toward the east, as I have suggested. Look at the
beautiful sky of azure and the white sand and the wild blue ocean.
Look at the whales. Think of all that you have instead of dwelling
upon your father's frightened inflexibility. Trouble finds us always
without our going to its house and asking it to come out and play
with us. Go for a swim. Save the power of your anger, which is
considerable, in case you did not know it, for a time in the present
when something real is threatening. Do not use it to fight a battle
that was over, won and lost, so long ago. Be nice to your father.

"No, Pa, I wouldn't have wanted to be brought up by a
stranger," I said. "But I can't help telling you that if strangers
had brought me up, they probably wouldn't have stayed
strangers for long." I went over to where he sat and leaned
down and kissed him on the cheek. He looked up at me like a
child trying to read an adult's face. I put my hand on his shoulder and he shifted around, but not away from my touch. "I'm
going for a swim," I said. "The waves are nice and high and the
water is warm." I took off my T-shirt and my sandals and went
down the steps from the porch and into the sand.

"Jake, I'm pleased to see that you're in such good shape,"
my father said.

Bear with me for just another minute, if you will, Mr. Singer, for
I cannot help telling you that I noticed your inability to refrain
from argument even while making amends. But, then, a chicken
that does not squawk at all is not a chicken, is it not, is it? While
you are at doing hard things that should be easy, why do you not
admit that for all your loud complaints you enjoy my company,
even when it is only hypothetical? I am smart, is it not? I am
funny, no? And I am interesting! That alone is a rarity, if you are
honest. Maybe I am the father you wish you had. After all, I am

constantly urging you to try harder. I watch out for you, as if it
were. Am I now opening my raincoat to show my own needs in a
sordid way? Maybe.

Be careful, now—you have read that last week there was an
undertone at this part of the bitch.

"It's wonderful to see you," Allegra said. She busied about
the kitchen, our main rendezvous of the previous spring, in an
uncharacteristically flustered and shy way, her usually unset-
tling gaze averted. It was the middle of September, a warm
night, except not so warm up here in the stratosphere over
Fifth Avenue, with the wide kitchen window open to the
breeze bringing the second or third hint of autumn in from the
Great Lakes and across the Central Park Reservoir. School had
started the week before, and Allegra had made this date with
me the day after she and her kids came back to the city. We
hadn't spoken since July, when she called me in Rockland and
offered the cottage on Fire Island to my father and me after his
surgery. "I was thinking about you and your father," she started
off. I hadn't known about the cottage until that moment. She
said she had never mentioned it because she associated it so
closely with her despair during her marriage. I wrote to thank
her afterward, and she wrote back a short letter saying we were
welcome and that she wished she could be with me.

Allegra was barefoot and had on white shorts and a white
tank-top shirt. The summer sun had replaced her statue's pallor
with an almond sheen. She looked sensational. "We had a
good time out there," she said. "Even I did, partly because I
could look forward to this all the time. I even managed to
laugh at the way my mother and father are. It's so obvious the
way they keep their psychological distance from me. Like
everyone else. I realized that without George I suddenly don't
have any real friends, except for you. My mother seems to

think it was bad manners of George to die. But they were nice enough to Georgie and Emily, and I felt like I could handle them. Jake, you have really helped me." She put our dinner down on the marble countertop, filled the two diaphanous wineglasses with diaphanous wine, and sat down across from me. "So when is Proctor going to announce that you're the next dean of the school?" she said with a little laugh, looking down at the table. "Gerry called to tell me he's leaving at the end of the year, and he thought you or Bill Daniels would be next in line. Of course he doesn't know about us, but he and George were—"

"Gerry's leaving?" I said. "That's news to me. But don't you think you're jumping the gun about me being dean? And by the way, how do you know it's wonderful to see me if you won't look at me?" I said.

She raised her beautiful blue eyes. "I'm nervous," she said. "I've been looking forward to this so much. I realized I enjoyed a lot of things because I imagined telling you about them. My mother would change what we were going to have for lunch for the third time in one morning and instead of despising her I would tell you about it in my mind and laugh. Thinking about you gave me a way to feel like I could be with my family, be in my closed life, and be outside of it, too. I imagined talking to you in bed, and that led to imagining everything else about being in bed. I have to tell you that I'm just completely in love with you, Jake. That's why I'm having trouble with how to act."

Now I looked down. "What a coincidence," I said, "because I—"

"No, don't—not as a reflex. I don't want any horse trading."

"You're giving me too much credit for the way you're feeling better and even feeling about me. I mean, you are in therapy, and we were separated for a couple of months."

"I've put off going back to therapy, for one thing. I think

she did everything for me that she could. I'm not sure that what's wrong with me can be fixed by talking about it. For another, you don't have to live up to anything—don't worry. You shouldn't feel any obligation to me. I realize that I'm damaged goods. You can get out of this anytime you want. I would be sad, I don't know what I'd do, but I wouldn't be angry."

She was her direct self again, her eyes level and her voice calm and quiet.

"I'm not going anywhere," I said. "I'd have to be a bigger idiot than I am if I did. Anyway, maybe your example will inspire me to dump Morales."

"I don't think you're an idiot. I think you're smart and funny and interesting."

"Well, that's settled, at any rate," I said.

"I don't know how long this physical longing for you is going to last, but, um, if you don't mind. Is this kitchen-to-bedroom routine getting routine?"

"No."

"It's embarrassing, but I've gotten this chair a little wet. Maybe we shouldn't go to the bedroom right away."

I went around the table and kissed her.

"Would you object if I took these off right here? And why not the rest of this?"

"I see it's still a problem to get a square meal at this place," I said.

"You don't have to kiss me," she said. "I know I'm supposed to want to be all romantic because we haven't seen each other for so long and all that. . . ."

"And one of these days would you think about letting me lead, maybe?"

"I'm sorry, Jake. Really. But could you hurry? I do love you so, and I am just steaming hot."

. . .

"EMILY HAS BEEN waking up and crying at three in the morning every three or four nights since we got back to New York," Allegra said. "Which means that you should leave before then. I'm sorry. She wants to sleep in here with me." We were lying naked on her bed, with the breeze making the gauzy white curtains billow away from the windows. "She was fine on the island. But being away from here and then coming back seems to make her aware that something is missing. Someone. George is lucky. He knows his father is gone. He would cry at the beach because the last couple of summers George would take him on his shoulders into the breakers. I'm not strong enough. You could do it. Georgie got mad at me and started crying, and then he'd just say, 'I want Dad.' Then he would be fine. Emily. I don't know. I want them to be all right. I hope she isn't going to be hurt by all of this. I keep thinking she's too young to be too affected. She's not even two."

"Don't most kids sometimes have sleep problems?" I asked.

"Yes, of course. That's the trouble. With adopted children you often can't untangle a normal problem from a special one."

"Until they're older, at least," I said. "I mean, some of the kids at school—it's clear by then. I think you need a lot more to go on than her just waking up from time to time to start worrying."

"But when you adopt a child you have this urgency to stay on top of things. To anticipate trouble. As if I had. Emily's adoption isn't even final yet."

"I can't imagine anyone being more conscientious than you are. Too conscientious, if anything. Just think of the lives you will give these children." I propped my head up on my hand and looked at Allegra. Even in the darkness—mitigated only by the faint blush cast by the night-light glowing on the luxurious Oriental runner down the hall near the children's rooms—I could see real fear in her face. *Lahbeel,* I heard in my mind's ear—Morales's way of saying "labile." I wondered if she would ever be happy or easy, and all at once it came to me that I was, at that moment, both—at least partly because this person, for all her wealth and intelligence, in some ways deferred to me as my students did, regarded me as a teacher. Which was a little bit of a joke, but I didn't correct her. I decided to be the counsellor.

"This thing about Emily's adoption—it's just a formality, right?"

"When George got sick and then when he died, the agency put off the court procedure. A message from my lawyer was waiting for me here when I got back. He said we should get it on the Family Court's calendar this fall and have it taken care of. I need to write a letter to the agency and to the judge, to say how things are going and to ask them to end the postponement."

"But it's just a formality."

"The agency technically still has custody. George's death has prolonged things, but probably nothing will happen. The judge and the agency both have to send a social worker for final home studies. I almost said autopsies. The lawyer was just reminding me. He said that we really should get the court to make it final."

"I've never in my life needed a lawyer."

"You have to have one when you're rich. His father was my grandfather's lawyer."

"*Mais oui.*"

"Cut it out. Jake, you don't think it's some kind of . . . error, do you?"

"What?"

"For me, for George and me to adopt these children."

"Well, it's too bad you weren't getting along. And of course it's too bad for the kids about what happened to George."

"You mean that he died. No, I mean the principle of it—of adoption."

"Someone else would have taken them, don't forget. They were not going to stay where they were, no matter what."

"Usually I think they were meant to be with me. I have no trouble thinking of them as my children. Then every now and then I do. It's funny, because that's when I love them the most. Or when I'm most aware of how much I love them. When they don't seem to be really mine. The night I read the letter from the lawyer, I dreamed about it—about the letter. I opened it and there was a black piece of paper in it with white letters cut out of newspapers glued onto it. It was like a ransom note. Only it was thanking me for having taken care of Emily so well. I was pleased, because the letter said such nice things. But then of course I went into this panic that she'd been taken away and I hadn't even realized it."

A small voice down the hall called out "Mama." It sounded like a ghost child's voice from offstage in a play.

"Oh, no—it's not even midnight yet," Allegra said. "This hasn't happened before."

"Maybe she senses that someone else is here," I said. As Allegra turned on the light next to the bed and went to the closet and put on a white, silk-looking bathrobe with big red flowers printed on it, I got up and picked up my clothes from where they lay on the floor and started getting dressed. "Actually, I was surprised that they never woke up when I was here last spring."

"I'm sorry, Jake," Allegra said. "I wish you could stay. We didn't even get to talk about anything. This situation won't go on forever if we keep seeing each other, I promise."

"Isn't it the man who is supposed to say something like that as he's going out the door in the middle of the night?" I said. "It's OK—I wouldn't know what to do with a crying baby anyway."

"Yes you would," Allegra said. "Can you let yourself out?"

She came to me where I stood with my shirt unbuttoned and my shoelaces untied and my belt unbuckled, and she opened her robe and embraced me. "You would be an excellent father," she said. "Although you would have to be careful about being too sarcastic."

"AND WHO IS this Hairy?" Dr. Morales asked after I had told him about my reunion with Allegra, leaving out the graphic details I knew he wanted most of all.

"Gerry. Gerald Grossman. He has been the dean of Coventry ever since I arrived. He's going to be headmaster at Trinity next year. At another school. He's very young to be a headmaster. About my age. Everyone figured he'd put in another ten years at Coventry and wait for Proctor to retire and then become headmaster. Trinity doesn't have the same kind of prestige. Maybe he's planning to come back later."

"But he will not be able to, will he?"

"Sure. Why not? It's probably a smart move on his part."

"But you will be the headmaster of Coventry then, and you will still be very young."

"Talk about jumping the gun."

"I may be jumping over the gun, Mr. Singer, but you refuse to jump over even a caps pistol. You are still stuck in the mud, in fact."

"Ah, it's so nice to be back. I've missed all this so much, and it's such a relief to hear your voice coming from outside my head instead of inside it. I feel less crazy already. Did you notice the leaves in Central Park? It's as though someone had lit them on fire, and when the wind blows through them they look even more like flames. How was your vacation, by the way? Mine was very nice. I wasn't aware of being depressed at all, by the way, though I must have been, because you said I would be. And I hope that by now you've forgiven me for not calling you to cancel my appointment on the day my father almost died. As you pointed out, it was really thoughtless of me to let eighteen hours go past like that, especially in comparison to the generosity you displayed in granting me phone sessions in July from Rockland, where I was helping my father to the toilet for a week before we went out to Fire Island. But what can I say? Here I am, stuck in the mud as always, even though I'm back on good terms with my father and my girlfriend is so in love with me that she takes all her clothes off in the kitchen while dinner is still on the table."

"She did this? You did not mention this."

"No, I didn't. I was saving it."

"For a raining day, perhaps?"

"Rainy. No, I was saving it to use when you got bored and started clearing your throat and shuffling papers around."

"Ah, Mr. Singer, and you actually believe that it is *you* who are glad to see *me*, that—"

" 'is glad.' "

"—that it is *you* who missèd *me*, when I have done nothing for the whole month of August but yairn for the opportunity to serve again as your trampoline, so that you can jump to new heights but only with me to provide the spring for your actions, as if it were, so that you can use me as something to step on and then escorn me and resent me for the service I have done for you. Yes, you have made progress, but when your lover and I mention a new opportunity for you in your profession, you pull on the reins and get down off the horse and accuse us of jumping over the gun that you have made sure to unload in advance."

"You'd better unload that metaphor. It's about to go off. And by the way, could you refer to my girlfriend as my girlfriend? 'Lover' is embarrassing."

"Mr. Singer, for you everything this morning is by the way. Such serious matters are now looming in front of you in your work and with your lover that you cannot face them head-on but only by the way, as if you desperately wish that the main road of your life were some stroll in the park to see the beautiful leaves. You want to stand still and shoot the breezes, as if it were, or at best hahmble about oh so casually and observe the seasons of the year, which do not ever go forward but always circle endlessly, because if you similarly have no destination, you can never fail to reach it. You are like the writer who so loves the decor of a room into which he has pushèd his characters or is so lazy or so afraid of what lies beyond that he cannot kick them out of it and into the action. You have masked your anxiety with disinterest, but you cannot fool me or yourself. Now. Let us try to pick up the litter you have so rudely thrown down around upon the floor of my office this morning, and to do that I shall have to ask you once again to answer my questions simply yes or no. Is there a chance that you could be the next dane?"

"Yes. Dean."

"Do you wish to be?"

"Yes."

"Is there a chance that you could be the next headmaster."

"I suppose—"

"Ah-ah, Mr. Singer—yes or no. I am like Aristotle and have excluded my middle to you. Either A or not-A, Mr. Singer. Alpha or not-Alpha."

"Yes."

"Would you like to be the next headmaster?"

"Yes."

"Are there rivals to be the next deeno?"

"Dean. Yes. One."

"Does he deserve to be the next dean more than you do?"

"No."

"You may expand. One sentence only."

"He is a sycophant and a schemer and a liar, and he steals all his ideas from others."

"And you, as we know, are pure of heart and a rebel and a genius."

"Yes."

"That was not a question. What is his name?"

"Bill Daniels."

"How did your lover know that Hairy was going to leave the school?"

"Gerry. Girlfriend. She knew because he graduated from Coventry with her husband and stayed friends with him until he died and is still sort of a friend of hers."

"Are you on good terms with him?"

"Yes, excellent—he and I and a few other teachers scrimmage together against the varsity during basketball season."

"Could your lover and Gerry help you to be the next dean or headmaster?"

"Probably."

"But that would make you a schemer, eh—like Daniel Bills?"

"Bills Daniel. I mean Bill. Yes."

"Still, it is how things are done, if you wish to avoid hiding your light under a bush until the batteries have run out completely. Now, our time is almost up, but there are still two aspects of what you have said here this morning that interest me. One is the wind. You mentioned it in the brief tour of the park you so kindly offered me, about the wind in the leaves. And before that you mentioned a wind blowing in the kitchen window of your lover's apartment, and the curtains in her bedroom in the wind. Why are you being so poetic? I wonder, and more specifically I wonder why all these zepheers and gusts are blowing through your conversation. The other matter is the sexual information that you saw it fitting to withhold from me in your account. You know how important it is, this aspect of the treatment, and in your flippant remarks about saving it for a time when I am bored, there of course like the nut inside the shell lay the truth. Things are going well for you, or better, and so you fear even more the losing of them. Your lover, who is, by the way—as you no doubt would put it, as it is so clearly not by the way—neither a girl nor a friend, is rich and in love with you, you have an opportunity for advancement in your work, and you have reestablished the contact with your father. You need me now more than ever, Mr. Singer, and so you truly do wish to guard against losing my interest. This is not only why you hoard the important intimate information but as you do so make your entire presentation of yourself and way of speaking into an emulation of what you perceive to be my cowstic personality. I accept the compliment and thank you for it, but I must tell you that it is at best a middle rong on the ladder out of your despair. And I shall also assure you now that even if like Aeolus at Zeus's behest you send not merely the winds but even hurricanes and typhones against me to test my allegiance, I shall not abandon you at this crucial time."

PAUL DID REAL-ESTATE law. He did a lot of the sales of big houses in Berkshire Heights, supervised dollar transfers of farm property from fathers to sons in New Berkshire, sold pasture-land to New Yorkers who wanted to build country houses, and had begun to help his father when he was involved with the purchase or sale of one of the estates around Stockbridge and Lenox. He remembered very little from Yale about family law and less than that about adoption law in particular—except that every state had its own rules. He knew that the states had recently agreed to something called the Interstate Compact, but he didn't know what it said. Without telling Sarah, he drove down to Norfolk, Connecticut, one day in the middle of September to talk to the lawyer who through a Berkshire County attorney had so effectively if ruthlessly handled his divorce for him–a Yale classmate named Richard Friedman.

Friedman's offices occupied half of the ground floor of his house–a handsome eyebrow colonial bought for him by his parents, who lived in New York on a family fortune made from the patenting and manufacturing of rotary nasal-hair clippers. Friedman himself had gotten fat, physically as well as financially, on nearly every high-priced and acrimonious divorce in Litchfield County. When Paul got there, Friedman was on the phone, but his secretary said he should go in anyway.

"Harry, we can't discuss this if Miss Brown doesn't know what she wants," Friedman said. He listened for about thirty seconds. "You're wasting your client's money. Why are we talking? She's going to oppose joint custody or she's not–one or the other. Let me know when she decides." He hung up. "What have we here?" he said, gesturing toward Paul with one arm, as if he had made a discovery. "It's either another marriage already on the rocks or a reunion of all the conservative law students from the Yale class of '68."

"No, it's something else," Paul said.

"So serious, Paul. If you don't learn how to relax you're going to snap someday."

"Well, this is serious," Paul said.

"Well, then, sit down. Tell me about it."

Paul sat, but only on the edge of the Eames chair across the big, modern mahogany desk from Friedman, ready to take physical action though there was none to take. "My wife Sarah had a daughter before we got married and gave her up for adoption. She feels sure the baby was a girl, even though she never saw it. I didn't know about it until just before we got married. Not that I wouldn't have married her anyway. But I think we should get this child back. I think it's upsetting Sarah."

"You're right—it is serious," Friedman said, resting his hands fondly on his big stomach.

The phone rang. Paul could hear Friedman's secretary murmuring in the outer office. "I'm not well versed in this field," Friedman said. "No one really is, unless he regularly works with the agencies or he's one of those sleazy baby buyers."

"It's Bailey McGrath," the secretary called out.

"Sorry, Paul—just a second," Friedman said. He picked up the phone and said, "Bailey, tell me which it is. Because if he didn't make that withdrawal, she has got to be lying." He listened. "Then she's lying. Good. I'll talk to you later." He hung up and apologized to Paul again, and then called out, "Deb, hold all my calls please, unless it's Harry about Miss Brown."

Friedman sat back in his handsome leather chair and folded his hands even more contentedly on his stomach. "In one very nasty divorce case I handled over in Lakeville a few years ago, the husband tried to avoid child support by saying that the adoption of his and his wife's two-year-old hadn't been finalized yet. It was a mess. The judge had to concede the husband's point but it made him mad as hell. I was representing the wife. She was mad, too, because the husband's tactics were a surprise and I wasn't prepared to deal with them. So I really don't know much."

"Is it possible to get a child back after one year or two?"

"Was the adoption in Massachusetts?"

"No, Sarah went over to Columbia County to have the baby. She thinks it's in New York City."

"Well, there's this new Interstate Compact about adoption which is supposed to make it all more uniform and easier for one state to accept a placement made in another. Or something like that."

"Maybe the adoption hasn't been finalized," Paul said.

"How old would the baby be now?"

"Just about two."

"It's probably finalized, then. But to tell you the truth, it probably doesn't make any difference. I'm suddenly remembering that New York has just recently formulated this best-interests-of-the-child rule. That's the way they're going to decide disputes about adoption. A couple of years ago they had a disaster—the adoptive parents had to take some little kid to Florida to hold on to him when it was clear that the law required putting him back with his biological mother and that that would have been a nightmare."

"This wouldn't be a nightmare. This child would have a—"

"How can you know that, Paul? It would certainly be a nightmare for the adoptive parents."

"It's a nightmare for Sarah now, but she doesn't even know it. She gets upset if I try to bring it up."

"That's not going to make it any easier."

"What do you mean?"

"It's not your kid in any way, Paul. Either Sarah wants to have the kid back and she says so, which sounds unlikely, or this is going nowhere."

"What if she did say so? Are there any legal grounds?"

"Well, I told you I don't know much, but I think the only chance would be some kind of fraud or malfeasance on the part of the agency, or a claim by Sarah that she was non compos when she made the decision. Or that she didn't have the legal counsel she needed when she made the decision."

Paul moved forward in the chair even farther. "That's it—that's what I told her. She couldn't have been in her right mind. The father of the child had just died in a terrible accident. They were going to get married. She already had a little boy to take care of and no money. She must have been beside herself. No wonder she doesn't want to talk about it now. She'll come around to it once we find out where the child is, I know it."

"Hey, take it easy, Paul—you're going to break your spring

if you're this wound up," Friedman said. "It looks to me like you're pretty upset yourself."

"Of course I want Sarah's child back—who knows what kind of people she ended up with?"

"I don't see any 'of course' about it. Most people would leave this kind of thing alone, especially if it wasn't their kid."

"But now I see that I'm doing it as much for Sarah and her child as for myself," Paul went on.

"I hope you're right. Anyway, as I said, it's not my field."

"Well, you can get me the name of a lawyer in New York who does know about it, and maybe the name of a good private detective," Paul said. "Don't you know a lot of those people?"

"No offense taken," Friedman said. "If I can find a lawyer to take the case on, he'll know the best investigator."

"I can't imagine what that child will go through as she grows up, not knowing who she really is," Paul said as he got up.

"I can," Friedman said, beaming, with his hands still comfortably confirming his girth.

"How can you possibly know anything about that kind of situation?" Paul asked.

"Didn't I ever tell you? I'm adopted. Either I didn't tell you or you forgot. It's interesting either way, because you certainly seem to believe that you know who *I* really am."

GEORGIE WAS ZEUS. He was going to carry lightning bolts made of cardboard that he and Allegra had painted yellow, and he wore a sheet and a false beard and sandals. Emily was a cat and wore black tights bulging with a diaper and a black turtleneck and tiny black ballet slippers and store-bought cat ears and whiskers that Allegra drew on with a charcoal pencil. Her tail was one leg of a defunct pair of Allegra's black stockings stuffed with rags and sewn to the back of the tights. Allegra helped the children put on their costumes while her parents and her in-laws and I watched.

Before we moved to Rockland, my mother took me to the doors of brownstones in the Village on Halloween. I barely remember it, though I do recall that some children begged for money in the streets as their parents looked on approvingly. In Rockland, it was standard suburban operations: door to door, crisp air, leaves falling down, dog shit in flaming bags, recluses yelling out curses from behind closed doors, highwayboys relieving small kids of their booty. My mother took me on these rounds until the terminal mischief was played on her and me and my father while kids outside were soaping car windows. After that, my poor father escorted me, in one nominal costume or another, like a security guard making a show of his diligence, until, when I was twelve or thirteen, the whole enterprise petered out.

Trick-or-treating in a lot of big New York apartment buildings is unique, in some of the same ways that the city itself stands out; it's vertical, rushed, expensive, and noisy. Between seven and eight in the evening, Batmen and Butt-heads, Peter Pans and princesses, Marilyns and Madonnas take service elevators up to the top floor and then zigzag down the back stairs like pinball balls, stopping to score modestly at attended candy outposts near kitchen doors and excessively at the vats of sweets that have been left unmanned by those who are trying to ride out the hour of misrule with a glass of wine in the den. The eleven- and twelve-year-old boys, whose costumes generally make no more than a nod toward their objective correlatives—a white garden glove and a porkpie hat signify Michael Jackson; a T-shirt with "23" scribbled on it with a red Magic Marker means Michael Jordan—like to think they know how to be louts. They spit down the stairwells, pillage the supplies, and deride the second-grade fairies and Supermen. Interlopers from the smaller building next door show up on a kind of guest pass.

The superintendent's teenagers surface from basement apartments but keep to themselves. The kids come back home, faces aflame from exertion and sugar highs. The younger ones stare in disbelief at the bounty they've reaped, the older ones barter less-favored items for more-favored, count up to see who got most, separate the junk according to kind or preference.

After Georgie and Emily got their costumes on, Allegra, with a backward glance of uncertainty and apology directed at me, ushered the kids out the kitchen door, which opened onto the back stairs. She was casting me adrift among her parents, the Herricks, and her in-laws, the Marshalls. I turned to face the four of them, standing evenly spaced around the kitchen table like a well-dressed, middle-aged doo-wop group: the Magna Cartas, maybe.

"Won't you have a drink, Jake?" Allegra's father asked me. "I know where she keeps the good Scotch. Hell, I gave her the good Scotch myself."

"For yourself, you mean," his wife said. "Allegra doesn't drink Scotch." She smiled sourly in my direction. She didn't appear to know that I knew anything much about her daughter. She and the other three thought I had agreed to be an occasional stand-in for the departed man of the house—a Coventry School Big Brother arrangement—after Allegra met me at the fund-raiser. She had called me on Tuesday and told me she was dreading Halloween and had come up with this scheme for having me there.

Allegra's father was tall, about six six. His purple jowls shook with chuckles above me, his one glass eye stared dully straight ahead while his good one looked down at me merrily.

"No, thanks, Mr. Herrick," I said.

"Well, it's six o'clock, so I'm going to just help myself here," he said. "And by the way, please call me Will. You're making me feel old." More jowls and laughter as he reached with a tremulous hand into a nearby cupboard for a glass, then into a higher cupboard for a bottle of Glensomething. "I *am* old. In fact, my habit of Scotch at six dates all the way back to the war, when they gave out—"

"Oh, no," Allegra's mother said.

"Six o'clock is when they gave out the rations of Scotch in London in 1944, to help get us through—"

"Will, is this necessary?"

"Jake, my bride always tells me not to talk about it, but this was a horrible situation—just terrifying. I was younger than you are now. Imagine."

A knock on the kitchen door was followed by a cry of "Trick or treat." I opened it on a dwarf rubber-mask-caricature Robert McNamara, complete with slicked-back hair and glinty fake specs, and scooped up some of the miniature Milky Ways and Butterfingers and Hershey bars which filled the wafer-thin china bowl that Allegra had put out for them. Georgie and I had dumped the candy in it together, and he had mixed it all up, like Scrooge McDuck laving himself in his hoarded ducats.

"Will, Mr. Singer is here to help Allegra with the children. He's got his hands full."

"Pretty good," I said to her as I dropped the candy into McNamara's shopping bag. "You have to promise never to bomb Cambodia again," I said to the kid.

"What?" Allegra's mother said.

"You know, he's McNamara. Cambodia. The war."

"No, I meant what did you mean when you said 'Pretty good'?"

"Oh—you had said I had my hands full," I said. "And they, um, were." I pointed at the candy.

"Oh, yes. I can't believe she's using that lovely bowl for this. It could break so easily. Here." She went into the pantry and got a big metal mixing bowl and poured the candy into it and put the china bowl away. She was tall, too, but angular and severe, a kind of stick figure of her daughter, complete with overlapping front teeth and straight black hair shot with no-nonsense gray. It looked as though anxiety over Allegra's wid-owhood had cost her twenty pounds and whatever good spirits she might have had. "No, wait," she said. "That doesn't look right. We should use the white one." She went back to the pantry and got a plain white bowl. "Claire, don't you think it was foolish to use one of her best bowls for Halloween candy?"

Allegra's mother-in-law, who was now also drinking Scotch, seized the opening. Earlier, she had been at Georgie about Zeus as he got his costume on, telling him in her broad Savannah accent that *her* momma had read the Greek myths to her and that Hermes had always been her favorite, well, maybe Minerva, and that the gods were always connected to certain places in Greece and that panic came from Pan, who was a god, or maybe the chief satyr—did he know about that—? and Pan was an old goat, just like your granddaddy Carter, standing right here, to which the taciturn Carter Marshall had said, "Oh, keep still, Claire, the poor boy has no idea what you're talking about." That had turned her faucet off until now. "My daddy broke my momma's momma's best vase. He was court-ing my momma at the time, and he had brought her some flowers, and my momma gave him this vase for them and he dropped it on the floor and it broke into a thousand pieces, but he was a smooth character. He apologized and said he was just so amazed at how beautiful they both looked and that's why he dropped it. Isn't that something?"

"Nobody cares about that, Claire, for heaven's sake—why don't you be quiet?" Carter said, but the Scotch had done its work.

"Now, Jake," she said, "aren't you glad you aren't courting, with the four of us old coots standing around?" A blowzy woman, the shortest of the Four Mayflowers, wearing a bright, blossomy dress, she had a slight speech defect which made her voice quack, as if she were talking with two invisible bird bills clapping together.

"Jake, you're a teacher, and it's so kind of you to be a friend to these children with my son gone. I'm sorry, we have two other boys, you know, but George was our oldest, and the only one with children and the only one living here in New York." Her eyes looked teary, and if she hadn't collected herself immediately, I might have started to come apart, too—she suddenly looked so grief-stricken. "Well, you know, it's like something out of the Bible, don't you think, this taking of the oldest son. Now, you're an English teacher, do you teach the Greek myths or the Bible to your classes? I think it really helps people to understand when terrible things happen to them if they have some great stories to fit them into and compare them with."

"I agree," I said. There was another knock on the kitchen door. "It's a great help. It's one of the reasons I like being a teacher."

"Claire, for heaven's sake, will you leave him alone," Carter said. He took off his camel's-hair sports coat and pushed his hand through his gray crew cut. "Will, I think I'll have to have some of that Scotch if my wife is going to go on like this."

"Be quiet yourself, Carter. Jake is a teacher, just as he says, and he's interested in intellectual things, even if you aren't."

At the door this time was a tiny, preverbal Elvis, attended by a young blond woman who smiled and said, "Tgick og Tgeat." She must have been a Scandinavian baby-sitter. Foreign au pairs formed a significant part of the building's demographics. I gave the tiny King some candy. A larger Long John Silver came with his mom close on Elvis's heels, and with the Episcotones going on behind me, the idea of a life at sea with rummies, villains, and sadists had a certain allure. "Har-har, matey," I said. "May I join yer crew?"

"Where is some candy?" said the bantam sailor of fortune at my kneecaps.

"Belay yourself and heave to," I said loudly. He backed up a few steps, and I turned over the booty.

"Jake, I was against the war, too," Claire Marshall said when I turned around. "I wasn't at first, but all those boys being killed and the South Vietnamese changing their corrupt government at the drop of a hat, and I just came to think it was just a great big mess."

"Good Lord, Claire, will you stop bothering him."

"That much sugar can't be good for them—Jake, could you give them less candy? I wish Allegra had bought some fruit instead."

"A drink might do you some good, too, my love."

ALLEGRA AND I oversaw the division of the Halloween spoils while sitting with Georgie and Emily at a wrought-iron, glass-covered table which Allegra's mother couldn't believe was out on the terrace in the first place, to say nothing of the children's being allowed to clamber around it. Nathalie, Allegra's French au pair, had gone down to the Village with some fellow-Continental baby-sitters to see the weird parade. It was still light out, on the balcony, and balmy for the end of October. This was where Allegra and I first met and I'd made my dead-husband gaffe. Spring had just smudged the trees with green then, and autumn was now performing its finale of splendor with those same leaves before lowering them to the ground—a splendor that I always found sad. It was when my mother dropped dead, as Dr. Morales might have put it. He was on my mind, because I hadn't had a chance to tell him I was meeting Allegra's family. I would pay for that, I knew.

Georgie was scrupulous in his candy trading. Wasn't the older one supposed to try to take advantage of the younger one? The Park Avenue Quartet watched the solemn and ethical transactions with strained smiles, Claire occasionally bursting out with some Joseph Campbell/Jung hodgepodge about All Souls' Eve. Allegra went into the kitchen to order a pizza for herself and the children.

Emily stood up in a chair in her diaper and the upper half of her cat costume counting her candy: "One, two, one two, one two," she said. Her daytime self didn't seem insecure in the least. Quite the opposite. I told her that she had dropped some candy and pointed to the floor, and while she was looking down I stole a piece and put it in my pocket. Georgie looked at me amazed. I knocked some of his goods onto the floor and apologized, and while he leaned over to pick them up, with a hitch of suspicion halfway down, I took a handful of his candy and stuffed it into my pocket. This time Emily looked astonished and pointed a finger at me. Carter Marshall smiled for the first time that evening and took a swig of his second Scotch.

Georgie straightened up and took note of his sister's finger-pointing. He examined his loot and then looked at me. "You took some," he said. "And you took some of hers."

"No, I didn't," I said, and then I took a lot more of his candy and stuck it into the now distended right pocket of my khakis.

"He took," Emily said.

"Sorry, but you're mistaken."

"I can prove it," George said.

"No, you can't," I said.

He got down from his chair and came around to my side of the table and pulled some candy out of my pocket. Then Emily did, too. She leaned up against me.

"Of course it's in your pocket," he said.

"How did that get in there?" I said.

"You," Emily said.

"I guess I have to go to jail."

"Yes, jail," she said.

"I confess I did it. I was hungry. Can you forgive me?"

Allegra came back out.

"He is hungry," Emily said to her.

"His name is Jake," Allegra said, sitting down. "And he's welcome to stay and eat with us. Would you like to, Jake?"

"Sure."

"Emily, come sit on my lap," Allegra said. "I'll cut up some pizza for you."

"We'd love to stay, too," her mother said. "Isn't it nice that we've all had such a good time? But it's time for us to leave, Will. Allegra, do you really want to use that nice platter when it could so easily get broken?"

"Carter and I should be running along, too," Claire said. "I remember what it's like trying to calm the children down after Halloween." Her eyes filled up again and she hurried over and kissed Allegra and the kids goodbye and shook my hand. "It's nice to meet such a nice young man," she said. It seemed to me that they all loved Allegra and her children but except maybe for Claire couldn't wait to get away, and I felt like an excuse, like relief in a tough duty to which they'd been assigned by a capricious sergeant. This was hardly the high life of luxury and security I'd been expecting not to fit into. It felt more fragile than my own.

"THE MOUSE," Emily said, pointing to the tiny white mouse on the first page of *Good Night Moon*, the book she asked me to read to her when she was ready for bed. When I turned the next page, I saw the mouse and put my thumb over it. "No mouse," I said. Emily looked at the picture and zeroed in on

my thumb. "Under," she said. "No, I don't think so," I said.
She lifted my thumb to reveal the mouse and I put on a star-
tled face while she looked vindicated. She had dark, curly hair
with dark-blue eyes and was small for her age, but she con-
ducted herself as if she owned the place. On the next page I
covered the mouse again and said, "No mouse," and made her
really work to get my thumb up.

We were sitting on a red plush couch in the immense living
room, a cavern of treasure. Allegra, pale and nervous—worn
out by the awkwardness of the grandparents, I thought—had
gone to the study to work on the letter that her lawyer had ad-
vised her to write to explain the delay in bringing Emily's
adoption before the court. The clacking of the electric type-
writer stopped a few minutes after it started. George lay on the
floor, drawing. He had brought his stuff out from his bedroom, which I saw for the first unsurreptitious time when
Emily took me on a tour of the whole establishment. He was
checking me out.

"OK, OK, there's the mouse," I said when we got to the
fourth page, "but in this picture for sure I happen to know
there are no mittens."

"Yes," Emily said, and pushed away my hand.

"OK, OK," I said. "In that case, if you're so smart, maybe
you can tell me where the elephant is."

Emily looked puzzled. She studied the picture and then
studied me.

"There are no elephants," Georgie said.

"Maybe there weren't any in the edition you read when
you were little," I said.

Georgie got up with a piece of paper in his hand and came
and stood beside the couch. "It's the exact same book," he
said. "There aren't any elephants, Emily." He looked at me and
said, "You play a lot of games."

"What are you drawing?" I said.

He showed me the picture, which was a pencil drawing of the head of a cougar or panther. It was good—not only with some modelling, which I guessed was unusual for a six-year-old, but with a real feeling of ferocity, surprising for a kid who seemed so quiet and calm. Or not surprising. What did I know? "It's excellent," I said.

"It's a black panther. They have one at the Bronx Zoo."

"I'd like to see that sometime," I said.

"I'll show it to you," George said. "I'm getting tired of drawing animals. I'd like to draw from comics, but I don't have any."

Allegra appeared in the doorway, diminished by the great proportions of the room and by her own anxious look. Even with a maid and another servant living somewhere in the apartment's steerage, the place dwarfed this accidental and accidentally reduced family. In looking at Allegra I was looking at myself as I had been before I knew her, and that irony—the irony that I had been so worried about fitting into what now turned out to be my own kind of lonely world instead of the world of lavish this and highly peopled that and chowder races and platform tennis which I expected to encounter—and a sudden and expansive feeling of diffused warmth around my heart which I now know is love checked my urge to flee. "I can't get anywhere with these letters," Allegra said.

"There's not very much you have to say, is there?" I said. "I mean, basically it's just can we please get on with it, isn't it?"

"Maybe you could help me with it on the weekend. We're going to the Metropolitan Museum to see the Rousseau exhibit on Sunday with Claire and Carter. The kids would like it. Maybe you could come over first and then go with us."

"Is Mr. Singer going to stay here now?" Georgie said.

"You can call me Jake, Georgie, and I'm just about to leave. It's a school night for all of us. That's one of the few things wrong with Halloween—it happens on a school night most of the time."

"That's right—I never thought of that," he said.

"I'll see you Sunday, though."

"MR. SINGER, I wish that you had not met your lover's family at this time, especially without discussing it with me before the hand," Dr. Morales said to me the next morning. For the first five or ten minutes of the session, I had described the evening as entertainingly as I could, hoping that he might spare me this lecture.

"But I couldn't talk to you about it," I said. "Allegra didn't ask me to come until Wednesday night."

"Then you should have declined the invitation. Now you have met the children, the parents, the in-laus. And you have made another date. It is obvious that you like the children and they like you, and by the way, from what you have told me, the mother-in-lau—how is it? Cher?—has already decided that you will be the rescuer of the damsell in distress, that you are the Lancelow."

"Lancelot."

"Lance*lot*. Entanglements of this kind are premature at this moment, I believe, and in any case you have made to me—and to yourself—a promise not to start down a new and important path without clearing the way in the treatment first."

"But I'm in love with her." If I hadn't been lying down already, I think I would have fallen down from surprise.

"You *love* her? Ho-ah, Betsy—don't kick down the fencing. Love is wonderful, but this exactly is the time for careful consideration of what you are becoming involvèd in, especially, since your lover may be more, um, troubled than was first evident."

"Hey, you pushed me into this, and now you're telling me to back off? Why do I get the feeling that you just don't want to let go of me? And if Allegra is fragile, I'm damaged goods, too. Who isn't?"

"There are quite a few people in one piece, Mr. Singer. This is something that my patients do not like to hear, but there are fish swimming in the ocean with all their fins and gills hitting on all eight cylinders, I can assure you. I have not forcèd you into any relationship, and all I am suggesting is that—"

"I throw this fish back. Look, give her a break. Her husband died, she has two adopted children, one of whom may be having problems of her own, and her parents and in-laws may be OK, but they aren't going to be much help to her emotionally."

"I must admit that it is gratifying to see how far you have come from the days of believing that this woman's wealth would absorb all of life's shocks for her and to watch it ascend the needle on the meter of real feeling that you are able to express. Still, we must analyze the idea of your making a commitment to this person."

"Analyze away, but I'm not running out on her now."

" 'DEAR WHOEVER: It has been almost a year since my husband's death, and Emily is almost two, so I'd like to make my adoption of her final as soon as possible. It would make our situation psychologically easier, I think, and it would be a natural part of getting on with our lives after a difficult time. My attorney, who will convey this letter to you, is ready to confirm a date in Family Court as soon as is convenient for you to write to the court and set one, though he has informed me that Packard-Weekes will have to do at least one further home study, and that when the request to the court is made, the city will send its own social worker for a home-study visit, as it did when we adopted George. I would welcome such visits at any time. Thank you very much for your attention. Emily is a wonderful child, and despite the very sad event of my husband's death this year, I feel fortunate that she and my son and my parents and my late husband's parents and I are all together as a family. Sincerely, Allegra Marshall.' How's that?"

"It's good," Allegra said. "Thanks, Jake. It sounds like you, but the people at the agency won't know that. And it's all true. Except that my parents and the Marshalls haven't been as much help as this implies." She kissed me on the cheek. It was Sunday and we were in the study, sitting on a small, royal-court-worthy sofa with deep-red upholstery and waiting to go to the museum with Claire.

"What sounds like me?"

" 'I would welcome these visits,' or whatever it was. 'Convey.' And some other formal things. When you talk, you go all the way from sounding like a little boy to being very ironic to sounding like a judge yourself. I'm not sure what your regular way of speaking is."

"Does anybody have a regular way of speaking?"

"I do."

"Yes, you do. Oh, well."

"But at least the letter's done, thanks to you. Really, thanks. But I still have this dread that something is going to happen, but I don't know why."

"I think it's lots of difficult things catching up with you, that's all," I said.

"We're ready," Claire Marshall called from the gorgeous hangar of a living room.

THE FIVE OF US went off to the Metropolitan, up Fifth Avenue through the bright early-November morning, the sun slanting down as it got ready to make itself scarce to the south.

Claire was so glad I'd come, she said—it was nice of me to spend one of my days off with the children. She was sorry that Carter couldn't make it. He had enjoyed meeting me the other night, but he just had too much work to do to come today. Didn't I think it was amazing that a customs officer like Rousseau had had the time to paint so many pictures? You know, he wasn't really a customs officer, I started to say but didn't. They're so mythic, she went on. Don't they remind you of the writing of the poet William Blake? I write poetry myself, she said, though I'm too embarrassed to show it to anybody. It's all about the South, probably just a lot of sentimental clap-trap. Do you write anything, Jake? I can't imagine how you would when you teach about all the great writers and have all those other voices swimming around in your head.

No, I don't write anything, I said. I used to write poetry in college, bad Dylan Thomas imitations, but I gave it up.

Georgie walked ahead of us. Emily held Allegra's hand and strolled along proprietarily, as if she were the city's Street Commissioner checking to make sure that the heavy pedestrian and vehicular traffic didn't jam up. She was a solid, athletic little girl. She didn't toddle or trip. She took my hand after half a block and said, "Swing," and Allegra and I lifted her up and she swung forward and landed decisively ahead of us on two feet. "Again."

You know, Claire said, I just think that the best thing about works of art is the way they take you out of yourself. Don't you agree, Jake? A great artist like Rousseau, why, he just put aside his mundane concerns and painted these mythical pictures. He had a tortured life but he got outside himself and travelled to different places in his imagination, and when I look at things like the pictures he painted, why, I can get outside myself, too, and even forget for a few minutes about things like what happened last winter. I know it just shows how old-fashioned I am, she said, but I really prefer the painters who paint things you can recognize, and writers who don't just write about themselves and their problems but who have grown beyond all that and can create a whole different world out of their imaginations. Don't you?

PART THREE

Why Are You Here?

A S WE CROSSED Fifth Avenue, the skin on the back of my neck prickled. I said to Allegra, "Uh, I'm going to go back to that vendor and get the kids a couple of hot pretzels." I dropped Emily's hand and turned around and almost crashed into a man who looked like a cross between a hippie and an amphibian. He wore cheap sandals and elephant-bell jeans that clung to his splayed, froglike legs, and an off-the-rack tie-dyed sweatshirt over his flattened-cylinder torso, and his head and neck came out of his shoulders in an almost undifferentiated slender tube, bald on the top, with a 270-degree brushy black tonsure. He was generally improbable, and as a bohemian impossible—too old and watchful-looking. "Sorry—excuse me," I said, staring at the guy. He at first looked away from me and seemed about to take off, but he hesitated and then put his hand on his smooth forehead, as if to shield himself from the sun that was in fact behind him, and turned back partway to me and said, halfheartedly, as if going through the motions, "Why don't you watch where you're going, buddy." He turned again, to go back in the direction he had come from, appeared to think better of it or remember where he was going, turned back again, and rushed past me.

"Did you see that guy?" I said to Allegra as I caught up to her, a few feet behind Claire and the kids near the foot of the museum's steps. "He was weird. He looked spooked when I turned around, as if he'd been following us. I think your paranoia is beginning to rub off on me."

"Jake, please don't say things like that," Allegra said. She started to take my arm but then realized she couldn't. "Where are the pretzels?"

"Don't worry, I'll protect you," I said. "Here—why don't you keep these until later for the kids."

"You will protect me? Do you promise?"

"Sure."

Allegra stopped and took my hand and fixed me with her unnerving stare. "Do you mean it?" she said.

"Let's go, the rest of you children," Claire sang from the steps, holding Georgie's and Emily's hands. She turned around and beamed at us. She had picked up on the hand-holding. "You're both too thin," she said, "though I know it's the fashion. I do wish Carter would spend more time with Georgie and Emily, they are so precious."

Claire herself seemed more interested in me than in her grandchildren. She wanted to stop and talk to me about every other painting and what it meant, especially if I knew, as she did, about Carl Jung and the collective unconscious. Allegra looked as dwarfed and distracted in the museum as she had to me in her apartment. Emily toddled through the galleries heedless of supervision and kidnappers, as though she were thinking about moving in, with not a trace of her midnight insecurities, and George gave the paintings that contained jungle animals a minute or so of intense study. Standing in front of *The Sleeping Gypsy*, with Emily about to disappear into the next room and Allegra wandering after her and Claire calling me over to look at a different painting, I said to Georgie, "So what do you think?"

"I like how he paints," Georgie said. "It's sharp and exact. I wish I could paint like that."

He walked away and over to another painting, as purposefully as if he were on assignment, and all at once I was in this very same gallery as a ten-year-old, during one of the ritual museum visits that my father took me on from time to time. We would drive almost silently in from Rockland on Sunday mornings, down the Palisades Parkway, find a parking place on Fifth in the Nineties, walk down to the Metropolitan, and speed through the oeil-tromping Cornells or the dramatic Géricaults or whatever other artist it was in a special exhibit that might appeal to a young boy. "Bring a friend with you," my father would say, probably as much in the hope of relieving some of the strain between us as out of generosity, but most of my friends went to church on Sundays, and nearly all of them came from families who hardly ever went to the city. It was before the Tappan Zee Bridge was built, and Rockland had not yet become a commuter town. Georgie came away from the painting and said to me, "Every single leaf has a pattern. I bet it took him more than a year to paint that." He looked around. "Where's Mom and Emily? I'm getting tired."

My father had restricted our viewing to exactly forty-five formal minutes, and then it was on to see a few particular favorites in the permanent collection—the Greek statues, the Egyptian stuff—and finally to the cafeteria, where we exchanged pleasantries like two strangers who find themselves sitting next to each other on a bus that has been delayed by an accident up ahead which they can't see. The museum visit was a routine that never varied in its elements or in its sense more of necessity than of pleasure, and that, I now realized with surprise as I looked down at Georgie, my father must have followed out of consideration for both of us rather than simply out of his inclination to quantify and limit everything, especially the time he spent with his son. How hard it must have been for my father, I said to myself, and I felt real sorrow, and then Georgie surprised me further by taking my hand. "You know, you and my father like the same kind of painting," I said. So maybe he did get something out of those museum marches for himself after all. "Would you like to meet him sometime?"

Georgie said, "Sure, I guess so."

"Maybe this afternoon," I said.

In the cafeteria, with Allegra and the children off to get some food, Claire and I sat down at an empty table, and she gabbled on about Rousseau, invoking Jung again, and Joseph Campbell again, and expressing amazement about Rousseau's having been so productive as a painter when his life was so hard—"He lost children, too, you know," she said, with tears welling up in *her* eyes—and considering that he had a regular job as a customs official.

"You know, he wasn't really a customs official," I said. "He had some other kind of job in the customs office, some kind of tax job, but they called him *le douanier* anyway."

"Well, now, that's fascinating," Claire said, sniffling and then blowing her nose.

"It would be as if people called me *le professeur.*"

"Where did you go to college, Jake?" Claire asked.

"Bristol."

"Now is that as hard a school as they say it is? You must have majored in art history. I wish I'd studied art at Emory."

"Actually, I minored in it. But I had a great modern-painting seminar with a Welshman who had a hobby of studying American accents. He might have even been able to guess that you're from the South, Mrs. Marshall."

"Oh, hush, Jake," Claire said. "And call me Claire."

"My father wanted me to go to Columbia, because he did. He didn't like Bristol at all. It was too unconventional for him. He didn't like all the folk-music records I brought home and played. And then I let him down by not going to medical school."

"Is that what he is—a doctor?"

"Yes. He's a cardiologist. He lives in Rockland, up on the Hudson, by himself—my mother died when I was six."

"How sad," Claire said. "But how wonderful that he's a doctor. I do wish I had made a career for myself. I believe it would have helped after George died to have some useful work to keep me going."

"It looks to me like you're doing OK."

"Not at night, when there's no one to talk to except someone who doesn't want to listen."

Allegra and the children came back to the table then, with yogurt and cinnamon buns and coffee and tea and milk.

"Jake was just telling me more about Rousseau," Claire said. She blew her nose again. "He's very good in art history."

"He never believed he was a simple painter," I said to Georgie. "He thought he was as fancy as any of the painters who went to college to study painting."

"Who?" Georgie said.

Emily stood up in her chair and gazed out across the cafeteria as if to survey her holdings. I saw myself in this same room with my father, both of us locked up inside ourselves, twenty-five years before, and then with Samira just a couple of years earlier—if I'd been a little readier to leave myself behind, I might easily be eating the sad Lebanese physician's kebab in New Jersey instead of drinking Metropolitan Museum coffee with this family. I envied Emily her assurance, the child's unaware assumption that her circumstances and her company were matters of necessity rather than the absolute contingency that I saw laced through everyone's life. For my part, I gazed around the table and saw it as an islet, with five passengers washed ashore arbitrarily and thrown together randomly by the Ocean of Chance. So-called family, because it wasn't a family, strictly speaking. Not even loosely speaking. None of the five had any genetic or legal relationship to any other, except for Georgie and Allegra, but here we were, together, making the best of our leases on life, trying to build a structure to replace earlier ones that chance had razed. Given the ragtag troubles that threw us together, I found it surprising to feel as at ease as I did. Start something and it just carries you along, I said to myself.

"I DON'T WANT to go," Robby said. He climbed into Sarah's lap. She was sitting downstairs in her bathrobe, feeling, as she often did, like a stranger in this big house on Berkshire Hills Road, in its living room with its fancy white swagged curtains over windows that had such a rich view of the town of Millbridge below, and with its gleaming floors and its silver-framed family pictures shining on the mantel over the fireplace with its heirloom and irons and its scrolled brass fender, and with its fine furniture that Robby had to be so careful of.

She was sick—she had slept badly because she had a fever and ached all over. Next to her Paul slept undisturbed. Early in the morning she dreamed him into an intruder who had happened by and decided to stay and rent the space next to her from a landlord who didn't care about her comfort. It's because I'm sick, she told herself, when she remembered the dream and when she looked around her and had no sense of belonging in this house.

"Robby, I'm sorry, sweetie," she said. "I feel too bad for you to be in my lap. Anyway, you shouldn't get so close. You'll catch my germs."

Robby got down and sat at her feet. "I want your germs," he said. "I don't want to go."

Sarah thought the aspirin she'd taken must be wearing off,

because she was having chills again, and everything she saw or heard, even Robby, seemed feeble or distorted, sick itself. The dark-green slipcover on the armchair where she sat looked putrid, her slippers felt like they had grown around her feet, the light from the lamp was a torture device, the pattern on the rug a mess. When you feel bad, she thought, everything around you looks bad.

Robby unwrapped a miniature Milky Way from his Halloween stash and ate it. The smell of it nauseated Sarah. "You haven't even had lunch yet. How much of that candy do you have left?"

"A lot. I hid it."

"Oh, great," Sarah said, shielding her eyes with her hand against the lamp's punishment.

Paul came down the stairs, wearing olive slacks with creases that looked planed and a tattersall shirt. He was holding his Deerfield letter sweater. He had won it in squash. He looked like a puppet, Sarah thought. Something you'd keep in a box when you weren't using it. But what would you use it for? She smiled. She remembered Paul silently clambering on top of her two nights before and then plugging away at her in his drill-like way. For the first time she had fantasized him into the first Paul, with his long legs and powerful shoulders and his naïve enthusiasm, and she had come when the real-life Paul did, and he was so happy about the whole thing that he began to tell her how he planned to expand his practice by taking on a partner or two. And then he said he would have another kind of very important news to tell her in a couple of weeks. It was sweet, in a way, but she lay there as lonely as if she were listening to the radio.

Paul put his sweater over his head smartly and then looked at Sarah. "I'm glad to see that you're smiling," he said. "You must be feeling better. Are you up to going to the game with us?"

"Actually, I feel worse," she said. "Just smiling at you. I can't go to the game."

"Well, buddy, it's just you and me, I guess," Paul said.

"I don't want to go," Robby said. "I hate football."

"He doesn't have to go," Sarah said. "Why don't you both stay here?"

"I want to go," Paul said. "And you're too sick to have him stay home with you. It's a big game today, Robby. Indian Hill has to win to stay in contention for a league championship again this year."

"I hate football today," Robby said, taking Sarah's hand. Sarah glanced down at him. His dark hair shone so much that for a moment it seemed fake.

"You go ahead," Sarah said. "Robby can stay home and watch television. I can rest."

"No, we're going, and that's that," Paul said. "We've got to support the team. Someday maybe Robby will be playing and he'll want people to come and watch him."

"I don't want to go today," Robby said.

"Get your coat, Robby-o," Paul said. "Your mom isn't feeling well. We should leave her alone so she'll feel better."

"Oh, fine," Robby said. He got up and went into the entrance hall and opened the closet door and jumped up to get his coat off the hook.

Sarah was too weak to get angry at Paul. "You look beautiful even when you're sick," he said to her, and she couldn't wait for him to get out. He turned around and followed Robby and put on his loden coat. He leaned over to take Robby's hand, but Robby dodged him by bending over to retie his shoelace.

After they'd left, Sarah wandered around from the living room to the kitchen, where the sight and the thought of food made her feel still worse, to the dining room, to the study, where everything was in aggressively rectangular order—the papers squared away on Paul's desk, the rug squared away on the floor, the tasteful local landscapes that Paul collected squared away on the walls, the two pistols he had competed with in college, flanked symmetrically by display cases of his wrestling ribbons, squarely in *their* case squarely in the middle of the mantel over the fireplace, in which the andirons stood squarely perpendicular to the chimney wall—and finally back to the living room, where she sat on the window seat before the bay window, which looked not east over the town but west, over the hills between Millbridge and Sisson Valley. The day was a bright, chilly-looking, windy one. A few shreds of white clouds strayed past in the painfully blue sky. The meadows were already tufty and tan from the frost, and the leaves that were still on the trees had lost their vivid colors. The hills rolled away toward the horizon, and Sarah sensed a benign indifference emanating from them to her, to everything, joining her, in its completeness, to her daughter—the immense, peaceful indifference of the huge rocky land, the entire rocky and watery earth as it turned, as it tilted toward winter, the blessed simplicity and unconcern of everything in the rock and the water of the real world outside consciousness.

"So NOW YOU have gone the entire hog in violating our agreement," Dr. Morales said. "Not only have you without consultation with me met your lover's children and her parents and her in-laus—twice, to boot it—but you have taken her and her children to meet your father in Rockleigh. You know, Mr. Singer, this is now more than a minor breach of the rules that you have promised to keep."

"Rockland," I said. "Rockland, Rockland, Rockland. So sue me. Allegra will pay my legal costs."

"Aha! You are feeling rich now, eh? You can act without heed of your promises and your lover will feet the bills."

"Foot," I said. "By the way, don't let me forget to tell you about this weird guy I ran into on Fifth Avenue and then saw again in Rockland."

"Foot. I may never find out about this weird guy or anything else from you, because I would certainly be within my rights to terminate our work immediately, you know. The rules have their reasons, Mr. Singer, and this wholesale disregard of them by you makes it very difficult to continue with analysis. You must not commit yourself before you're sure who it is that you are and what it is that you want, and whether the path you are taking will lead you to it."

"More of your empty threats," I said. "You couldn't get along without me, and you know it. But maybe you've done better and quicker work than you think. Give yourself credit instead of being so ready to blame me." I turned my head and looked across Dr. Morales's cluttered office, with its columns of book piles and ground cover of papers and files and its big brown boulder of a desk, and out the window at the backs of other brownstones. A rod of what I knew had started out as brilliant sunshine struggled through the glass and the dust and grime in an effort to brighten this pit into which so much quotidian misery and real anguish and intractable self-loathing and grandiosity had been dumped, but by the time it hit the floor it looked less like the result of titanic nuclear activity, which had blasted its bright product across ninety-three million miles of space and through a dense rind of atmosphere to bring the gift of life to earth, than a urine stain.

"By the way, so long as you are anticipating court costs, I may mention that you have not told me, I believe, exactly how rich your lover is. It is clear to me that you have gone a great distance from the station where you thought her resources were a block of the road, to the place where you enjoy riding in the luxury vehicle and wish to rave its engine to show off to the lookers-on."

"Aha! yourself," I said. "You'd love to see her portfolio, I'm sure. You could probably give her investment guy some good advice. Of course you want me to proceed with caution now, now that I'm with this rich dame who might someday be willing to bankroll my visits to see you, especially since she has quit her own treatment."

"She has?"

"Yes. Or at least for the time being. She doesn't think she needs it, now that she's found the cure for her disease."

"Mr. Singer. Oh, Mr. Singer, Mr. Singer, Mr. Singer. If you were an upstanding comedian, the owdience would oblige you very quickly to sit down, I can assure you. You would have rotted tomatoes dripping down about your face as the hooker came out from the wings and yanked you off the stage by your scrawny neck. This is how unfunny you are as you try to esquirm away as always from . . ."

I looked out the window again, feeling a great surge of affection and sympathy for this man whose work with me would never be done, and a great desire to lie there and cross swords with him forever. "You know," I said, "it's a genuine relief and refuge to come here to see you, instead of the torture session it used to be. I've fallen so far short of your goals for me for so long that I've learned that I have to make do with the best I can do. Which has been a great lesson."

"You are not listening to me—how do you know where you have fallen, short or long?"

"You listen—I am back on good terms with my boss and with my father. I have a beautiful, rich girlfriend. She *is* very rich, by the way, to answer your question. The one thing I know about her wealth is that she holds one percent of all the AT&T common stock that there is, and that's just the beginning. She told me that in bed just after I teased her for being cheap for having only two phones in her whole gigantic apartment and just before she asked me if I wanted to watch her masturbate. My anxiety and depression have lifted. I'm even willing to give your slice-and-dice analysis method some of the credit, maybe even a lot of the credit. But in any case I think I can make some important decisions on my own now."

"The Declaration of Independence!" Dr. Morales said. "Next you will be liberating Cuba so that I can return. All right, I can see that you are too full of yourself this morning to allow room for real insight to rent any espace, but I shall still ask you to put off the Tea Party for some time yet, until you may come down from the heights of this misleading self-assurance and understand that the exit of being a Wise Guy along the superhighway may be a good place to stop and have a soda pop, and it may be a more congenial environment than the twin cities of Anxiety and Depression, but it is not the same as the destination of Maturity. In this regard, and speaking of travels, perhaps you can tell me just a little about how it went with your father when you took the laws of analysis into your own hands and visited him with your lover and her children yesterday, but first, did you watch her?"

"Did I watch her what?"

"Did you watch her masturbate?" Dr. Morales asked, his voice taking on the caramelized tone he drizzled over words in discussing sex. "You, ah, mentioned that she has invited you to watch her, so I am now asking you if you did."

"Yes."

"And?"

"And what?"

"So now you are teasing me. I have told you and told you how important it is to be frank and candid about sexual matters, but here you are still the croquette."

Allegra had taken the covers off and drawn her knees up and opened her legs, I recalled. She turned her head into the pillow, and with her mouth slightly open and with the middle and ring fingers of her right hand, like a pastry chef buttering the bottom of a shallow muffin cup, she rubbed herself in a small circle, and her hand moved with delicacy and tension. I looked at her face then, because it was so wonderful to watch her lose herself, and in a few minutes, after she began kneading her breasts with her left hand, she said, "I'm almost there," and turned on her other side, away from me, and said, "Please." When I started to enter her, she canted her hips forward and down and said, "There, please."

"Well, she went to the refrigerator and came back to the bedroom with a zucchini," I said to Dr. Morales, "and then she dipped it into a jar filled with Mazola oil, and then she—"

"She did not," Dr. Morales said, with what I thought was a hint of hope-against-hope glowing through his skepticism.

"No, you're right, she didn't. In fact, I haven't watched her masturbate at all—I was just trying to rave your engine."

"Why is it, Mr. Singer, that I am beginning to suspect that I liked you more when you were more unhappy? Please tell me about the visit to your father, unless that, too, is a fiction."

"It's because I was nicer then," I said. I went ahead and told about the visit, to humor Dr. Morales—I felt for the first time ever—instead of to submit to him.

AFTER WE LEFT the Metropolitan Museum, and after Claire, for all her incipient matchmaking, had beaten what seemed to me another hasty retreat, I suggested to Allegra that we call my father and get her car, her Jip, out of the garage and go and visit him. The fall color would be beautiful along the Palisades Parkway and the Hudson River. The kids were willing—Emily was always up for anything, and Georgie seemed interested in the idea that, as I told him, my father had held human hearts in his hands.

I called from one of Allegra's two phones, after Allegra called the garage to tell them I could pick her Jeep up. "It would be nice to meet your friend, Jacob," my father said, "but I'm a little busy today. I have to rake the leaves. And then I'm going to dinner at the Wassermans', I'm afraid."

"I'll rake the leaves for you," I said, "and we'll only stay a couple of hours, I promise. I want to take Georgie to that baseball-card and comic-book store on Main Street. You'll really like Allegra, I promise."

"I'm sure I would, but maybe another—"

"We'll see you in about an hour, then," I said, and then I said goodbye.

"THAT WAS EARL Taylor and the Clinch Mountain Boys singing Bill Monroe's great bluegrass classic 'Uncle Pen,' " the student disc jockey said, in a thick New York accent. "Mr. Monroe composed that song about his own Uncle Penrod, who played the fiddle and was such a profound influence on the development of Mr. Monroe's music. As you know, everyone calls him Mr. Monroe because everyone has such great respect for him. He is the real thing, and the real thing is what we try to bring you here every Sunday afternoon on 'City Pickin',' here on WKCR, the voice of Columbia University, here in New York City."

I looked over at Allegra. "This or the NFL or the Knicks or doubleheaders was Sunday afternoon for me until today," I said. "That band has a great guitar."

"You mean the way he plays it?" Allegra asked.

"No. Well, yes. But I meant the guitar itself."

"What kind is it?"

"It's called a Martin Dreadnought. It's probably worth ten thousand bucks. It's so bright it sounds like a bell." I got into the right lane to exit from the parkway at Rockland. "At least the music goes with this scenery better than it goes with West End Avenue."

"Look at the trees, Emily and Georgie," Allegra said. "Aren't they beautiful?"

In the backseat of the Jeep, Georgie said to Emily, "I finished my pretzel—can I have some of yours?" Emily broke off a piece and gave it to him. "Thanks," he said. "Stop looking at me. Hey, Mom, Emily's looking at me, and she's getting on my side of the seat."

"She just gave you some of her pretzel," I said.

"So?" Georgie said. "I still don't want her to look at me. She's not my real sister, anyway."

"She looks real to me," I said.

"I don't mean that," Georgie said. "I mean we're both adopted."

"Tell me, what would you do if you saw some kid being mean to her?"

"I'd kill them," Georgie said.

"Look how beautiful the trees are," Allegra said.

"Yeah, they're great," Georgie said.

"Here's the exit," I said, "and here's an idiot swerving in front of me. Jesus."

EMILY USED A very small rake that I remembered using when I was a little kid. I found it in the back of my father's garage. She assiduously raked up a five-by-five quadrant at the corner of the lawn, near the Russian olive tree that, in my mind's eye, I could see my mother planting. It had been her height then and was now forty feet. Its thin, green-silver leaves had curled and turned all silver and fallen; they were just the right size for the little rake. Emily worked with patience and intensity—she looked like an industrious dwarf from a fairy tale—as I used the regular rake and made a big pile in the middle of the lawn and Allegra looked on, and looked out across the street and over at the Hudson River, which lay like a broad band of blue cloth

against the low hills of Tarrytown to the east. The sun made her
black hair glisten. When I finished, I picked up the old sheet
that I was going to load up with leaves three or four times and
take to the compost pile at the back of the immaculate garden,
now tidily bare except for a few areas of monkshood and phlox
and cosmos, but Allegra said, "Wait—don't you know what we
have to do first?" She went over to where Emily was now down
on all fours, scouring the grass for individual leaves that had
somehow escaped her diligence, took her by the hand, and led
her over to the big pile. Emily said, "No, Mommy," and
pointed to her junior heap in the corner. I went over and put
the sheet down next to the small pile and pulled it onto the
sheet, then wrapped the leaves up in a big version of a hobo's
handkerchief pouch and walked back to the big pile, where I
spilled Emily's leaves on the top. "OK," Allegra said, and she
turned her back to the pile of leaves and fell backward into it
and laughed, that musical laugh that I had heard so rarely. I
went around to the other side of the pile and got down on my
stomach and tunnelled through it. I grabbed Emily by the
waist when I got to her, and she screamed with delight. Then
we all lay there looking up at the blue nothingness above us.

We had left Georgie in the house with my father, who
acted awkward and grouchy when they first arrived. "Jacob, I
was trying to tell you about my schedule," he began as he came
out of the back door and we got out of the Jeep. "This is Allegra
and Georgie and Emily Marshall," I said. "Don't worry, we
won't stay long. Are the rakes still in the garage?" My father,
whose first close look at Allegra seemed to restore his manners,
said, "It was very generous of you to let me recuperate at your
beautiful cottage on Fire Island. You must forgive me for not
being so hospitable right now, but as I tried to tell Jake on the
telephone . . ." Allegra put out her hand for that strong handshake, and my father looked suddenly smitten. I realized that I
had seen Allegra only under very restricted circumstances, and

watching my father's reaction to her reminded me of how striking and compelling her presence was. Then Georgie shook hands and said, "Where is the heart, Dr. Singer? He said you have a big model of a heart that you can take apart. Could I see it, please?"

My father took us all inside. As we followed him, Allegra whispered to me, "It's breathtaking, your resemblance to him." He made some tea for us and gave us some sugar cookies that he said he had made himself a few nights earlier for trick-or-treaters. "Now I'll do the lawn," I said, and Allegra and Emily went with me, through the front part of the house, where my father's office was. "Here is the heart my son has told you about," my father said to Georgie, pointing to the model on a shelf in the office. It was a new heart, much larger than the one I recalled sitting there years and years earlier, and it was liver-and-pink-and-fuchsia in color, an asymmetrical set of chambers and valves which in this representation, with significant sections of the aorta and vena cava and other vessels sticking up from it at the top, not only seemed to me a marvel of hydraulic engineering and an amazing evolutionary elaboration of the primitive vascular thickening and pulsation that were all the heart that an invertebrate needed but also looked like a root bole—arboreal. "Would you like to see how it works?" my father said to Georgie.

We left them behind and went and got the rakes. And when we were finished tumbling in the leaves and throwing them up in the air and reraking them and after I had dragged the airy, bulbous sheetfuls back to the compost, I took Georgie on the short walk up to the village to go to the comic-book store. Georgie put out his hand to be held halfway up Blauvelt Avenue, and when we crossed the street, I had to pull him back as a car filled with Rockland High kids screeched around the corner from Main Street. When we got back, in forty-five minutes, I noticed a nondescript gray car parked across from my father's house which I realized I had seen while I was raking the leaves, and before the person inside the car put a newspaper up in front of his face, I was sure that I recognized the frog-hippie I had almost collided with on Fifth Avenue a couple of hours earlier. I didn't tell Allegra about it.

We left with my father smiling broadly, thanking me for taking care of the leaves, inviting us to come back anytime. "Try to give me a bit more warning," he said, "so I can have something better than leftover cookies to give to the children." On the trip back, Emily slept and Georgie looked at his comic book in the backseat, while in the front Allegra told me about her conversation with my father. "I told him how beautiful the house and garden were," she said. "It felt lonely there, almost frozen, but at least he has kept things up. He asked how we met, and I told him about George's having gone to Coventry and your coming to lunch to speak that day. He seemed proud. When I said that he and I had something else, something sad, in common even before I met you, he said yes, he knew, and he had sympathy for me. Then he said, 'As for me, that sadness is long in the past,' but your mother could have died yesterday, her absence in that house was still that strong. And that made me think of you, Jake—how hard this all must have been for you. Must be still. And then I found my way naturally back to Emily and Georgie. And then to myself, selfishly, and now I'm sorry, but I think I'm going to have to say that I need you."

"SHE IS MORE correct than she knows, eh?" Dr. Morales said, at the end of the next morning's session. "Forgive me, Mr. Singer, but that weirdo you have mentioned crossing Fifth Avenue and putting your father's house up on the stakeout could not be interested in you—you have nothing to offer, unless you have led a secret life of sabotage or subversion or screwing another rich wife whose husband is not as dead as is your lover's husband or are supplying your students with windowshade acid. Something you have not told me about. He must be interested in your lover, or maybe her association with you, and I am thinking that her recent anxiety about her situation and her children may be anchored in reality, as well as in the sea of bereavement and an earlier family situation that from your brief description of her mother sounded to me as if it must have suffered from overprotection and the partner in crime of overprotection, which is judgmentalism. Because I cannot imagine why she married at such a young age, and in addition someone so different from herself, ultimately, if not, at least in part, to escape from that mother. But it is you, not she, who has the good fortune to be my patient, so it is to you that I must say please be careful."

I thought I could hear excitement in Dr. Morales's voice—enthusiasm and curiosity that nullified whatever concern his words expressed. And I found myself half hoping that something would happen, that I would at least see the salamander man again.

I CALLED ALLEGRA during a free period that afternoon. As usual, it took five or six rings to get someone to pick up—one of the phones was in the study, one in Allegra's bedroom, both places a few leagues from where anyone spent any substantial amount of time during the day. It was Nathalie, the French au pair—"ow pair," as Dr. Morales had once said—who finally answered. As a weekend and holiday and surreptitious night visitor, I still hadn't met her. "Mrs. Marshall is wiz Emily, eating launch," she said. "Juz a minute, I will get hair."

"If you're with Emily, what does Nathalie do all day?" I said when Allegra finally came to the phone.

"I started feeling anxious and worried again. I wanted to stay close to her."

"You seemed OK yesterday afternoon. Now everyone has met everyone, and we never have to worry about them again."

"You made it easy to make that visit," Allegra said.

"No, you're the one who made things easy. I think my father thinks I've finally done something right. I wish I could have gone home with you." I remembered again what I had remembered in Dr. Morales's office a few hours earlier—Allegra's mouth open, her eyes hooded with arousal, the way she lowered her hips to refuse one incursion and ask for another—and I felt my heart speed up and my blood beginning to redistribute itself. Some kids from my freshman class went by the school office where I was using the phone and waved at me, and I felt some redistributing blood rush to my face. One of the boys, Billy Glass, a short, nasty prig with short blond hair so wavy that it looked marcelled, wearing his customary horn-rimmed glasses and camel's-hair sports jacket and carrying a briefcase, reappeared in the doorway, stopped, and said, "Sir, about the grade on this last composition." He looked and acted just like his mother, I thought—rigid, interventionist, a complainer who constantly interrupted me and her husband during parent-teacher conferences and whom I suspected of having snooped into my grade book when Proctor called me out into the hall during Open House, in September. I pointed to the phone and waved Billy away.

"You don't understand," Allegra said. "I was glad to see your father, but I meant that I've begun having a hard time even leaving the apartment, I've been feeling so anxious, and you made it easy for me yesterday, I feel that comfortable with you. This morning I had a committee meeting, something for Central Park that George was doing and I agreed to take over, but I didn't want to go out."

"I'm worried, too," I said. I almost added, "Someone is following you," but stopped myself and instead said, "Because you're so worried. I want to see you this afternoon. Can I take Georgie home?"

"Just think—it's not much more than six months since you brought him home that day when he was sick."

"And the plot has so thickened. Call the school office and tell them that I'm going to take Georgie home and that he won't be on the bus."

"You don't mind that people will start talking?" Allegra said.

"Everyone's going to catch on sooner or later, anyway, if we keep seeing each other. Claire's already wise to us, I'm sure."

"YOUR DAD LET me pick up one of those knives doctors use to cut people open," Georgie said, after we got settled in our seats on the crosstown bus. He took off his backpack first and gave it to me to hold.

"Wow," I said. "Those things are sharp. He must have thought you were pretty grown-up to let you hold one of those."

"He did," Georgie said. "What do you call them?"

"Scalpels."

"That's right—scalpels. Your dad is nice."

"I'm glad you like him."

"Do you have fights with him?"

"Yeah, we've had some pretty bad arguments."

"I know," Georgie said. "My dad and I used to argue when he tried to get me to eat stuff I didn't like, like beets. I hate beets."

"You might get to like them someday," I said.

"I won't," Georgie said. "Believe me you, I won't. I miss my dad."

. . .

THE MINUTE I saw her, I realized that though I thought I'd seen Allegra really upset before, I hadn't. She opened the door and put her hand out to hold on to me and it was shaking. I glanced down at Georgie so as to remind Allegra of his presence, and she hesitated for a second and then said "Jake" and took my hand anyway. It felt cold and damp, and her face was as white as milk. Georgie looked up at us. "Georgie, Nathalie bought some of those cookies with jelly in them that you like," she said. Her voice sounded so normal that I felt the effort behind it. "She and Emily are down in the kitchen. Why don't you go have one?"

"Actually, they're beet cookies," I said.

"No, they're not," Georgie said. "That's just one of your jokes. They're called Linzer tortes. Mom doesn't realize I know the name. She thinks I'm a baby like Emily." He threw his backpack on the floor and ran off down the long hall toward the kitchen.

"Georgie, don't talk so rudely," Allegra halfheartedly called out after him.

"It's a compliment," I said. "What is the matter with you? You look as if—"

"Come with me," Allegra said. She clung to my hand and led me through the foyer and the vast living room and into the study. "The agency called about an hour ago. Emily's mother is trying to get her back."

"What do you mean? You're her mother."

"Her biological mother," Allegra said. "Or it's a couple, the agency said. So maybe it's her mother and her father. I don't know." She seemed even whiter in this dark room, as if her anxiety were emitting lunar light from within. "I have to sit down—I feel really faint."

"Who are these people?"

"I told you—I don't know. But they know who I am, and they know Emily's name and where we live. And they know who you are, and they know about us."

"How do you know all that?"

"Because the agency told me. They said that they'd had a call and a letter from a lawyer here in New York who's trying to block the finalization and get Emily back to her biological mother."

"But that's ridiculous. She's almost two years old. What's the agency going to do?"

"They went to the Family Court immediately and asked for finalization."

"Well, so it will be all right, then. Listen, that kid isn't going anywhere. It's absurd. They can't just tear a family apart after two years."

"The court will have to get a new home study, because of the changed circumstances of George's death, and so will the agency. This is just so terrifying."

"But the agency is on your side. Listen, Allegra, Emily is your daughter, period."

I sat down next to her on the small, royal-red sofa and put my arm around her shoulders. "What is the law on this—do you know?"

"My lawyer's not an expert in adoption law, but he thinks it's a new rule that this sort of dispute has to be settled in the best interests of the child."

"Well, then, that takes care of that. Try to calm down. You've got to think of Emily, and of Georgie, too."

"I know—you're right, but I feel completely alone, except for you, and now I can't see you anymore, either." Tears started running down her face and onto my shoulder.

"Of course you can see me."

"No, I can't. The agency said that this other lawyer might try to use our relationship against me as a fit mother. He even knows I was seeing a psychiatrist."

"But neither of those things is so awful. The only thing that's awful is that you can't see me—that would be awful for anyone."

"Shut up, Jake," Allegra said, laughing through her tears. "I can't do this on my own."

"You can," I said. "You'll get hold of yourself, and then you'll get up and go down to your kids and be your usual excellent parent. Anyway, at least we'll be able to talk on the phone, won't we? And you can certainly get the best legal help, right?"

"My lawyer is seeing to that right away," Allegra said, crying less hard now. "We can talk on the phone. It can't go that far. I'll have to ask. I knew something was wrong. I just felt it."

Emily appeared in the study's doorway in bare feet, a diaper, and a white undershirt embellished with red jelly stains. A hoar of powdered sugar adhered to her chin and flecked her curly, dark hair, and her hands were covered with a sugar-jelly compound. Allegra quickly swiped her teary face with her arm and pulled away from me. "Where are you going, sweetie?" she asked.

"To play," Emily said.

"You can't go in the living room without washing your hands and face," Allegra said as she stood up.

"Going to play," Emily said.

"OK, but after you wash up in the kitchen, OK?"

"OK."

"Where's Nathalie?"

"In the bathroom," Emily said.

"Oh, I see. Well, come back with me to the kitchen and we'll get you washed up, OK?"

"OK."

I got up, too. "I should be leaving, I guess," I said. "I mean, considering."

"No, wait here," Allegra said. "I'll be back in a minute. You don't have to go right away."

"Bye," Emily said. She sauntered back toward the kitchen.

"I'll come say goodbye. Wait here, all right? Of course we can talk on the phone. I'll need to talk to you."

Allegra turned and followed Emily down the runway of the hall. I sat back down on the sofa. Georgie came in a minute later holding a piece of paper in his hand. "Look," he said. "From the comics you got me." I looked at the colored-pencil drawing, which was of Batman and Spiderman back-to-back, facing away from each other, with Spiderman battle-ready in his semicontorted way and Batman standing tall—as if they were both about to be assaulted by formidable foes. Behind them was a sketchy, phantasmagorical cityscape, with dark buildings looming out of a smudgy mist. "I made up the idea," Georgie said.

"It's really good," I said. "I wish I could draw this well. It's one thing I've never been able to do. This is really impressive, Georgie."

"I'll teach you," Georgie said. He took the drawing back and left.

The phone rang. I realized that everyone in the place was miles away from both phones, and, thinking, Everyone knows about everything anyway, I picked it up and said hello.

"Hello, is this the Marshall residence?" It was a woman's voice, young and, I thought immediately, antagonistic.

"Yes, it is."

"May I speak to Allegra Marshall?"

"Well, Mrs. Marshall is busy at the moment. Can I take a message?"

"My name is Jennifer Petroski—P-e-t-r-o-s-k-i. I'm a CSW from the Family Court of Manhattan. I'm calling to make an appointment with Mrs. Marshall for a home study. It's some kind of urgent thing. I don't know why, and it's sort of an inconvenient thing for me, but I could manage to—"

"Uh, listen, maybe I should just take your number and have Mrs. Marshall call you back."

"No, I've got to go out on a follow-up child-neglect thing. You know, it's a really serious kind of a case, not like some simple adoption visit, which is why I can't understand what's so urgent. But I can be there tomorrow. What time does the son get home from school? Mrs. Marshall and both children have to be there for me to do the home study."

"You know, I don't think I should speak for Mrs. Marshall."

"Are you a relative?"

"No, I'm just a friend. I'm a teacher at Mrs. Marshall's son's school."

"So you know when the son gets home from school."

"By four at the latest, I think."

"Well, that's one good thing. Please give Mrs. Marshall the message that I called and that unless I hear something else from her, I'm going to be there at four-thirty. My name is Jennifer Petroski—P-e-t-r-o-s-k-i," and she gave her number. "I certainly hope that Mrs. Marshall will be able to see me then. It's kind of a disruption. Just let me check off a few things, if you know the family well. It will save me some time with the paperwork stuff before the visit. I can just check a few things off to make sure I have them right. Mr. Marshall died on one January—is that correct?"

"Yes, I think so. Listen, I'm not sure I should—"

"The son, George—George the Second—is also adopted, is that right?"

"Yes."

"Packard-Weekes also, right?"

"Uh, yes."

"The address of the apartment is 1067 Fifth Avenue, and it's on the fourteenth floor. What's the apartment number?"

"It's the only one on the fourteenth floor. I don't think it has a number."

"Mrs. Marshall's full name is Allegra Randolph Herrick Marshall—is that correct?"

"Randolph?" I said.

"That's what I have here."

"Well, OK. Now I really think—"

"The child's name is Emily Grace Marshall."

"Grace? Look, this is why I think you should check this with Mrs. Marshall."

"That's all right—I just want to fill some of these things out ahead of time. The agency is also Packard-Weekes?"

"Um, yes."

"And the son is through Packard-Weekes?"

"Yes, definitely," I said, laughing a little.

"You know, I'm just trying to expedite this thing, as I was asked to do."

"OK," Jake said. "I'm sure Mrs. Marshall would appreciate that, Ms. Petrowski."

"It's 'Petroski'—P-e-t-r-o-s-k-i. Now, the biological mother's name is Sarah Gibson."

"What did you say?"

"Sarah Gibson, of—what is this? Is this a real address? Hat Cherry—what is this name here?—Hat Cherry Road, New Berkshire, Massachusetts?"

"New Berkshire? Listen, I really think you shouldn't—"

"Just forget that. Mrs. Marshall wouldn't know that. Of course not. I just realized that."

"Yes, that's right." I took a piece of paper out of the wastepaper basket next to the sofa and wrote down "Sarah Gibson, Hat Cherry Road, New Berkshire, Mass." on it.

"Well, all right, I'll be there at 4:30 p.m. tomorrow."

"I'll tell Mrs. Marshall, and I'll give her your number so she can call you if there's some problem with that time."

"I certainly hope there won't be."

"I do, too."

After I hung up, I folded up the piece of paper and put it in the inside pocket of my sports jacket. Allegra came back down the hall a few seconds later. She looked more composed. I told her about the call and the appointment, which made her shaky all over again, and it was then that the quandary I had just been pushed into was resolved. While I was trying to calm Allegra down, I was thinking that whoever was on the other side of this battle had gotten information about Allegra and Emily and me; I didn't know how, but it almost had to have been illicit, at least about Emily's whereabouts. It seemed to me that to turn over this name and address to Allegra or to anyone else would at best accomplish nothing and at worst make Allegra even more distraught and, if the adoption lawyer Allegra hired was himself unscrupulous, lead to more unscrupulousness, which Allegra would never want to be part of. So I shut up.

"Jake, I guess you had better go now," Allegra said. "I want you to call me tonight. At about nine-thirty. Would you do that?"

"Of course. Are you going to tell your parents and the Marshalls about this?"

"I have to," she said. "It will just set them back more, but they should know."

"If I were you, I'd ask at least one of them to be here tomorrow when that social worker shows up. I'd get Claire—she's the warmest, to tell you the truth. It would look like support, even if she wasn't part of the formal interview."

"Yes, that's a good idea," Allegra said. "That might really help. Thank you, Jake. I do have to ask you to help me through this. I'm sorry."

"I want to. I just wish I could be here myself. But since I

can't, here's how I would handle the social worker if I were you, since I talked to her. Mainly, don't act rich. It doesn't matter what you do, actually, as long as you don't insult her or something like that. She just considers this an imposition but routine. I don't think she even knows about the other side."

"Do I act rich?"

"Well, you can, sometimes you can't help it, but now you're like anyone else would be. You'll be fine. Be gracious, ask her about her work, if you can wedge it in. I got a hint from what she said that she's very idealistic."

WHEN I LEFT Allegra's building it was dusk, and what do you know?—there was the amphibian, his pate catching a beam from a streetlight. He was leaning against the side of a doorway of a brownstone on Eighty-fourth Street, just off Fifth, wearing a pure central-casting trenchcoat—maybe he had rotated his surveillance costumes away from hippie to movies—and pretending to read a newspaper. I pretended not to see him and was surprised but pleased when the guy started following me. There was almost surely wrongdoing somewhere on the other side of this matter, I told myself again. I remembered this fellow's guilty behavior when he almost ran into me near the museum. Newton, I decided to call him, as I hatched a plan of action of my own.

I walked briskly down Fifth and turned east on Seventy-sixth Street, toward the big foreign embassy on that block between Madison and Park. There were always cops hanging around there. When I was about fifty yards away, I could make out some blue uniforms killing time near the embassy's entrance, and, having crossed Madison Avenue, I took my wallet out of my pocket and turned around suddenly and walked right at Newton. This took him by surprise, and he hesitated, but then he kept on walking, as he had the other time. Just as I was about to pass him, I checked to try to make sure that no one was looking directly at us, which no one seemed to be, and then veered into Newton's path and crashed into him as hard as I could. "What the fuck," Newton said, as we fell down on the sidewalk.

"Help, thief!" I yelled. "He stole my wallet!"

"What are you doing?" the guy said. "I'll break your fucking head."

"Try it," I said under my breath. We started punching each other, and I managed to smash him full in the face with all my strength. "Help—police!" I shouted. Newton, shaken by the punch and looking scared, saw the cops starting to run toward us and got up quickly. "You cocksucker," he said.

I stood up and faced him, my heart hammering with anger. I dropped my wallet at Newton's feet. "If I ever see you again, I'll kill you," I said quietly. "I have terminal cancer and I have absolutely nothing to lose. So believe me, I'll kill you." Then I yelled, "He stole my wallet!"

Newton took off. One of the cops stopped to see if I was all right. The other ran halfheartedly after Newton. "Yeah, I'm fine," I said. "Look—he dropped it."

"They always do that," the cop said. "I don't think we're going to get him. He had too much of a head start."

"That's all right," I said. I leaned over with my hands on my knees to catch my breath. "I appreciate the effort. I wouldn't have pressed charges anyway, now that I've got this back." I straightened up and opened the wallet for the cop to see. "Look—it even has the money still in it."

"You're lucky," the cop said. "It looked like you got a pretty good shot in. Maybe he'll stop his life of crime."

As I went on my way a few minutes later, I felt the adrenaline leaching out of my bloodstream and started to shake. I walked through the park, pleased with myself and crying, as I've noticed many people do after they've had a fight.

SARAH WAS FEELING better by the time Robby got home from school on Monday, two days after Paul took him to the football game, but the air in the house tasted almost metallic from the tension that ran through it. At the game, Robby had run away from Paul and crawled under the stands. Paul had to ask the student on the PA system to announce a missing kid, and when a woman found Robby and brought him to the scorer's table, where Paul was waiting, he took the boy by the hand and in his anger slapped the top of his head. Then he dragged him back to the stands and held his hand tightly as he sat and tried to watch the game, and Robby kept on saying, "You're hurting me," which made other people look at them, and Paul finally gave up and left at the end of the third quarter. When they got home, Robby ran to Sarah, sick as she was, and told her what had happened—so honestly, even about running away, that Paul didn't even have the adult satisfaction of amending his account, and all he could say was "We're going to have to correct this situation." Sarah had managed to fight through the batting of her fever and say to Paul, "Don't you ever lay a hand on my son again."

Now they were at dinner, and Robby wouldn't look at Paul, wouldn't respond to his flat-toned instructions to sit up and use his napkin and not eat with his fingers and eat his carrots. "I said eat your carrots," Paul said. "Your mother grew them just for you." Sarah said, "No, I didn't. Why do you say things like that? He doesn't have to eat them if he doesn't want to." And Robby said, "It's OK, Mom—I'll eat some." He took a big mouthful of the sliced boiled carrots and for the first time that entire evening turned and looked at Paul, who said, "That's better, son," whereupon Robby made a kind of choking, gagging sound and opened his mouth and showed Paul its bright, mealy contents. Paul reached out and grabbed the boy's

hand and got up from the table and said, "You just bought
yourself a spanking, young man."

"Get your hands off him," Sarah said evenly. She felt as
though she were at the very earliest stages of waking from a
dream, when you begin to understand that what you're looking at—the pig with wheels, the walls with ears, the river of fire—
can't be real.

"As long as he's living in my house he has got to learn to respect me," Paul said. "He has to learn to get along with me."

"You're going to beat it into him. That makes a lot of
sense."

Sarah got up and went around the table and took Robby's
other hand while Paul tried to pull him away. "You made a
good point about as long as we're all living in your house," she
said. "So let's not."

"You had better behave yourself, too," Paul said.

"What? What did you say? Let go of him, or I'll call the police." She meant what she was saying, but it still sounded coun-
terfeit to her.

Paul dropped Robby's hand and glared at Sarah and the
boy as if they had just cheated him out of something he had
won. "Go ahead," he said. "But don't forget that I'm an officer
of the court."

"What are you talking about?" Sarah said.

"He's an officer in a court," Robby said pompously, sticking close to Sarah's side and beginning to wheeze.

"Let's get out of here," Sarah said.

UPSTAIRS, SHE PACKED some things for her and Robby.
Paul went up a few minutes later. He caught her by the arm as
she came out of the bathroom, with toothbrushes, toothpaste,
and shampoo in her hand. "Don't be silly," he said. "He just
went too far, and I—"

"You what?" Sarah said. She pulled away from him and looked at him. She went into Robby's room. He was sitting on the bed like a little man waiting to leave his hotel room. She could hear that his breath had the beginning of an asthmatic hiss. She took his hand again, went downstairs, got their coats and hats from the closet, and walked out into the clear, cold November night. She opened the door of the gray Escort that she had backed into the first Paul's pickup truck, and threw her bags into the backseat and told Robby to get in. She said to Paul, "Call me when you're ready to really apologize and we'll see," she said.

"Yeah, we'll see," Robby said.

THE HOUSE STOOD loftily above William's Lake Road, behind mock-orange and lilac bushes that had grown wild. It was barn red, with black trim, and with black-framed storm windows. The paint was flaking, the handsome gray slate shingles of the roof were crumbling, the chimney lacked some bricks at the top, and above the foundation of the huge barn just north of the house the siding bellied out with fatigue. But in the light, postcard snow that was now falling, the place still had a baronial aspect, lording it over the road, tucked beneath an even higher hill behind it, with enormous thorn locusts framing it and with a big, octagonal window, an oversize and valuable coin, set just under the roof's peak. As with many New England farmhouses, its industrious successive farmers had successively added on to it, front to back, each of its three later sections smaller than the last, with the final structure, a milk house, built over an underground stream and looking like the ultimate box in a Chinese puzzle.

I stopped the Jeep at the bottom of the driveway. I had never been in the Berkshires before. I had only heard Dave Leonard at Bristol tell stories about the Communists who swarmed up from the city and into these Massachusetts hills, his uncle—who owned this house—chief among them, a red beacon for other red and then nostalgically pink summer settlers. Still, I could have sworn I'd driven up this same driveway and through these same snowflakes before—I felt as though I were practicing some old habit, as I had during the flurry-dusted drive up Route 67 and through the Litchfield Hills, following the directions Dave had given me, and the guy who filled the car with gas at Renny's on Route 6 in Ridgefield said, "Don't I see you fishing on William's Lake in the summers?" And even though I told him that I wasn't from the area, the guy said, "Hey, if you're short of cash, why don't you catch me later, if you got any other errands to run?" Just as I left the gas station, an eighteen-wheeler with a Grand Union logo on the side jammed on its brakes at the stop sign coming out of County Road and skidded out onto Route 6, which made the car going south speed up suddenly. I had to mash the brakes on to avoid being hit. The snow tires on the Jeep helped to stop the car in time.

At the top of the driveway at Dave's uncle's place stood a small unpainted barn with white doors. To the left was a garage with its white doors closed and locked. To the right was the house, grand for a farmhouse—grand and dark in the gathering dusk and snow. I walked up onto the side porch and, as Dave had told me to do, slid to the side the right-hand pane of the second window next to the door. I squeezed backward through the window and ended up sitting in the kitchen sink. I swivelled around and jumped down to the floor.

Overhead, fluorescent lights went on. A short, thin, bald old man with a frigate's keel of a nose and Dumboid ears stood in the kitchen doorway as if conjured out of thin air. He had on a vintage plaid shirt and corduroy pants of equal yore, blunt brown shoes, and an oversize, aged earth-tone cardigan. "You're early," he said. "Dinner isn't until seven."

"Uh, I'm Jake Singer," I said. "I'm a friend of Dave Leonard's. He said it would be all right to stay here. I have to try to see someone here in New Berkshire. Dave said no one would be here. I'm sorry to disturb you. I'll just leave and find a motel or something." I turned back toward the sink, then, realizing how weird it would be to go back out through the window, I stopped myself. I didn't know what to do.

"You look just like that lousy nephew of mine," the old man said. "I hope your character is better."

I glanced around the kitchen. The sink I'd sat in was one of two, built into a stain-dappled thirties-looking structure of metal drawers and cupboards that bore the name Shirley on a metal plaque at its center. The refrigerator, yellowed-white, and with rounded corners, was dieseling away in one corner, and the stove, a black behemoth six-burner double-oven Garland, lurked in the other. Behind the old man I could see a wood-panelled dining room, in the middle of which was a mahogany table surrounded by bentwood chairs. On the far side of that room was an upright piano, black against the red-tan wide-plank pine floor. Two windows at the other end of the room looked out onto a frosted back lawn at the end of which loomed the big barn I'd seen from the road. Clouds purple with snow filled the sky behind the barn.

"He can't wait to get his hands on this place—I know it," the old man said. "He's practicing."

"I'm really sorry to disturb you. If you're Sol Leonard, Dave said you'd left for Mexico yesterday and you wouldn't mind if I stayed here."

"And if I'm not?"

"If you're not what? I'm sorry, I don't understand."

"The hell with it. All his other friends and their grandmothers use my place, so why shouldn't you? He probably runs a white-slave ring out of here every winter."

"Uh, you are Sol Leonard, right?"

"Yes."

"Well, I owe you a debt of gratitude."

"My, how fancy we are," the old man said. "A debt of gratitude." He turned around and walked through the dining room
and into the living room beyond, as if people dropped in
through his kitchen window all the time. The living room was
in the main part of the house, the biggest part, and it had
lighter panelling on the walls and a blonder floor. Two old
couches stood near a big fireplace, and two big Mexican rugs
covered the wide pine floorboards. Opposite the fireplace, in
front of three large windows that gave onto the driveway and
the smaller barn and the garage, was an X-based pine table. The
old man sat down on the couch nearest the fireplace. "And
what debt of gratitude do you owe me?" he said.

"Dave sold me one of the guitars that you bring back from
Mexico. It's wonderful."

"That was back when he was fencing stolen goods, I guess,"
the old man said. "Before he got into white-slaving. What's
your name, boy?"

"Jake Singer."

"You a journalist like Davey?"

"No, I'm a schoolteacher."

"You teach second-story work?"

"English."

"Where?"

"In Manhattan—a place called the Coventry School."

"Oh, yes—a pretty swell joint, as I recall."

"Well, yes, it is mainly for rich kids."

"While the poor don't even have decent textbooks. You
know, things are getting very bad in the inner cities, and there's
going to be a day of reckoning—mark my words. The riots were
only a taste. This system is going to collapse from its own con-
tradictions sooner or later. Tell me, why doesn't a nice young

person like you go and teach where you can do some real good?"

"That's a good question. I sometimes ask myself the same thing."

"Well, then, answer it. In the meantime, make yourself at home here. The Blooms are arriving at any minute, and I have to get some more things together. They were supposed to pick me up yesterday, but Joe had a bad tooth."

He got up and teetered for a few seconds and then walked toward another room, a gloomy bedroom off the living room.

"No, really, Mr. Leonard, I think it would be better if I—"

"Oh, shuh tup, will you?" the old man said. "And call me Sol. And here, take this guitar and show me what you can do. But do it in the living room. I have to change my clothes."

He handed me a bigger and much more elaborately decorated version of the same guitar that I had at home.

"You keep the good stuff for yourself, I see," I said.

The old man came back out of the bedroom and looked me up and down. "And you're a smart aleck just like my nephew, too. Go ahead and play."

Half an hour later, what must have been the Blooms, tiny and old but a bit younger than their ancient passenger, pulled up in the driveway in one of those huge Oldsmobile boats that dwarf even larger elderly drivers, and I carried three suitcases—one of them string-bound—out to the car. "Next time you play for me, try to sing less twangy," the old man said. "You'd never pass as a hillbilly."

The little lady in the front passenger seat rolled down the window. "Come on, Sol," she said. "Joe says we can beat the storm to New York if we start south now."

"Ida, I'd like you to meet Whoosie here."

"Jake," I said.

"Jake," the old man said. "Jake Whatsis."

"Jake Singer."

"Jake Singer. He's a friend of Davey's, but he seems to have a pretty good sense of values anyway. These are the Blooms—Joe and Ida."

"Very pleased to meet you," the teensy driver said. "Now come on, Sol."

The old man turned to me. "Come back and visit me sometime," he said. "I'll show you how to really play the guitar." He creaked into the backseat. "You should live so long and be so lucky," he added, before pulling the door closed. A fin of blue from the wool swamp of his overcoat hung down outside the car.

The barge backed down the driveway, just missing one of the locusts. I watched as it wove away from the house, pointed roughly toward the equator, the blue triangle flapping away. Then I went back inside.

Go ahead, build a fire, the old man had said. The wood is out in the woodshed—ain't that a surprise?—on the other side of where you did your breaking and entering. The thermostat is right over here. The phone is in the hall here. Sleep upstairs—not in my room, if you please. The front bedroom is the nicest, right at the top of the stairs. I usually reserve it for the quality, but there's no one else here, so I guess you can have it. Go up and take a look around. Clean sheets are in the bottom of the dresser drawer. There's a bathroom right off the hall up there. Make sure the toilet doesn't keep running. Use a match to light the stove—it's not one of those fancy new ones—it works good. The furnace goes on and off with a wallop, so don't be surprised. Someone will plow the driveway if it snows hard—you might want to move that contraption you're driving across the road. The guy who does the plowing is an old friend and hunts on our land, so he's used to strangers staying here.

After I moved the Jeep across the road and got settled and—sipping from a glass of red wine from an already open bottle to which the old man had told me to help myself—looked around the handsome old place, with its brown ceramic doorknobs, its hand-painted dressers and brass bedsteads in the five upstairs rooms, the Pop Hart drawings and family photographs and Rivera prints on the walls, the jumble of lamps and blankets and old radios and thrift-shop-looking clothes and old shoes in the closets, the general sense of personal history that stuffed the house, I started the fire, whose construction the old man had so critically supervised. "You shouldn't need more than one piece of newspaper. Put the kindling in a grid—no, not like that, you eejit: put the short pieces across the long. It takes three logs to make a fire—didn't your grandpa ever teach you that? If you use more than one match, I'll know—I've counted every one in the box." When the ordeal was over, I said, "Thanks, Dr. Morales." The old man chuckled and asked who Dr. Morales was, and I said, "I remind you of your nephew, and you remind me of Dr. Morales."

I sat down in front of the fire and wondered what I was doing there. After I left Allegra's apartment, with Allegra still fighting off tears, I'd gone straight home and sat down at the desk in the living room and looked up Dave Leonard's number in the phone book. I knew he lived on the West Side, because I ran into him from time to time and we had sidewalk conversations. "Isn't your uncle's house in Massachusetts in New Berkshire?" I said, after a minute of catching up. "Yeah," Dave said. "Why?" I said, "I think I may need to go up there. Someone I want to meet lives there, and I thought I remembered the name of the town from the stories you told about your uncle." Dave said, "Where do they live?" I took out the slip of paper and said, "Well, that's another thing. I'm not quite sure. Hat Cherry Road. Something like that." Dave laughed. "Hatchery," he said. "Not Hat Cherry. Hatchery Road. There's a fish hatchery on it—part of the National Park Service. It's very close to my uncle's place, in fact. Why don't you stay there? You'd really like it. There's all these old folk-song books all over the place. He left for Mexico yesterday. He's always telling me to use the place or let my friends stay there, because he thinks when it sits empty, people will break in. You should really stay there."

As Dave spoke, I focussed on what I'd absently been staring at on the desk—the extra set of keys to Allegra's Jeep, which I'd forgotten to give back to her after we got home from Rockland and put the car in the garage on the East Side. Their being there sealed it. I would call the school in the morning and say there was an emergency, go over and get the car, and drive up to New Berkshire. Allegra almost never used the car and certainly wouldn't be using it during the next day or two, in her awful anxiety, with the social worker coming, in her near-agoraphobia, and she had told the people at the garage that I could take it out anytime. The idea of going on this indeterminate mission seemed inevitable, as if I'd been given a quest to pursue in order to win the hand of the fair maiden. I called Allegra at nine-thirty, as I said I would. Both of the children were asleep, Emily in Allegra's bed—her own request, she admitted, not Emily's. I said, "Everything will be all right," "Don't worry," "Nothing bad is going to happen," at the right times, but I wasn't really listening.

Now, what would I have for dinner? The old man had said I could help myself to whatever I found in the freezer in the cellar, but when I had gone down the perilous, tilted steps to take a look I found that all the foil-wrapped lumps in the thing bore handwritten stickers that dated back at least to the Johnson presidency. The old man had also invited me to finish a bottle of good red wine that other visitors had brought two days earlier and that now stood on the clever kitchen table which could be hidden away in the sideboard behind it. The old man told me that he had designed and built the table and sideboard himself, and then picked up the wine and said, They brought the wine for me but they hardly poured me a drap. I had found a cache of magically thin and beautiful crystal wineglasses in a nearly secret cupboard I found in the panelling in the dining room right after the Blooms and their fragile cargo departed, and sitting there in front of the fire, which I had to admit was burning as perfectly as the Yule log I'd pathetically spent the last three or four Christmas Eves staring at on WPIX in New York, and drinking the fragrant and peppery wine, I found myself thinking that what I was to do would come to me one way or another. Teach us to sit still. Well, I hadn't found the wineglasses right after their departure, because the first thing I'd done was look up Sarah Gibson in the Berkshire County phone book that was under the phone in the downstairs hall. There she was, on Hatchery Road.

I picked up the magnificent guitar and played some songs from an issue of *Sing Out!* even older than the freezer food. It was a special number devoted to songs of the Spanish Civil War, and I remembered that Dave Leonard had told me that his uncle had fought in that war, with the Lincoln Brigade. I wished that my father and mother hadn't so thoroughly forsaken the political idealism that had propelled *their* parents to America. I sang "Peat Bog Soldiers," "Freiheit," "Hans Beimler," "Viva la Quince Brigada," and the guitar was so easy to play that it seemed to play itself, as if it had the tunes by heart. The old house creaked in the wind. I didn't feel hungry anymore. I would drive down to the town and have a big breakfast in the morning, before doing whatever it was I was going to do.

I was just putting the guitar back into its case and thinking about how long and complicated the last two days had been, and how at this same time forty-eight hours earlier Newton and I had had our run-in, when I heard a car come up the driveway. I found the switch for the outside porch light in the dining room, beside the door I had yet to use, and turned it on. There was a gray, dented Escort, chuffing out a white tail of exhaust in what had grown into a pretty serious snowfall. A young woman got out of the driver's side and a little boy got out of the other door. They walked toward the porch, and I opened the door.

"Is Mr. Leonard here?" the woman asked. The boy was holding her hand.

"No, I'm sorry. He left an hour or so ago and won't be back for a while."

"Sorry to disturb you, but I know Mr. Leonard a little and I was hoping I could use his phone."

"Well, I don't mind, and I'm sure he wouldn't," I said. "Come in."

"Hope I'm not bothering you," the woman said, stepping inside the house with her son.

"It's fine," I said. "I'm just visiting for a day or two. I'm a friend of Mr. Leonard's nephew. Are you having car trouble?"

"No, I just need to call the phone company. I've, uh, been away from my house for a while and the phone service has been cut off, and now I'm going back. I just was hoping that I could call them and get them to turn the phone on, with all this snow they say is coming. Though it's after business hours. I know this special number you can call. It's supposed to be only for the company's workers. The phones always go out after the storm is over. Don't know why."

"Sure, go ahead. Do you know where the phone is?"

"I've been here a couple of times before. My—well, I don't know what to call him, late fiancé, I guess—used to do some work for Mr. Leonard. Phone's in the hall, right? this way?"

"Right," I said, and I followed her and the little boy through the living room.

She turned around and said to the boy, "Robby, stay in

here by the fire for a minute—get nice and warm. I'll be right back."

"OK," the boy said. I noticed that he was wheezing—working at breathing. "Are we going back to be with him, Mom?"

"No, don't worry—we're going to *our* house," the woman said.

I looked at her and saw she was very pretty—small and, I guessed, dainty under her heavy coat, with wisps of shiny brown hair straying across her face as she took off her dark-blue wool hat. Then she took off her gloves and I saw how delicate her wrists were. Her brown eyes were clear and big, her skin light and clear, her cheeks wide. "Can't dial the phone with my gloves on," she said, and she laughed, but I thought she looked upset and wondered what was going on with her.

"Can you play that?" the boy asked, pointing to the guitar, lying on the floor in the still open case.

"Yes," I said.

"Play it now?" he said.

"Don't be a nuisance, Robby," the woman said.

"It's OK," I said. "You go ahead and make your call. How about if you play something?" I said to the boy. "I'll hold the guitar and make the chords and you strum the strings."

I have told you to be careful, and this is how you have responded—like one of the carbuncular adolescents into whose oily-haired heads you attempt to hammer poetry and punctuation, is it not? By disregarding common sense and plunging yourself into a situation so far over your head it is like the Marianas Trench. You are driving down a road with your eyes closed again, eh? It's fun, is it not, but will you equally enjoy the ride when your head goes through the windshield as the car you are blindly not steering fails to pass magically through the tree you are headed for? And by the way, Mr. Singer, the

*reason that you do not know what you are doing, as you have
at least had the honesty to admit to yourself, is that you do not
want to let yourself understand it, and that is because it is so
irrational that to recognize it would preclude your taking this to
you thrilling but potentially very dangerous ride—dangerous, if
not physically, then legally. Why are you here? You are looking
for your mommy, you are a piece of bruised fruit looking for the
tree that it has fallen from or that fell down away from it and
left it dangling in middle-air. You are trying to find it so that
you can jump up from the ground, hoopsee-dacey, and reattach
your cute little estem to it. You would try to laugh at my
metaphor of fruit so as to avoid the core of truth at its heart,
would you not? But think about it, if that excellent burgundy,
whose nose and complexity the old Communist would have
understood and appreciated even less than you do, has not too
thickly clouded your brain: This woman who has just been here
but you did not know who she was had a child, whom she gave
up. To that child, as perhaps a person of my vocation will
someday have to show her, the woman who carried her in her
womb died, abandoned her, as she may someday see it. She may
also perceive it as her fault, as her brother, Jorge, may already see
the death of his father, and as you see the departure of your
mother, from a stroke of bad luck. I am sorry, I am sorry. The
temptation of a pun in English, no matter how primitive, is one
that I cannot easily resist, even with so dire a topic. You think
vaguely that you will resolve somehow the situation about the
lawyers and the adoption, or that you will at least espy out some
information, but underneath you are trying to push time back
and restore something that cannot be restored. Thank the good
Christ, I must admit that you do truly care about your lover's
children, when you could so easily turn away from them as if
from a time-wharp mirror of your own situation. You
sympathize with them as you do not yet sympathize with
yourself. It is complicated—Emilia has two mothers and no*

*father, you have no mother and half a father. The whole thing is
whirling you around as if in a tornado, but as you have just
shown with this sad little boy who is, if you had known it,
Emilia's half brother, do not forget, as you have just shown by
letting him play the chords of "La Bamba"—what a fascinating
choice of songs, wouldn't you say, Mr. Singer, with its linguistic
suggestions of infancy?—as you have just shown, you have
sympathy for these bereft mirrors of yourself as a child, when you
could so easily turn away from them. As you do, also, I have no
doubt, for those pimply boys who are your students, who are
similarly, if only because of hormonal estorms of their own, in a
crisis, however normal. And now, speaking as I would be, if I
were really speaking, of abandonment and departures, you have
left me behind, and I would wonder if you are even going to call
my answering machine tonight or tomorrow morning bright and
early to tell me that you may miss our Wednesday session on
account of your determination to get yourself into trouble, despite
my warnings, because you did not come to me first about this
Berkshyer odyssey, this journey with its psychological destination
so sockèd in with fog that even I cannot entirely penetrate it, and
its physical destination, round hills and dense forest, snow-
covered mounds and tangled underbrush, so evocative of the
woman's body you seek, perhaps even to apply for reentry, no?
I can hear you now what you would reply if you heard this,
"Maybe it's just life, Dr. Morales," and maybe I would
agree with you. I still wish you had come to me first. I cannot
physically stand over you, as did the old Communist who
reminded you of me—I cannot stand over you, as he did when
he showed you how to build a fire correctly. It is a delightful
fire, as you have said. Often people who have some experience
can keep you from making mistakes. Though I should like to
have a chance to cure that old man of the reverence he almost
certainly entertains for my country's despote Infidel Castro,
as I call him.*

Allegra told me later that she slept that night with Emily in her bed again, but in her sleep she held her daughter so tightly that the little girl woke up and wriggled away from her and then went peacefully back to a dream about the snow falling over Central Park. For her part, Allegra dreamed of skiing on a brilliant day with Emily and Georgie skiing beside her. She realized they were heading toward the edge of a miles-high sheer cliff, and she and Georgie were able to stop, but Emily wasn't. She disappeared silently, the top of her curly-haired head winking out of sight like the sun sinking below the horizon. Horrified, Allegra leaned over the cliff and saw that Emily had landed safely on a ledge a hundred feet below. Relief immediately gave way to new despair when she saw someone else on the ledge, someone in a Merlin costume, not walking but unnaturally gliding along the ledge toward her daughter. He was going to take her away.

MY FATHER TOLD me later that he had had dinner with the positive Wassermans that night. And I imagined that for the first time in a long time he had something besides pleasantries and medical tales to offer against the professor's complaints about the high-school kids who drag-raced on Broadway late at night and his wife's denunciations of the music of Stravinsky and all the tone-deaf composers who came after him. I imagined that he talked about me and Allegra and her children. He didn't say they were adopted, though he thought about it as he talked. Because he had met them and been charmed by them, he now found the idea more mysterious than troubling. How we get where we are, he might have said to himself. I hope. How contingent it does seem, as Jake says. He usually didn't think about such things. And the mother—so beautiful. He would have told about how the boy put his fingers into the vena cava and the aorta of the model heart and held it up like a misshapen bowling ball. He would have laughed, and the Wassermans would have taken time out from their complaining to laugh with him. When he showed the daughter his examining room, where the heart had been restored to its proper place, she had looked up at her mother and said, No shots.

The Wassermans lived a few blocks away, on Kuyper Avenue, right on the Hudson, and my father would have walked there from his house. On the way home, heavy snow would have been falling through the darkness, and the cars going down Grandview Street would have been driving slowly and carefully. Don't worry, Professor, I hear my father saying to himself, no drag-racing tonight. Up ahead, kids were sledding down the steep hill of Nyack Avenue between Broadway and Grandview. All clear, Mike? a boy's voice called from the top of the hill. All clear, another boy, standing in the middle of the street, shouted back. Ten seconds later, a sled shot out from the bottom of Nyack onto Grandview and cornered sharply, making twenty or thirty yards farther on the flat road. A record, Mikey! the small boy shouted. A record! He ran past my father, reminding my father of me at that age, and gave the sled to the other boy, who started running back up the hill with it. When my father got home, the house that had been so quiet for so long must have felt animated by the energy that Allegra and her kids had left behind them, and by his earlier conversation about us, and spruced up by Allegra's beauty.

I SLEPT A DEEP, quiet sleep in the bedroom at the front of the house which the old man had granted me. It had two big windows facing north and two more facing east, and it seemed to me, before I closed my eyes, like the prow of a ship as the wind and the now heavy snow swept around it. I woke up only once—from a dream that at the end had me on an island facing a muffled nautical cannonade—when the scraping rumble of a snowplow went past. A single car followed, almost silently, a minute later, before I fell asleep again, and I saw out one of the windows the snow falling in merry chaos through the headlights' jumpy beams, which, like kliegs, for a few seconds turned the storm into a formless but majestic staging of haphazardness.

When I woke up, more than a foot of snow had fallen and a light snow was still blowing around in a gusty wind through the gray air. Having accomplished its random, slipshod journey, in its famous supposed infinite particularity, the snow that had come to rest now lay with great art over everything, commenting on every line horizontal enough to bear it, taking everything that had formerly stood apart and connecting it to everything else, joking about every shape by reshaping it on top of itself—an ermine stole for this grand limb, a bolster for that hummock—and arbitrating yesterday's Balkan landscape into one with invisible borders, common purposes, and a single white currency.

I decided to call Dr. Morales to say that I might not be able to make the next morning's session. I timed the call so that I could leave a message on the answering machine. If I waited too long, Dr. Morales, having dismissed the five-day-a-week seven-o'clock patient—after three years still the Rich Amazing Cryer—would pick up the phone himself and hector me about cancelling and warn me away from whatever vague mission I might be on. Also, I was hungry, and I knew I had to make three calls to New York altogether, and I didn't want the grouchy old uncle to see the financial result of a Dr. Morales diatribe, which he would no doubt assume was just a wastrel long-distance chat. Who knew—maybe I would come back to this beautiful house someday. "This is Jake Singer," I said to the machine. It sounded foolishly existential in the big old place, with nature making its own huge, mute declaration outside. "I probably won't be able to come to tomorrow morning's session. I'm sorry. I'll see you on Friday." Then I called Coventry to remind them that I'd be out for the day and was told by a teacher who happened to be going past the receptionist's phone that the school was closed because of the snow. I hung up, then picked up the phone again to call Allegra, but this time the call didn't go through. I imagined her alone with the children and hoped that Claire would be arriving soon, to help her wait for Ms. P-e-t-r-o-s-k-i, and my heart went out to her.

The Jeep had little trouble with what without four-wheel drive and the right tires would have been dangerous driving on William's Lake Road. Route 32 had been plowed and sanded. I turned left onto it, and drove down toward the town of Mill-bridge. The small ski area I went past, a place called Pinewood Basin, was enjoying a minor November bonanza. The parking lot was already half full, and the parentheses and exclamation marks of skiers punctuated the slopes amid the swirling snow. Smoke billowed out of the chimney of the lodge at the base of the main chairlift; cars peeled off the road and into the area; some kids, probably from houses very nearby, were even walking in with skis and poles on their shoulders, pushing each other and laughing. Of course—the schools are closed here, too, I thought.

Friendly's, where I had breakfast, was very busy, too. I sat at the counter, next to a heavy young guy with a crew cut and a round face. All the men in the place had short hair and fifties clothes. Everyone seemed to know everyone else. The fleece of my sheepskin coat looked cloudy in this clean-cut atmosphere. The *New York Times,* which I had bought at the Shell station just across from the restaurant, might have been *Pravda,* to judge by the glances it got. Oh, well. I had bacon and eggs, white toast and butter, a big glass of orange juice, and two cups of coffee while performing the New Yorker's trick of folding the paper into a slender, readable back-and-front four columns and listening to the banter swirling around me. "Debbie, you look like you had a hard night last night," the heavy young guy sitting next to me said to our waitress. "Hope it was fun at least."

"Yeah, a lot of fun," Debbie said, stifling a yawn and pouring me a second cup of coffee. I looked up at her, and she gave me the nicest tired smile. She looked like a buck-toothed Loretta Lynn with permanent and deep fatigue lines around her mouth and eyes, though she couldn't have been much more than thirty.

"Old Jay won't leave you alone, I guess. I wouldn't, if you was my wife."

"Get out of here, Ernie."

"I wouldn't, I swear. Tell you what, let's me and you run off."

"At the mouth is the only running off you are capable of," Debbie said. "I'm going to tell Nancy how you flirt with everyone."

"I only flirt with you, and that's because you're so pretty," Ernie said. He turned toward me and said, "Isn't she pretty?"

"Very," I said.

"This man's trying to read his paper," Debbie said, but she was smiling again at me. "Why don't you leave him alone?"

"See, even a liberal thinks you're beautiful, Debbie," Ernie said, gesturing toward the newspaper. "No offense," he added.

"None taken," I said.

"I am too tired for your nonsense," Debbie said. "Anything else, hon?" she said to me.

"No thanks."

"I'll just give you your check. Ernie, why don't you go open your store a couple of hours early this morning, or go back home and help Nancy shovel the snow and take care of those kids? There's no school today, I heard. How do you get away with coming down here so early every morning when you don't open till eleven, anyway?"

"I got all the slicing to do, all the preparation. You know how it is. Slice the mozzarella, the ham, the other cheese, the salami, slice the Coke, the Pepsi, the mayo, the mustard, the this, the that. There's a lot of work in getting a sub shop ready to open, and I got to clean up, too. Mop up the floor, the walls, the ceiling, the parking lot, the etcetera. That uniform really shows up your figure, Deb."

The waitress waved at him to be quiet while she wrote out my bill. Just as she handed it to me, I remembered that I had spent almost all my money on gas on the drive up from New York the day before.

"Um, uh-oh," I said. I took out my wallet and confirmed that the single dollar bill left in it had not magically replicated itself overnight.

"Hey, McGinley, fill up the sink," Ernie called to the store manager, who was frying bacon on the grill a few feet away. "You got yourself a dishwasher."

"Ernie, will you shut up," Debbie said.

"No offense intended," Ernie said, putting his hand on my shoulder.

"Uh, none taken again," I said. "Listen," I said to the waitress, "I can go get some traveller's checks at a bank—is that OK? I have an American Express card here. Do you accept traveller's checks?"

"Sure. We get a million tourists here in the summer."

"Well, I could leave something behind."

"Hey, relax, this ain't New York City," Ernie said. "He don't have to do that, does he, Debbie?"

"Course not," she said. "He's a lot more respectable-looking than you are, and he's a gentleman, which is more than I can say for you."

"Well, thanks, then," I said, getting up. "I'll be back as soon as I can. Where's the nearest bank?"

"First Aggie, on Main Street," Ernie said. "But tell you

what, you don't have to rush. Let me pay your bill now and you come by my sub shop whenever you're ready–it's called Jonesy's, right up the road here, across from the bowling alley."

"That's nice of you," I said. "I passed your place on the way, right?"

"Yep," Ernie said. "Here, Deb." He gave the waitress a twenty.

"Well, I'll probably come right back to your place anyway," I said.

"OK. But I'm not open for a little while yet, so just knock on the door if it's locked. I'll be in there slicing."

"And eating, from the look of you," Debbie said.

"See what I get?" Ernie appealed to me. "I give her a compliment and help out a stranger to impress her and what do I get for it but an insult? Oh, I am doomed to be her unrequited lover."

"Yeah, and on the next shift you'll be Betsey's."

AT THE BANK, I fumbled in my wallet at the teller's window to find my American Express card, the one connection to my father that had remained in place during our long estrangement. I hadn't used it a single time since I paid for dinner with it at the restaurant with Samira, so long ago. When I found it and looked up, I saw that the triangular nameplate in front of the mousy, pale, utterly flat-chested, disapproving-looking young woman standing behind the counter read "Sarah Gibson."

"Can I help you, sir?" the woman said, giving my coat and the *Times* a severe inspection.

"What?" I said.

"Can I help you?"

"Uh, yes, sure," I said. I handed her the credit card. "I'd like three ten-dollar traveller's . . ."

"Traveller's checks? Is something wrong?"

"No, um, Mrs. Gibson."

"What?"

"Nothing's wrong. Yes, three ten-dollar traveller's checks, please. Uh, would you have a few minutes to talk now, or maybe later? Lunchtime or something?"

"What?"

"I was wondering if you might have a chance to talk to me sometime today," I said. "I should introduce myself—I'm sorry. My name is—"

"I know your name," the woman said.

"What?"

"I know who you are. You're Jacob Singer. Listen, I'm a married woman—"

"I know that. But how do you know I am, uh, who I am?"

The woman held up my American Express card in her right hand. "These things have the person's name on it, remember?" she said. "Just like you know I'm a married woman because of this." She held up her left hand with an engagement ring whose diamond was the size of a peppercorn and a filamental gold wedding ring.

"But that's not how I knew you're married, Mrs., um, Gibson."

"Now look, I'm going to have to call the manager over here. Mrs.—who did you say?"

"Mrs. Gibson."

"Oh, *now* I get it," the woman said, after following my gaze toward the brass nameplate. "You think I'm Sarah Gibson because of this." She handed back the credit card and picked up the triangular bar and allowed her narrow lips a tiny smile of relief. "I guess Sarah forgot to put it away yesterday afternoon, and I don't have my own out here yet. You know, technically, she's not Mrs. Gibson. That's her maiden name. Her husband's name is Winship—Paul Winship." She leaned down and put the bar under the counter and brought out a new one and set it down. "Lorilee Tietz," it read. "Sarah's not coming in today," she said. "She called just a few minutes ago. There's no school and she has to stay with Robby, and the snow is terrible over in New Berkshire, and anyways Robby's sick with the asthma. I can't imagine why she's over there and not in town. She had to have gone out there last night. How do you know her, anyway?"

"I don't," I said. "But I'd like to talk to her. Doesn't she live on Hatchery Road?"

"Not for quite a while now," Mrs. Tietz said. "But she's out there today, I guess."

"Well, thanks," I said. "Mrs. Tietz," I added, commanding my eyes not to descend below the woman's pinched face.

"It's 'Tites,' " the woman said.

"Tites?"

"Tites."

"Tites," I said.

"Can I give Sarah some kind of a message if she gets through again? The phone cut out just when I was going to ask her if she was OK and why was she out there. Is this some kind of an emergency? I don't know if her husband is in at his office or not, but he has his office right up on Station Street. Maybe you'd want to talk to him. He'd be getting in in about half an hour."

"No, that's OK. Maybe I'll stop in here tomorrow. Thank you."

I finished the paperwork the woman had given me and fled.

AT JONESY'S, I paid Ernie back with one of the traveller's checks. "Can you tell me where a road called Hatchery Road is?" I asked.

"Can but I won't," Ernie said. He handed me the change.

"What?"

"Just kidding. I'll tell you, but the hatchery ain't open in the wintertime, you know."

"That's OK," I said.

"You looking for anything in particular?"

"Well, there's a house I'm interested in."

"You looking to buy?"

"Uh, not really. Just looking."

"OK, now Hatchery Road. Go up 32—you know where that is?"

"Yes."

"Go east on 32 past Pinewood, and at the top of that hill there's William's Lake Road."

"Yes, I know that road. I'm staying in a house on William's Lake Road."

"Not over at the Leonard house?"

"Yes. How did you know?"

"He's always having someone to stay there. It's like a hotel. A friend of mine who passed away a couple of years ago used to do some landscaping for old man Leonard."

"Well, small world," I said.

"He was a good friend, too. He was about to get married to this nice lady he met. She was pregnant. Had to give the kid up for adoption when it was born. He was a good friend, like I said." These remarks restored my bewilderment, which had begun to ease a little since it had nearly overwhelmed me during the conversation in the bank with Mrs. Tietz. Meanwhile, Ernie's eyes were filling up, and he turned away for a moment, picked up a napkin, and wiped the tears away. "Anyways," he went on, "since you know that road, turn back down William's Lake Road and don't go over on 32, because you might end up in Monterey. Sorry about this. I get a little emotional. My wife tells me I should have been a woman. Anyways, go back down past Leonard's house and bear left at the Y a half a mile further on, go down around to the left on this big hill, and then go straight over a small bridge till where you run into 44. Turn left and then turn right right away and that's Hatchery Road. Be careful, though. The roads are probably pretty bad still, though I see the snow has stopped, and isn't that the sun over there in the east?"

"Anyway, I've got a Jeep out there, with snow tires," I said. I repeated the directions to make sure I had them right.

"Right," Ernie said. "Come back and have a sub for lunch."

"Maybe I will," I said. "Thanks for the loan."

MY GUESS IS that Paul tried to call Sarah just after the phones in New Berkshire went out. So he drove his BMW, which was just the right size for him, down to the bank to see if she had somehow managed to come in to work. He was going too fast, I'm sure, and slid around a little on Castle Heights Avenue as he drove down from Berkshire Heights, and where it came out onto Main Street he slid through the red light and out into the traffic, which, luckily, was light and slow. He hadn't slept at all. He was angry at Sarah and Robby, and he kept mistaking his humiliation for how much he loved her. When he got to the bank, Lorilee told him that Sarah had called before the phones went dead to say that she wasn't coming in. What's going on, Paul? she said. Why is she out there? She had to check something at the house, Paul said. Well, someone was in here about ten minutes ago looking for her, the woman said. Who? Paul said. Do you know who it was? Hey, take it easy, Lorilee said. Yeah, I know the guy's name. I gave him some traveller's checks, so I saw his American— What was his name? Paul said. Jacob Singer, Lorilee answered, and he— Did you say—did you tell him where she was? Paul said. Well, he seemed confused concerning where Sarah and you live, but— *Did you tell him where Sarah was?* Paul said again. I told him she had called from over on Hatchery Road— Well, what *is* going on here, she said to herself after Paul turned around abruptly and left. He drove back up Christian Hill Avenue. He was furious about the pace of the sander in front of him, even though he knew that he probably wouldn't have been getting back up the steep hill without the sand it was spreading. He went into the house and got one of the pearl-handled pistols from its display case and got back in the car. Then he got out again and went back into the house and tried to call Sarah, but all he got was a busy-circuit signal.

I HEADED BACK up 32, past the skiers, turned south onto William's Lake Road, and drove along distractedly, still bewildered by the encounters and conversations I had just had in town—incidents that began to call back to my memory the overdetermination of everything that had happened to me, in sessions with Dr. Morales and in real life, before I'd been knifed in the locker room by Walter Cooper. That event had led directly to Proctor's sentimental embrace, which had led to my presence at Allegra's house, which had led to my being here now. Interpreting Ms. Petroski's indiscretion and my need for traveller's checks and the bank nameplate and Ernie's reference to adoption as signs of fate or meaning didn't have much over the zodiac or rune-casting or pawing through a pigeon's guts in search of the future, I realized, but I couldn't help it. I still didn't know what I would say when and if I found Sarah Gibson, but I couldn't help feeling pointed in her direction.

The sun was coming out, but snow was blowing in the air, and a thick flurry from a dark-gray cloud remnant almost blinded me as I went past a dirt road on the left with a sign on the tree near it that said "Camp North Wind," and I had to stop gathering ontological wool and turn my full attention to

the road. Instead of driving past the old man's house and following Ernie's directions right away, I pulled into the driveway
and went in and looked up Sarah Gibson's number in the
phone book again and, not allowing myself to think about
anything, I picked up the phone. There was no dial tone at all
now. I went back out to the car and stopped still when I saw a
line of thirteen or fourteen fat gremlins trudging through a
blurred dust devil of snow being whipped up in the orchard
south of the house by the suddenly icy wind that was blowing.
The sun was shining where I stood, and brilliant particles of ice
fell down around me like a shower of silver, and the gremlins
plodded along through the snow-obscured orchard. What *are*
those things? I said out loud. Instead of getting into the car
and going on around to Hatchery Road, I walked out toward
the orchard a few yards. The ground storm of snow subsided,
and the gremlins turned into turkeys, wild turkeys, parading
through the sunlight and the silver crystals and looking hilari-
ously like the picture on the bourbon bottle. They picked up
some speed as I approached, and then they began running like
tailbacks and melted into the woods beyond the orchard, leaving not a trace behind except for their Euclidean footprints in
the snow.

Now I got into the Jeep. I backed out of the driveway and
turned south on William's Lake Road. I passed another snow-
covered road on the left, then another, marked by another
sign, "Camp He-To-No." Below the Y Ernie had described farther down the road stood an ancient gray building that looked
like a horse barn, part of which appeared to have been con-
verted into living quarters. An old man with a distracted air,
dressed only in boxer underwear and an undershirt in the frigid
cold, walked a few steps up the driveway and waved at me. A
door opened behind him just as I was about to slow down to
see if he was all right and a fat, ugly woman, wearing something that looked like a huge laundry bag, came out and led

him inside. On I went, past a boarded-up farmstand. "See you in July—Fred and Freddie" the sign on the farmstand said. Down around the hill I drove, past another small road off to the left, with, to one side of its entrance, a stand of mailboxes. Snow sat on all of them except one, which had been brushed off and proclaimed "Barbara Marks" in big, handsome letters. Across a small bridge I went, and on between two flat meadows of snow. I came to the intersection with Route 44, which looked less like a route than a lane. Here I was delayed again for a minute or so as a snowplow sander lumbered by. I turned left, saw the sign for Hatchery Road on the right, and turned right. This road hadn't been plowed and bore only a few tire tracks. It was even narrower than 44.

Snug, well-kept houses dotted both sides of the road. Behind the houses on the left I caught glimpses of a winding stream, some of it ice-covered, some of it open. On the right, a hundred yards away, a ridge thick with sentinel evergreens frosted with white ran parallel to the road. Sunlight filtered through the trees and set everything sparkling. The Jeep made almost no noise as it wound along through the deep snow.

More mailboxes covered with snow. As I went by a small goat farm on the left and realized that the houses were growing sparser, I decided to turn around the next chance I had and go back to the old man's place and wait for the phones to start working. Or maybe just bag the whole thing. The force of circumstance that just ten minutes earlier had seemed so powerful weakened here, in this impenetrably picture-perfect scenery.

SARAH WAS IN her house, glad that the phone had gone out while she was talking to Lorilee, so that Paul couldn't call her up and so that she would have time to think things over. Maybe her leaving last night would shake him up and help him get along better with Robby. She doubted it. The house felt the right size for her and Robby. He had slept fitfully at first, with labored breathing, and he was still wheezing a little when she woke up at around six, but it eased off a lot in the next hour, as if Paul's influence was lifting away from him, and when he got up she patched a breakfast together out of oatmeal and frozen orange juice, and then he wanted to go out into the snow immediately. Sarah bundled him up and sent him out into the backyard, while she made herself some coffee.

A CAR, A BMW, appeared in the Jeep's rearview mirror just after I started looking for somewhere to turn around. It came up close behind me. The driver, who I could see was wearing a business overcoat and a striped tie, started honking his horn and gesturing for me to pull over. I tapped the brakes to warn the guy to drop back. It didn't work. He pulled out as if to try to pass, but when he saw the road was too narrow he got behind me again, honking and tailgating. I was about to stop and pull over and let the lunatic pass when I rounded a sharp curve and found a line of frantic wild turkeys zipping across the road thirty yards in front of me. At the end of the line, running after the turkeys, was a child. I jammed on the brakes and the tires slipped a little and then held, and the Jeep had almost come to a stop when the BMW smashed into it from behind and pushed it forward toward the boy, who was now standing paralyzed in the middle of the road. When both cars finally stopped, the Jeep's bumper was three feet away from the little boy.

I jumped out of the car, ran up to the kid, and picked him up. "Are you OK?" I asked. I carried him to the side of the road and stood there with him. "You don't look like a turkey," I said, and the boy smiled a weak smile, and I could feel his rigid body relax a little inside the heavy parka he had on.

"Put him down," said a voice behind me.

"Hey, don't I know you?" I said. "Aren't you the boy who taught me how to play the guitar last night? Robby?"

"Yes," Robby said.

"I said put him down," the voice behind me said. I turned around and found the BMW's crazed suit glaring at me.

"If you were in such a hurry to pass, why did you stop?" I said. I looked at Robby. "He's scared. I'm just trying to calm him down."

"I said put him down, Singer," the short but, I now noticed, compact and powerful-looking guy said.

"How do you know my name?"

"Put him down and get back into that Jeep and get out of here, unless you want to get hurt."

I put the boy down and squared up to Paul.

"Go inside to your mother, Robby," Paul said. "How do you know his name, Singer?"

"He and his mother stopped by where I'm staying last night—what's it to you, anyway? Why don't you clear out of here, come to think of it. I'll give you a break on rear-ending me."

"You don't have any idea what you're messing around with here," Paul said. "Go inside, Robby," he said again.

The boy didn't move. "You're not the boss of me," he said. "You're not my *father.*"

"Why don't you just take off and come back later, if you have any business here," I said. "You're frightening this kid."

"I'm married to his mother," Paul said, stepping up close to me. "His mother is my wife, and I know who you are, Singer, and my very strong advice to you is to leave while you can."

"You're not my father," Robby said again, weakly.

Paul stepped even closer to me. "Get out," he said.

"Fuck you," I said. I could feel the fight coming but knew I could start it if I wanted to. "Fuck you and the BMW you rode in on. Come to think of it, fuck yourself and keep the baby. I'm taking this boy inside his house."

Paul raised his hands and pushed me backward by the shoulders. I bumped into the mailbox behind me, and some of the snow fell from it with a thump. Trying to regain my balance, I turned around and saw the letters "son" on the mailbox. Paul pushed me against it again and the rest of the snow fell off. "S. Gibson."

"Holy shit," I said. "Sarah Gibson lives here. You're her husband?" I smiled and extended my hand. "Listen, I'm sorry. How *do* you know my name, anyway? Listen, I think we have some things to talk over."

This change in my demeanor took Paul by surprise, and he stepped back and dropped his hands, at which point I stepped forward and hit him hard in the face. "Don't push me, asshole," I said. "I don't care who you are. You're the one who's causing the trouble here. What are you—some kind of maniac?"

Paul held his face with his right hand. Blood was dripping out of his nose and staining the snow where he stood. "Hit him again," Robby said.

Paul said, "Fistfights are for children." He turned around and got back into his car as Robby and I watched him. Then he got out again, holding the pearl-handled pistol. "Get into your car," he said.

I felt my knees weaken instantly before the gun, and I said, "Hey, hold on."

"Get into your car and drive away while you still can."

Sarah burst out of the house. "Oh, Robby, thank God— here you are!" she cried. "I told you to stay in the backyard. I was looking all over for you back there. I thought you'd fallen into the river. You *know* better than to play in the road."

"There were some turkeys," Robby said. "He has a gun."

Sarah picked him up and held him and only then took in

what was going on. "Paul, what's this all about? Oh, put that gun away, for God's sake. There's a child here."

I had to sit down in the snow, my knees were so weak and I felt so faint with fear and confusion. "You're Sarah Gibson?" I said. "I met you last night. This can't actually be happening."

"It certainly is happening, Singer," Paul said. "Get up and get into your car. Sarah, if you don't want Robby out here with this gun, take him inside. This Jew is here to spy on you, and he assaulted me. Do you want him being the father to your daughter? This is for your own good—I'll explain it all later."

"My daughter! What are you talking about?"

"Get into the house right now!" Paul shouted. For a second it looked as though he might turn the gun on Sarah. She took Robby and went back inside the house.

"Get up, Singer," Paul said. "Get out of here."

I got to my feet shakily and walked past Paul toward the Jeep. Paul followed me. As he did, Sarah must have come back out of the house holding the twenty-two rifle that the first Paul had given her and then walked up behind Paul silently and stuck the barrel into the back of his coat. "That's enough, Paul," I heard her say. "Robby told me what happened with the cars here. This man was just trying to help my son. I'm glad you came out here. Now I know I've had enough of you. Put that down and leave and don't come back. We're through."

"Sarah, you don't know what I'm trying to do for—"

"I don't care what you're trying to do for me. It's for you, whatever it is. I don't want you running my life anymore."

I STAYED FOR three hours. With tears in her eyes as we sat down in the kitchen, Sarah asked me, "What's my little girl's name?" She made some more coffee, and while Robby played outside and then came in and watched TV in the living room and made do with some more oatmeal, she and I sat in the kitchen looking out on the brook in back and talked. The day grew more brilliant as the sun ascended, and its light danced off the ice and water of the brook, whose rushing water sounded like children laughing a long way away. "I'm crying just like some woman," Sarah said after I told her about Emily and Allegra and their lives, and before she told me about hers. "You're not some woman," I said. "You're Annie Oakley." Sarah laughed and said, "The rifle wasn't even loaded," and then she covered her eyes with her hands. "How did I ever get hooked up with him?" she said. She didn't see me start to lean forward to put my arm around her and then sit back. "Emily's like you," I said.

Hoops! Mr. Singer, you have been hasty before and almost paid for it dearly, so why don't you stop and consider what has happened here before you go? I heard my onboard Dr. Morales say. *You have put your feet admirably into this lovely young woman's small snow boots, so why don't you try on the wingtips of her lousy husband for a minute. He is out there somewhere with that gun of his, no? He knows where you are staying, is it not? You have humiliated him, have you not? OK, OK, you are right. His wife has humiliated him more. ALL THE WORSE! She cut his little testicles off and held them up for you to see, correct? You were the one who had been sitting down with your bowels located somewhere near your weak knees. Some hero you are, by the way, is what you may be thinking. But don't forget that you have built a bridge between this woman's life, on the one hand, and the lives of the little girl she gave birth to and of your lover, on the other. In any case, do you think this man will release you back to your fellow Semites in New York entirely scot-free? No! He must attempt to relocate and reattach his testicles! So do for me and for yourself a favor and this time for once keep an eye on your own cojones. Yes, it*

*would be a favor to me, too—not because I have forgiven you for
taking such serious matters into your own hands this way, and
as a result because of it nearly purchased the farm, but because I
don't want to lose a paying customer. Yes, that is why I am
warning you! There is no other reason, no matter whether you
believe me or not.*

I asked Sarah if I could try her phone. But the phones still
weren't working. She said, You're thinking he'll be looking for
you? I said yes. You're right, she said—I know him. He knows
where you're staying. Were you going to call the police? I said
yes. Well, just go to them, then, Sarah said. Ask for Ed Andruss, and tell Ed I told you to. Turn right onto 44 and just
drive into Millbridge. He wouldn't be waiting on the open
road somewhere.

I drove the damaged Jeep into town and went to the police.
I drove back to the old man's house half an hour later, rehearsing how I would tell Allegra that she could stop worrying
about Emily, as soon as I could talk to her. When I got to the
house I pulled a little way up the driveway and stopped. Paul
was waiting in his car, with its battered bumper and shattered
headlight. He got out holding his gun. In the police car that
had been following me out from town, Officer Ed Andruss
pulled in right behind me. Paul said, It's not loaded.

I DROVE BACK to New York that afternoon, stopping at every
public phone I could find in Massachusetts and then northwest Connecticut until I found one that worked, in Sharon. I
stood in the snow outside a 7-Eleven on Route 34 and rushed
Allegra through a chaotic account of what had happened but
managed to get the news across that Emily would stay right
where she was. I said, "Call your lawyer or is it lawyers now and
make an appointment with them tomorrow morning. I'll go

with you. There's nothing more for them to do, but they should know about what happened, probably. All Sarah wants is some news about Emily from time to time, and maybe she'll get to meet her someday, and maybe you, too. She knows Emily's in good hands. I swear, I can't tell you how weird everything that happened up there was. People were lending me money, people knew my name and I didn't know how they knew it, a guy I met at a counter eating breakfast told me about Emily's biological father without the faintest clue that I had anything to do with her. I'll tell you about him when I see you—he died in an accident. It's pretty sad. If I hadn't stopped to look at some turkeys in an orchard, I might never have met this woman. Oh, yeah—your Jeep's rear end is a little banged up. I'm sorry. Anyway, Sarah had nothing to do with trying to get Emily back—it was her husband, and she didn't even know about it. You'd have never had to go to court anyway, probably, unless you want to arrest me for stealing your car." I yammered on and then heard myself yammering on and then stopped and said, "How was Miss Petroski?"

"I was so worried when I didn't hear from you," Allegra said. "I thought you'd run out on me. I wouldn't have blamed you. I half hoped you had, for your sake. Why should you get mixed up in this mess I've made? Instead you were trying to help me."

"You didn't make a mess. Did Miss Petroski come?"

"Yes, and I was so nervous at first, I was sure she thought I was just arrogant, just as you feared would happen. Claire was here, and she was charming, but I sat there paralyzed, and Georgie wouldn't say a word, but Emily rescued me. She went to her room and found a book she'd been asking me to read to her before the social worker came but there wasn't time. She came back into the living room and got up on the couch next to her and told her if she was thirsty, I would get her some coffee. I'd forgotten to offer her anything, I was so anxious. I said, 'Oh, I'm sorry, would you like anything?' and when she said no thank you, Emily said to her, 'Would you read?' I said, 'No, sweetie, she can't read to you right now, but I will, I promise, in a few minutes,' and she got down from the couch and then came and sat in my lap, holding the book, waiting patiently, and the minute she touched me I relaxed. I began to believe that I would be able to keep her. She said, 'Mommy will read later,' and held up the book up like a prize."

I TOLD DR. MORALES that Allegra and I were going to get married. "So why, then, are you here, Mr. Singer?" he asked icily. He appeared to have chilled down completely on the trip from inside to outside my head. I had once again invented a kinder, gentler version of him for myself, I realized, sort of like trying to give a comic impression of Genghis Khan. It was Friday morning, early, before school started, with a bitter-cold rain falling outside from nickel-colored skies. I was sure that the same weather was taking the form of snow again, rather than rain, in the Berkshires. I'd spent the first twenty minutes of the session describing to a stone-still Dr. Morales what had happened there, after leading off with another apology for missing the session on Wednesday morning, which I had spent with Allegra at her lawyer's office, recounting the same events. An adoption-law expert sat in with us.

"Allegra has calmed down about Emily now," I said to Dr. Morales, ignoring his question, "but you were right about her being more fragile than I thought she was. She has this constant precarious intensity about her."

"I ask you again, since you have in the last month repeatedly broken the agreement between us to consult with me about any important decisions you make, why are you here?" Dr. Morales said. "Especially since you have managed to blame your unilateral abrogation of our contract on me. Here you have almost gotten yourself killed, you have made a lifelong commitment to a woman whose psychological problems have done nothing but grow more manifest from the day you first put your penis in her. Why did you not cancel this session, too, and all the rest?"

"You might congratulate me," I said.

"You believe that that is why you are here—to receive my congratulations?"

"And to show you that you might want to congratulate yourself, for a job well done."

"Do not patronize me, Mr. Singer, as if I were a plumber in beeb overhauls who had fixed your backèd-up toilet for you. Do not toss over your shoulder to me some decayed bone such as 'You were right about her' and 'You have done such a good job' and expect me to wag my tail in gratitude. Especially since I strongly suspect that if you indeed think that you have found your way out of the morass your life was in when we first started the treatment, you also think you would have done it without me."

"Maybe."

" 'Maybe.' You see, we are back where we began. You are trying to destroy what we have been building as casually as in the Apocrypha God destroys the men he has just created from sand. And just in case you never figure it out, the answer to the question I have asked about why you are here is this: You are begging me to stop you. Listen to what you have said about this woman you have just met and how you admired her, how her courage and beauty impressed you. I heard no irony, no skepticism, but only enthusiasm and respect when you spoke of her. I must tell you that I am nearly in the professional equivalent of despair, but I suppose that it is my duty to try to accommodate this unconscious plea to remove you once again from the tracks you have tied yourself down to, as the train whose freight may well not include your own best interests bears down upon you."

"That's enough," I said. "This will be endless. Get the rich girl, you as much as tell me. Ah-ah, she's crazy. What about this one with a gun in the sticks? Let's talk about her. I came here again today to see what you had to say about what has happened to me and what I've done—"

"This is precisely what I am trying to tell you, Mr. Singer."

"—but what I find is the same old dragging-out, anger, disappointment, and sarcasm. It's personal despair that you feel. You see me acting on my own, and you don't want to let me go. You are like a parent whose kid has been nearly run over crossing the street—you're trying to turn your fear of losing me into anger."

"Mr. Singer, you have made progress, even great progress, in overcoming your passivity and in your relationships, but in your heart of hearts the motive is still *your* anger and *your* rebellion—to show me that I am wrong about what I now see as your potentially lethal impulsiveness, to show me that you do not need me as much as you in fact do need me. This buried pollution of defiance, the waste matter from your self-hatred and guilt—we must continue to dig down to it until we can flush it entirely from your system."

"I don't have time," I said, resisting the temptation to point out to Dr. Morales that he had just donned beeb overhauls without any assistance from me. "If you can't see what I've accomplished, perhaps with your help, however cruel, then of course no one can make you see it. You've given me all of what you could give me, which was at the very least a lot to think about, and that's not nothing. I've had enough."

I got up from the couch and extended my hand to Dr. Morales, who sat there as immobile as the bronze Christ on the crucifix behind him.

PART FOUR

The Last Freudian

T HE FATES STAND for storytelling–beginnings, middles, and ends–and for death, and that's why guns, and before them knives, arrows, clubs, slingshots, jaws of asses, etc., have played such important parts in eight or nine of the twelve stories some wit once said are available to us. Lo, we Spear-Danes. *Arma virumque cano.* When the creator of a narrative puts a lethal weapon into it, he's putting himself into it, or an important part of himself: the power to end the lives that he has invented. Anyone who has had a serious gun held on him which he thinks is loaded believes in a way he'll never forget that his life has continued at the mercy of *something,* even if that something is nothing but luck.

Today is the seventh anniversary of the day Paul Winship held a gun on me in the snow. He has a new wife now, Sarah has told me. A blond one from a rich family in Egremont. He no longer uses the First Agricultural Bank, never speaks to her, she says. He tried to persuade her to come back to him–even after she demanded a divorce–but he surreptitiously got in touch with Richard Friedman down in Norfolk just in case, and finally gave up and stopped talking to her when Friedman turned him down, called Sarah, and offered to pay his colleague in Massachusetts to represent her. No charges were brought against Paul, by me or the cop, and he still has a practice, though it's getting smaller all the time and he had to give a considerable settlement to Sarah to avoid a nasty court fight. Good thing his parents and his wife's are rich, Sarah said once. She hasn't touched the settlement money and hopes not to have to, and she won't accept child support. It's always a comfort to have the villains in one's life turn out to be guilty of anti-Semitism—it's a kind of made-to-order evil—but still, I almost feel sorry for Paul. *Oh, please, Mr. Singer, give me some small essemblance of a break,* says the Morales chip in my brain.

Sarah has been promoted twice at the bank, and she thinks that Robby, who is in eighth grade, may get an athletic scholarship for college. Turns out to be a good football player, she told me a couple of years back, with a grin on her face. He and Sarah still live in the little house on Hat Cherry Road, and she goes out with a flight instructor from the Great Barrington airport, who proposed to her as she first took the controls and flew his little plane over Squaw Peak, but she has no intention of getting married again. I go up to see her a couple of weekends every year—usually in the middle of October and at the end of April, the times of year when that beautiful place is at its most beautiful. I bring her pictures of Emily, and we have a conversation, and if it's nice out, we take a walk. She does the opposite of what Allegra does when she's talking intensely—she looks down, she looks away—and that's when I most want to take her hand, but of course I don't. Not only am I married but she wouldn't be interested in me anyway, I tell myself. Not in that way. A few times when I've let out some obsessiveness or intensity in her company, I've caught her looking at me with bafflement—a normal person disbelieving an autochthonous New Yorker. We tend to sow bewilderment wherever we go. I stay with Sol Leonard, and sometimes Dave makes it a point to be there, and we sing the old songs, the musical remnants of a century's worth of demotic idealism, and the old man keeps trying to get us both to play a seventh note when we play a dominant chord and to sing with a less rustic accent, and we immediately get twangier, just to annoy him and make him laugh. Dave has become a friend—we're different enough now—and so has Mac Preston, whom I appointed dean when I became headmaster. Mac is leaving Coventry in January, to start a storefront school of his own, funded by himself, in Harlem. Allegra and I are giving a fund-raiser buffet for Mac's school tomorrow night, Friday, with all the Coventry upper-school parents invited, and Mac will be the guest of honor. Once it gets under way, Allegra will be fine—frank and charming—and with her help I've learned how to get through them, too, and even have a good time.

The gun wasn't loaded and even if it had been I don't think Paul would ever have pulled the trigger, but, then, we threads here on earth never know when Atropos will start snipping. It has made the first week in November even more of an anniversary than it had been before, I realize, especially when I have a little time on my hands, as I do this afternoon, sitting in my vast office—the foredeck that Proctor abandoned to me for the helm of Lawrenceville—waiting for a parent to come in and complain about her son's grade in English, and especially when there's a big snowstorm on the way, as there's supposed to be now.

How could the board at Lawrenceville have fallen for Proctor's act? How did Coventry's board fall for mine? Allegra's money helped, but it's not impossible that I would have made it anyway, I like to hear her tell me and I like to tell myself. Proctor made me dean for the last two years he spent here, and we got along well. He had hardly a thought in his head, but he did run a tight ship, and a tight ship was what the seventies called for. Most of the parents seem happy with me, but not all—some distrust the more relaxed atmosphere of their grand old school, are sorry to have seen the dress rules eased to include blue jeans, aren't too pleased with the community-service requirements, but on this matter they don't dare grumble too loudly for fear of looking mean. Especially since I go with the students when they do their volunteer work at the Salvation Army nursing home around the corner or clean up Riverside Park. I don't love it myself, to be honest—I'm too selfish to love that kind of thing. But I feel obliged to do what I can to give the boys some immunity to the lawyer-doctor fever that has seized the almost and definitely rich kids and their families under Reagan, and they still get into Harvard and Yale and Amherst and Williams in constant numbers, and they still score just as well on all the tests, and the drug situation has eased, so no one is complaining about me too much. The boys still like me, or so it seems. I still scrimmage with the basketball team and score a few points, though I'm just about to turn forty and have lost a step. Galgano has mellowed—either that or he's kowtowing to me. And are the kids letting me score? It's not always easy for a boss to feel it when his ass is being kissed. And I am the boss. I make decisions quickly and firmly, sometimes impulsively and even curtly. I've joined the club after all, I suppose, though I try to be less of a martinet than Proctor, less limited than my father, and less maniacal than Dr. Morales. I don't play politics—which, when you get results, is the best politics you can play. I fired a popular gym teacher for cuffing a kid, and I've thrown two kids out of school, one for cheating—twice—and another for writing vicious anonymous threats to boys he thought were gay. I can afford a certain audacity, since my living doesn't depend on this job or any other, but I often feel a kind of profound pointlessness lurking beneath the thin ice of principle and bravado I'm skating over. I sometimes feel it's all an act, a performance.

Mrs. Glass is going to be late, I can tell. "You go on home, Lauren," I call to my assistant. "It's starting to snow. There's no reason for both of us to be stuck here."

I stand up and go to look out the huge window over the Hudson. The snow has started to blur the bright trees over on the Jersey shore. Mrs. Glass's second boy, Stevie, a senior, is an even nastier kid than his older brother, Billy, was. He's pathetic, really. He has taken his brother's political conservatism to a caricatured extreme. I had to stop him once as he was reading an essay in my class about how much he disliked what he referred to as Negroid features. His briefcase is even snappier and shinier than Billy's was. He runs a baby-sitting service but has never done any baby-sitting himself. He farms out the work to his classmates and takes a percentage. Mrs. Glass's husband, Herb, died over the summer of a heart attack at the age of fifty-five—Dr. Morales would have said he wanted out of his marriage, I'm sure—and she has grown more impossible than ever, if you ask me. Every time I see her or hear from her, her control-freakism seems more out of control. She has complained about the school's lunch menu, about phys-ed requirements for seniors, about my own advanced-placement English class, which she thinks should concern British literature, not American. Now she wants to whine at me about Stevie's grade in that class. I gave him a C for the first trimester, with some remorse, because the colleges always look at first-trimester grades of senior year particularly closely, and the boy in his nasty, mechanical way *has* tried very hard to get hold of the more psychological and artistic aspects of what we've been reading—Cotton Mather, Hawthorne, Melville. But he's hopelessly literal-minded when it comes to fiction, for all his brilliance in other subjects, not only math and science but history and even political science. And he takes relentless issue with the very idea of interpretation. "Maybe Melville makes Ishmael say so many things about the whiteness of the whale because he wants to make fun of interpretation—sir," Stevie said the other day. Not a bad idea for him to come up with on his own, but it was offered as an insult, not a thesis. I look for some sign of imagination and spontaneity and involvement with the reading in the kids I teach, and Stevie is the only boy in his class who has none. I think of the C almost as a gift. Mrs. Glass has incessantly told me that she wants Stevie to go to Harvard, like his father, who confided to me last year at the fund-raiser we always hold around now that he wished he'd gone to the Oberlin Conservatory and become a clarinettist instead of the management consultant he'd so remuneratively become. He blamed some of his kids' reactionary politics on the kind of work he did.

Emily and Georgie are growing up nicely. Georgie calls me Jake, which is fine, and Emily calls me Pop, which makes me proud. She has Sarah's independence and strong will in every matter. She learned to tie her shoes before she was three—she tied them for the first time just before the little wedding that Allegra and I had at St. Paul's Chapel, on the campus of Columbia. She taught herself her times tables when she was eight, begged me for driving lessons on the back roads around Sag Harbor when she was nine, and took to the water in the ocean nearby and in the Caribbean in the winter like a fish. Georgie is a terrific artist for his age, studying drawing at the Metropolitan and earning the respect of his Coventry classmates with his work. He designed the eighth grade's yearbook page this year. He's the only kid I've ever known who has gotten blonder as he's grown older. He's handsome, he has a lot of friends, and he settles disputes for them in an almost undetectable way. I know this because I eavesdrop on them when they're in Georgie's room cursing manfully and trying to decide whether to watch the Knicks or a movie on TV. Like Twain's father, I know nothing, as far as this thirteen-year-old is concerned. "Heed me, my children—yea, I have indeed completed my tasks," he says to his mother and me when we finish dinner and ask him if he's done his homework.

And Allegra. She has never overcome the anxiety set off by the crisis with Emily. They now think that this nervous condition she has was probably lying nascent in her all along, and that if the fear of losing her daughter hadn't brought it out, something else would have. She's prone to panic and gets anxious about social events—as I used to—and meeting new people or trying anything new. She's fine about going to Fire Island and Sag Harbor and visiting my father in Rockland. She'll be great tomorrow night at the party, though she'll also be terrifically worried about it before the first guest arrives. My father doesn't know about this problem—it's a secret—and he dotes on her and her kids, to the point of making me jealous, I realize for the first time, standing here and waiting for Mrs. Glass. He attends to Allegra with a courtliness I've never seen in him before, and he takes a grandparent's pleasure in having presents and food on hand every time the kids visit, and he treats me with respect bordering on deference, which I find preferable to silent disapproval but not wildly so. I wouldn't mind a few snacks and presents myself, but there's no going back.

Allegra understands her problems and how they limit her, and she talks to me about it with repeated apologies and complete candor—about how helpless it makes her feel, and how grateful she is to have me to take the children out of the routines she's so mired in. I took them both to Tuscany for two weeks last summer. Allegra just couldn't do it. I tell her again and again that I can't forgive her because there's nothing to forgive her for. We still have a wonderful kind of intimacy, and she is still direct and sensual, but it can be debilitating to worry so much for her sake about ordinary life, and I can see that she can see in my eyes that this commitment to her is at least in part just that. But what is commitment to someone if it isn't sometimes just commitment?

What does she sacrifice in her commitment to me? I'm elusive and would-be wise, and, as Dr. Morales has just told me from his secure internal perch, "understanding" to a fault, at least outside of business hours, and as he always said in real life, overironical—which is better than the sarcasm I used to trade in so heavily—overintellectual, too amused and bemused by what should engage me directly. *Too much of a Buddhist of convenience, and a movie critic of your life, Mr. Gautama St. Francis Pauline Kael Singer,* Dr. Morales concludes. It's a quiet household, our huge apartment, and when Georgie and Emily and their lively friends leave to go to college themselves, I'm not sure what Allegra and I will do—how we'll do. Claire can come over and brighten things with her chatter only so many times and only for so long. Her husband and Allegra's parents seldom pay us more than limited and ceremonial visits. They all seem relieved to have me around. Well, that's only natural.

So much death accounts for the way my life has turned out—my mother, Allegra's husband, Paul Sullivan, even the schemer Bill Daniels died, by his own hand, a few years ago. And now I'm waiting for the Widow Glass, come to think of it.

Herb Glass is   . That's the way it should be written. That's the way it should be said. To use a word to describe what someone is when he is no longer alive is to confer upon the adjective and its noun form, "death," an existential dignity that neither deserves. Herb Glass isn't anything anymore— there is no predicate that will do for a sentence about his state of being, because he has none. Merely to think the word   is to propel one's thoughts headlong into absurdity.   be not proud.   is no brother to sleep.   has no family at all.   is not a leveller.   is not inevitable. Whatever was coming for the Archbishop, it couldn't have been   , because that's nothing. There isn't even a first   , to say nothing of any other after it. Sin has no paycheck whatsoever, if its wages are what Christ promised in his contract with sinners. Pledge wouldn't have helped Macbeth find his way any more easily. Patrick Henry staked his claim to posterity on a nondichotomy. If Emily Dickinson had stopped, her horses wouldn't have had to pull any harder, and had only her neurasthenic weight to pull when he stopped for her. I shall not see my mother or anyone else or anything more, I won't know anything, touch anything, be aware of anything at all, even the halt itself, when my life is over. If death is in fact the mother of beauty, she's pretty mean to her kids.

I conjure with this terrifying zero from time to time—*timor mortis conturbat me*—in addition to mulling about the arbitrary string of occurrences that precede it. I think about sitting there in the snow and facing the mouth of the narrow tunnel of a gun barrel that might have introduced me to my maker, the big fat Nullity. I try to conjure—I put my hand into the hat and come up with absolutely nothing every single time. Except now, when what's not in that hat or anywhere else suddenly turns even more cataclysmically intolerable to my mind, because I understand that with the end of every life comes the end of the world. *That* is the way the world ends—chronically, relentlessly, routinely, thousands upon thousands of times a day.

"Ahem—Mr. Singer?"

"Oh, hello, Mrs. Glass. I was just wool-gathering over here. Please come in and sit down."

"Isn't someone supposed to be at the desk out there?"

"I let Lauren go home—the snow is getting pretty heavy."

She takes her coat off—camel's hair appears to run in the family—and we sit down in the two chairs in front of my desk.

She is dressed perfectly but still looks deranged—almost daffy—with intensity and determination. If only her lipstick were a little off, her hair a little messed up. She looks like she might crack in despair at any moment.

"Now, you know why I'm here," she says. "Or at least one of the reasons. Stevie works very hard, and he needs at least a B in English for college applications, and I think your grade isn't fair. And he thinks you have something against him because he's more mature than the other boys."

"OK, B it is," I say.

"I beg your pardon?"

"I'm changing his grade to a B. But he has to do something for it in return."

"Extra credit—of course he'll do that."

"No, not extra credit—he has to tutor math and reading in the middle school two hours every week for the rest of the year."

"But that hasn't got anything to do with his own studies."

"No, but that's the deal I'm offering. I wish it was as much for the sake of the kids he'll be helping as it is for his, but it isn't. Even so, it's the deal. And the deal is off if anyone else finds out about it. I shouldn't make it and you shouldn't accept it, but still it's the deal."

"This is most irregular."

"It's not entirely fair to the other kids, but we'll all survive. What was the other thing you wanted to talk about?"

"Another irregularity, I'm afraid—one that, however unfortunately, heightened my concern about your relationship with Stevie and your position in general. Dr. Ernesto Morales spoke of you to me."

"What?"

"For two or three weeks after Herb died, I was very upset, and I went to the school psychologist, and she recommended I see Dr. Ernesto Morales—"

"I'm firing her tomorrow."

"—and I saw him only once. He was such a horrible man. I tried to talk to him about Herb and Stevie, but he seemed to be completely bored. Except when I mentioned Coventry. That's when he said that you had been his patient."

"That is outrageous. What else did he say?"

"He said that you had stopped the treatment before you should have and had made a bad marriage as a consequence and he hoped that your unresolved conflicts wouldn't affect your judgment in this job. I knew he was out of order, but I have to say that what he told me about you raised questions—"

"He talked about Allegra?"

"He said—"

"Wait a minute—were you going to try to use this somehow about Stevie's grade?"

"Only if I had—"

"Actually, Mrs. Glass, I don't want to know. Get out of here and do whatever you like. I hope you'll have the decency to keep whatever private information you've learned about me and my family to yourself. As for Dr. Morales, I'll deal with him directly. Your son still gets his B, but now he has to tutor three hours a week instead of two."

"ESUE ME," DR. MORALES says the next day. The snow has stopped, but Coventry and every other school in the city are closed, for the first time since I met Sarah for the first time, so as Allegra nervously began to get ready for the party and George and Emily ran outside to the playland of the park with Jeanne, this year's au pair, another French girl, I called Dr. Morales and asked to see him. He had many different times available, which was a kind of preliminary comfort against his treachery. He used to be completely booked up.

He has also moved his office. It is now one of four in a

Sheetrock suite on the top floor of a brownstone in one of the shabbier parts of Chelsea—though even that neighborhood looks pretty picturesque beneath its white blanket under a sparkling sun. A Tourette's sufferer sits with me in the cheaply furnished waiting room—at least I extrapolate that that was his problem when his practitioner comes out to get him and he says, "Hi, fuckshit Scott." Dr. Morales looks exactly the same, except for a gray strand or two in his black beard. His quarters are smaller and even more cluttered than they were on the East Side.

"You're lucky I don't beat your ass in for you here and now," I say. "Violating our privacy. I just want you to know that if it weren't for the issue of privacy I'd take action against you with the New York Psychoanalytic Society. I'm ashamed of myself for ever saying anything at all about Allegra or her children to you."

"I assure you the situation is not what this deeply disturbed woman has told you it is," Dr. Morales says. "But I shall not defend myself. I shall not tell you how I found her pausing through my files during the single session I had with her when I had to run out of the office because down there on the street—you see out this window?—they were towing my car away, when it, like me, had violated no laws. I shall not tell you that this woman saw me only once because I threw her out, this horrible woman. It is all so improbable that you will not believe me and would not believe it. This woman is not neurotic, she is not in mourning, she is entirely demented by the rage that no doubt led her husband to flee her and into oblivion and that increased with his doing so. I shall confess only one thing to you—that when she told me that her unfortunate sons attended your school, I mentioned that you were an acquaintance of mine. Perhaps from that she surmisèd that you had been my patient and looked in the files when I had to go down the stairs to retrieve my car from the brownshirts who were trying to tow it. In fact, she has obliged me at this very moment to violate the confidentiality between me and her, which I will tell you is the only time in my career that I have done such a thing. In vengeance to me, because I told her to get out when I caught her in the act, she has gone to you—I had no idea what she had seen in that file drawer until you have shown up here so ready as always to do battle with me."

"And is that what it says in the files about me?"

"Yes. There is a summary of your case at the front of the file with your name on it. But that should not be a surprise to you. I never hid this opinion of mine from you. You know that I believe that you terminated the treatment before you should have. You know what you have told me about your wife, about Emilia and her biological mother. I regret this accidental breach of confidence—if you go over to those files at this moment, you will see that my file drawers are now lockèd at all times—but I ask you to examine how ready you were, how eager, to believe the worst about me. Does it not prove my point?"

"After this, can I believe anything besides the worst about you? Why isn't it equally likely that you spoke to her on purpose so that I would come to see you again?"

"No. You became so angry so that you have an excuse, a steed of rage, on which to ride back to *me*. It is always the same and always will be with you, I fear."

"Well, when it comes to making mistakes that can be avoided, there are no accidents, as the master taught me. You at the very least invited this woman to look through your files by negligently leaving them open, and so—"

"And so shut up now, Mr. Singer, and do as I ask—esue me—if you do not believe what I say." Dr. Morales stands up, and veins begin to stand out on his neck and forehead. His shoulders outside his vest look bulgier than ever, and he holds his hands stiff at his sides. Light from the window glances off his glasses, rendering him eyeless-looking.

"You couldn't get along without—"

"You! Listen to your ignorant prattle. You think you can esize me up and dress me down! You are a half-finished esculpture in the corner of my work's atelier, Mr. Singer. Something so lockèd with recalcitrance that Buonarroti himself could not have freed the rest of your obdurate psyche from the block of Oedipal marble in which it is immured. You do not know how lucky you are to have gotten as far as you have. You would be dead if it were not for me, Mr. Singer. You would be dead. I am the last Freudian, Mr. Singer! I am the last Freudian! I am the last of a line that estretches from Moses to Aristotle through Cicero to our good Lord Jesus Christ and Aquinas and Maimonides and Shakespeare and Montaigne and finally to Freud and then to me. A line of fascination with and respect for the dignity, the very concept, of the human soul. Do you know what will happen here in this country, and for that matter around the globe, now, Mr. Singer? Do you know what trouble the idea of the soul is in, by any remote eeyota of a chance, Mr. Singer? Let me tell you. *Close that door, Escott!*"

He is suddenly looking over my shoulder. The door has opened, I see when I turn my head, and the man who is treating the Tourettist is in the doorway with his fingers to his lips.

"Close the door! I must listen to the mindless obscenities of the miserable creatures whom you call patients all day long. It will not hurt you to hear what I am saying. After all, I never keep my confidences in any case, so what difference does it make?"

The door closes. Dr. Morales sits down.

"Mr. Singer, this man Reagan will spend the Soviets into oblivion, believe me. I know economics, it may come as some surprise to you to hear. Or not. Because that is right—you are the one who always felt you could hide from me behind financial smoke screens, as if it were. Reagan will spend the Soviets into Chapter Eleven, and then free-market capitalism will have free rein throughout the world, which should be music to the ears of a man like myself but is not. Because then the flight from mystery and meaning in this country will be complete—in fact, the literature that you love so well will begin to fall into desuetude as well. We shall have won the political and economic war and thereby lost. Look at the retreat I myself am in here in this office." In fact, I find that I have grown oblivious of our surroundings. There is something about Dr. Morales's voice, which has now descended into an oracular portentousness, that makes both of us seem abstract, disembodied—like opposed principles instead of two angry people. "Along with these hollow external victories will come the development in the medical world of the psychopharmacopoeia which Freud so astutely predicted," Dr. Morales continued. "Treatment will no longer consist of explorations of significance and spirit and mystery but quick fixes, twelve steps, behavioral adjustment, and pills. Freud will die, as Marx will die. And all that will be left of those nineteenth-century giants of intellect will be the unpityingly neutral doctrines of Sharles Darwin. Darwin is the man who must bear the responsibility for the end of meaning, Mr. Singer. Darwin. Instead of trying to get me thrown out of my profession, whatever may be left of it, you should be thanking me for doing my best to give your life whatever may be left of meaning, Mr. Singer. Mr. Singer.

"Mr. Singer, I had some dim hope that you might be the Hawk's-eye to my Chinkaja–Chinaka–however you say it. That you might take an interest in analysis and pursue it as an adjunct to your work as a teacher. Because if nothing else you did show an interest similar to mine in these matters of meaning. And you were young enough. But no. You could go only so far down that road before bailing out, as if it were. You didn't have what it takes for a real analysis. You failed. Unlike you, I can press on in my concern for the soul, because beyond and above all these intellectual matters I have my faith, which is a shield against the chaos which you are so ready to accept. You see, the greatest good that Christ has done for us is not to save our souls—though that is indeed of course a great gift, a great service that cost him his very life here on earth—but to give our lives a *context* in which they can be lived. He says, 'It matters what you do not only to yourself and to other human beings but to *me*.' He gives our lives meaning and, as if it were, another dimension of significance.

"Because you see, whether you realize it or do not, you and your godless kind are waiting for Something to Happen. All humanity has always wished for Something to Happen—something from above, as if it were, or perhaps it would be better to say something from outside, to provide a garment woven from plan and purpose for our poor and otherwise naked selves. Miracles are the metaphor for this yairning: the division of the sea, all the supernatural kinds of rain that you may read about—the frogs, the blood, the locusts, and et cetera—and the bread and the seafood, the walking upon the water, and et cetera. When we do not see these events that crack the dome of our earthly enclosure from without, we attempt to breach it from within, to make Something Happen by building ourselves and our artifacts up, with war, with art, with escience, with the skyscraper, in the hope that the membrane will at last be piercèd. The 'Ode to Joy,' the orgasm, the intercontinental ballistic missile, the four-minute mile, the bombing of the town until it lies beaten flat, the rebuilding of the town—all of this in the effort of overcoming our limits, of making Something Happen. For me, you see, It has already Happened. The two perpendicular boards of wood wrought in brass behind me represent that very gracious visitation of the supernatural into the natural of which I am speaking—the sending to the earth and into flesh and blood the idea behind the flesh and blood in the first place, as if it were, into the very play itself the dramaturge. That is the true generosity of God. For you, Mr. Singer, that grace will not be available, nor will even the pagan pleasure of a life fully lived—the kind of life made possible from the inside by the kind of work I was trying to do with you—because by stopping the treatment you have denied yourself even secular maturity.

"Now, you may not believe this, but the occasional serious and conscientious patient does come in to see me from time to time, still, and so you will have to excuse me.

"Speechless, Mr. Singer? A first for you, who, it always seemed to me, subscribed to your poetic paragon Yeets's indefensible doctrine that words alone are certain good. But you must open your mouth one more time here today, Mr. Singer, for whether or not I see you in court or before the review board of the society or never again, you must tell me your new address so I can know where to send the bill for this session, is it not?"

"I TOLD HIM Brigadoon and walked out the door," I say to Allegra. We're in bed in the dark, in the room where for a while almost a decade ago I felt like such a stranger. Now it's a retreat—a kind of opulent treehouse—where we can find the solitude, or is it isolation, that we both seek out as often as we can. Though I still tend to fold my clothes and put them away and straighten up my side of the room, while Allegra's territory remains disordered until the maid takes care of it—one of her very few rich traits. Tonight the park below is cold and silent, with its lamps casting circles of light on the snow like pearls strewn on gray velvet. "I was thinking about not telling you about this, but that didn't seem right. I feel much worse about the invasion of your privacy than I do about myself, except maybe for the embarrassment of ever having entrusted any confidences to this guy. To say nothing of seven years' worth. 'The treatment.' A great name for the whole thing, when you think about it."

"You got something from it. You've grown up a lot."

"Well, I *am* seven years older."

"I think you grew up faster than you would have without him if only to be able to escape him."

"For which he punished me. You know, I'm amazed that Mrs. Glass had the nerve to show up here tonight."

"Oh, she's so desperate, and she doesn't even realize it. And she really believes that she's doing everything she does for the sake of her kids."

"I'm glad I didn't tell you about her and Morales before the party. You were so nice to her."

"Do you think I wouldn't have been nice to her anyway? Don't you know me better by now? That's part of my trouble, I think—I don't really know how to get angry. Especially at anyone who is a parent."

"It's true. Even my heart didn't go out to Nixon like yours did on account of how he must have felt in front of his daughters when he made his resignation speech."

"She's so miserable," Allegra says. "Her husband just died and her children are such prigs. Think how desperate she was to go looking through his files, if that's what happened. Or how pathetic he was if he told her these things because you stopped seeing him when he didn't think you should have. You shouldn't have worried about telling me. I don't really care what those two people think they know about me. It can't hurt me. It hurts them, to act like that."

She turns on the small lamp next to her side of the bed and sits up. She's wearing a pair of my boxers, plain blue, and a white undershirt, mine also, looking elegantly overcrowded at the top and on the sides. I sit up against the headboard, too. "What's the trouble?" I say.

"Just a little anxious, as usual," she says. "I felt disembodied, talking in the dark like that. I wanted to see you."

"I didn't know that Mac could play the piano," I say.

"I didn't either."

"I hope Emily will keep up with her lessons."

"Me, too."

"Emmylou Harris is lucky that she looks a little like you."

"Thank you, Jake."

"I'm going to take these covers all the way off and make you less anxious."

"Wait, wait, wait—I wasn't going to give you this until Christmas, but watching Mac play and seeing Emily join the singing, and then even Georgie, made me realize that you don't use the one you have often enough." She sits forward, and her fall of dark hair falls across her face. "And to top it all off, you talk about Emmylou Harris. And who knows what will happen? Who ever knows? Look under the bed."

"Huh? What are you talking about?"

"Actually, all you have to do is put your hand down and feel around under the bed on your side. I've been looking for one for a while."

I fish around under the bed, where my hand immediately runs into a hard, leathery-feeling thing. At first I think it's a briefcase, but when I pull it out, slowly because of the awkwardness, I can tell that it's much bigger than a briefcase, and oddly shaped. I swivel around on the bed and put my feet on the floor and look down.

It's a guitar case—a black behemoth of nearly celloesque proportions. I open it up and take the guitar out. "But it's a Martin Dreadnought," I say. "It's excellent." I hold the guitar toward the light and look inside it and read the code. "Jeez, it's at least forty years old. But it's in perfect condition. These things go for—"

"It's the thought that counts, especially when you have a lot of money."

"How nice of you, Legs."

"You've almost stopped playing." She sits up straight and fixes me with her eyes. "You know, I know you and I love you, Jake, but I still can't—I don't know. I can't really know who you are. Even though I can seem so sympathetic, as you were saying, I still can't really get outside myself. That's what I feel when I'm feeling anxious. Everything is such a mystery to me. Everyone is a mystery to me, even you are, but I only worry about it when I love the person. Like the kids. And you. Such mysteries. When someone says he had someone in sex, I think it means something like the same thing as having something by heart. It's inside you. You actually know the person for that time, if it's any good—like knowing a song—and that's why it's sad when it's over. In the Bible, that's why it says that so-and-so knew so-and-so. I like it so much when you play and sing. I feel like when you lose yourself I find you."

I turn around and put the guitar back in the case, and then turn all the way back around to face Allegra. "I'm going to take lessons," I say. "But not right at this very moment." I push her hair back and kiss her where it was falling.

"Lovely, Jake," she says. "Hurt me a little bit, would you please?"

I do, and she whimpers. I sit back up to look at her, and in the low light from the lamp her dark hair shimmers, her eyes, still holding me, now almost apologetically, glow with heat. She raises her arms and I lift the undershirt away. "Talk about lovely," I say. "You can't possibly be forty. Look at you."

Her lips are parted, her eyes, though still fixed on me, have the beginning of the sexual trance in them that I always take as such a compliment. "You just don't notice what's happening," she says, close to indistinctly. "Like the little girl who lifted the cow every day."

"Cow, eh?" I say. I kiss her breasts and then take off my own undershirt and boxers. "Little girl, eh?"

THE BED IS a fair mess, and Allegra, still naked and splendidly messy herself, is in a profound sleep beside me. With a murmur of "Thank you, Jake," she drifted right off, evidently without the sadness she'd spoken of—the return to unsynchronized life and our unsynchronized selves. "We aim to please," I say now.

I reach across her to turn off the lamp, and just as I do, a light goes on down the corridor. I can't tell if it's from Emily's room or from Georgie's. Then it goes off. I get up and get my bathrobe out of the closet and put it on and go out into the hall. Georgie's room is first, but he's sound asleep, I can see in the faint illumination from the night-light in the hall. It's there more for Allegra now than it is for the kids. He's lying on his back with his arms up over his head—a prince, without a care. He's such an iconoclast right now, so touchingly scornful of adult conduct. He asked us why we were straightening up this evening before people began arriving—"It's just sucking up to the guests," he said, before we had a chance to answer. He went back to his room trailing disdain, with me laughing quietly to myself and Allegra momentarily losing her nervousness, but later he came out and stood next to us, proudly, it seemed to me, as we welcomed people. He looks so handsome and serious in his sleep.

Back out into the hall and next door to Emily's room. I can tell that her eyes are open.

"Are you OK, Emmy?" I ask.

"Oh, yeah," she says, with midnight rascality.

"But you just had your light on."

"Oh, yeah, Pops," she says. "I had a bad dream."

"What was the dream about?"

"I don't want to tell you."

"OK. I know how that is. Are you all right now?"

"Oh, yeah. See, I was in some big house all by myself, but I heard noises coming from everywhere. So I had to wake up and make sure I was where I'm supposed to be."

"And?"

"And what?"

"Are you where you're supposed to be?"

"Of course."

"Well, good."

"Tell me a story, Popsy."

"I'm not very good at stories—you know that."

"Then rub my back."

"OK."

I sit down on the side of the bed and rub her back, so narrow and strong. She's asleep within a minute, but I keep on a while longer, for my own selfish sake, as if in the hope that the naturalness of her could come up from her through my hands and arms and into my heart.

I get up, finally, and wander out into the cavernous living room, where I look out again over the ghostly park, and I think of my old snow parade with Dr. Morales—surely worth a short article in the *Journal of American Bizarro Psychoanalysis*. I remember his determined gait, his chitinous red coat, his emotional brick wall. And I recall the high-school kids playing around us in the snow so heedlessly, so immersed in the moment. They're in college now. No, they've graduated.

Speaking of Dr. M.: Where are you? Shouldn't you be weighing in right about now? Speechless, Dr. Morales? A first for you. I've been thinking about what you said, and I must admit that I wouldn't mind seeing a brief shower of bread or gold fall on Fifth Avenue. Some undoubtable sign. I wouldn't mind even just believing in the possibility of such a thing. I'd mind even less believing that Emily's father knows and sees how excellent she is, and that I shall see my mother again someday. That all the circles broken by death or chance will someday be unbroken.

ACKNOWLEDGMENTS

Thank you to Charles McGrath, who so astutely and forbearingly edited the *New Yorker* stories on which part of this novel is based; to Sonny Mehta and Jordan Pavlin, and all the others at Knopf, for their unexampled expertise and encouragement; and to Esther Newberg and Heather Schroeder at ICM, similarly unexampled. Thank you to Minna Fyer and to Lauren MacIntyre, and to Aaron Britvan for his generous counsel about adoption law. And to William and Elizabeth Menaker—talk about unexampled!